OCTAVIAN NOTHING

—◆—

VOLUME I

The

ASTONISHING

LIFE

of

OCTAVIAN NOTHING

TRAITOR TO THE NATION

❧❧❧❧❧❧❧❧❧❧

TAKEN FROM ACCOUNTS BY HIS OWN HAND

AND OTHER SUNDRY SOURCES

COLLECTED BY

MR. M. T. ANDERSON

OF BOSTON

VOLUME I

THE POX PARTY

❧

PRINTED AT THE SIGN OF THE BEAR AND FLAME
BY CANDLEWICK PRESS
2067 MASSACHUSETTS AVENUE
CAMBRIDGE, MASSACHUSETTS
MMVI

First edition 2006

Library of Congress Cataloging-in-Publication Data
Anderson, M. T.
The Pox party / taken from accounts by [Octavian Nothing's] own hand and other sundry sources ; collected by Mr. M. T. Anderson of Boston.
p.   cm. — (The astonishing life of Octavian Nothing, traitor to the nation ; v. 1)
Summary: Various diaries, letters, and other manuscripts chronicle the experiences of Octavian, from birth to age sixteen, as he is brought up as part of a science experiment in the years leading up to and during the Revolutionary War.
ISBN-10: 0-7636-2402-0
ISBN-13: 978-0-7636-2402-6
[1. Freedom—Fiction. 2. Slavery—Fiction. 3. Science—Experiments—Fiction.
4. African Americans—Fiction. 5. Massachusetts—History—Revolution, 1775–1783—Fiction.
6. United States—History—Revolution, 1775–1783—Fiction.] I. Title.
PZ7.A54395Pox 2006
[Fic]—dc22   2006043170

2   4   6   8   10   9   7   5   3

Printed in the United States of America

This book was typeset in Caslon and Archetype.

Candlewick Press
2067 Massachusetts Avenue
Cambridge, Massachusetts 02140

visit us at www.candlewick.com

[TABLE OF CONTENTS]

I.

THE TRANSIT
OF VENUS

—1—

II.

THE POX PARTY

—117—

III.

LIBERTY
& PROPERTY

—235—

IV.

THE GREAT
CHAIN OF BEING

—307—

[I.]

THE TRANSIT
OF VENUS

=========

drawn Primarily from
the Manuscript Testimony
of the Boy *Octavian*

———

With an anxious air, I say to him, "My dear Émile, what shall
we do to get out of here?"

Émile: I don't know. I'm tired; I'm thirsty; I'm hungry;
I can't go on.

Myself: Do you think I'm in any better state than you? Don't
you think I would cry too, if I could dine on tears?

     —Jean-Jacques Rousseau, *Émile, or On Education*

I was raised in a gaunt house with a garden; my earliest recollections are of floating lights in the apple-trees.

I recall, in the orchard behind the house, orbs of flames rising through the black boughs and branches; they climbed, spirit-ous, and flickered out; my mother squeezed my hand with delight. We stood near the door to the ice-chamber.

By the well, servants lit bubbles of gas on fire, clad in frock-coats of asbestos.

Around the orchard and gardens stood a wall of some height, designed to repel the glance of idle curiosity and to keep us all from slipping away and running for freedom; though that, of course, I did not yet understand.

How doth all that seeks to rise burn itself to nothing.

The men who raised me were lords of matter, and in the dim chambers I watched as they traced the spinning of bodies celestial in vast, iron courses, and bid sparks to dance upon their hands; they read the bodies of fish as if each dying trout or shad was a fresh Biblical Testament, the wet and twitching volume of a new-born Pentateuch. They burned holes in the air, wrote poems of love, sucked the venom from sores, painted landscapes of gloom, and made metal sing; they dissected fire like newts.

I did not find it strange that I was raised with no one father, nor did I marvel at the singularity of any other article in my upbringing. It is ever the lot of children to accept their circumstances as universal, and their particularities as general.

So I did not ask why I was raised in a house by many men, none of whom claimed blood relation to me. I thought not to inquire why my mother stayed in this house, or why we alone were given names — mine, Octavian; hers, Cassiopeia — when all the others in the house were designated by number.

The owner of the house, Mr. Gitney, or as he styled himself, 03-01, had a large head and little hair and a dollop of a nose. He rarely dressed if he did not have to go out, but shuffled most of the time through his mansion in a banyan-robe and undress cap, shaking out his hands as if he'd washed them newly. He did not see to my instruction directly, but required that the others spend some hours a day teaching me my Latin and Greek, my mathematics, scraps of botany, and the science of music, which grew to be my first love.

The other men came and went. They did not live in the house, but came of an afternoon, or stayed there often for some weeks to perform their virtuosic experiments, and then leave. Most were philosophers, and inquired into the workings of time and memory, natural history, the properties of light, heat, and petrifaction. There were musicians among them as well, and painters and poets.

My mother, being of great beauty, was often painted. Once, she and I were clad as Venus, goddess of love, and her son Cupid, and we reclined in a bower. At other times, they made portraits of her dressed in the finest silks of the age, smiling behind a fan, or leaning on a pillar; and on another occasion, when she was sixteen, they drew her nude, for an engraving, with lines and letters that identified places upon her body.

The house was large and commodious, though often drafty. In its many rooms, the men read their odes, or played the violin, or performed their philosophical exercises. They combined chemical compounds and stirred them. They cut apart birds to trace the structure of the avian skeleton, and, masked in leather hoods, they dissected a skunk. They kept cages full of fireflies. They coaxed reptiles with mice. From the uppermost story of the house, they surveyed the city and the bay through spy-glasses, and noted the ships that arrived from far corners of the Empire, the direction of winds and the migration of clouds across the waters and, on its tawny isle, spotted with shadow, the Castle.

Amidst their many experimental chambers, there was one door that I was not allowed to pass. One of the painters sketched a little skull-and-crossbones on paper, endowed not with a skull, but with my face, my mouth open in a gasp; and this warning they hung upon that interdicted door as a reminder. They meant it doubtless as a jest, but to me, the door was terrible, as ghastly in its secrets as legendary Bluebeard's door, behind which his dead, white wives sat at table, streaked with blood from their slit throats.

We did not venture much out of the house and its grounds into the city that surrounded us. In the garden, we could hear its bustle, the horseshoes on stone cobbles and dirt, the conversation of sailors, the crying of onions and oysters in passageways. The men of that house feared that too much interaction with the world would corrupt me, and so I was, in the main, hidden away for my earliest years, as the infant Jove, snatched out of the gullet of Time, was reared by his horned nurse on Mount Ida in profoundest secrecy.

When we did go abroad, Mr. 03-01 warned me that I should not lean out at the window of the carriage, and should not show my face. He told me that, should I ever run away into the city, I would not return, but would be snatched up by evil men who would take me forever away from my mother. This was, I know now, but a half-lie.

I imagine that I was a silent and solemn child—as solemn as my mother was smiling and gay. The appearance of solemnity was much increased by the fact that, from my earliest youth, my head was shaved, and I was made to wear white wigs, so that even in childhood, I had the look of age. I was told that the hair for my wigs, and for my mother's—for she too was shaved and wore white wigs, though hers were towering, and marked with jet-black ribbons—that this hair came from a pensioners' home in Prague, where hair was farmed in exchange for soup and bread. Such wigs could not have been inexpensive; but they were simply one of the extravagant customs of that place, and I found them unsurprising.

In the parlance of that house, the master, Mr. Gitney, was called 03-01 because he was the head (and so 01) of the third family enumerated (that is, the Gitneys). He was attempting to introduce a numerical system of naming, with the idea that it would rationalize human relations. 01-01, therefore, was our glorious majesty the King—the initial 01 signifying His Majesty's family, the House of Hanover. The Queen was 01-02; George Augustus Frederick, Prince of Wales, 01-03; and so on. 02-01 was His Lordship the Earl of Cheldthorpe, a very Mæcenas whose generous patronage allowed our household its investigations, and whose portrait hung, stained yellow from flares and exudations, in one of the experimental chambers.

In the years as I grew, my mother must have perceived the peculiarity of our situation; but though she may have noted, she did not discover its irregularities to me by word, look, or gesture.

Or, by God—I reckon now, now that it is all gone—yea—mayhap she did discover it to me, in every gesture, in all looks, in the space between each word—and I, never knowing her elsewhere, did not know how to parse her warnings and subtility.

How would her smile have appeared, did we not live in that house? Would it have been the one I know as hers—the which I saw slow-spreading across her soft and radiant features to greet each gentleman who attended our musical *soirées,* of an evening? (For when the gentry would gather to hear her play upon the harpsichord, and hear me, no taller than her waist, play upon the violin, she smiled upon each and every one of them as they watched, wigged and fingering their canes.)

I did not ask why we were not numbered, as the others were; I suspected that it was due to my mother's royal blood—for I was told from my earliest youth that she was a princess in her own kingdom, could she but get back to it from her exile. In her bearing, she was still a queen.

They called themselves the Novanglian College of Lucidity, and devoted themselves to divining the secrets of the universe, so praising the Creator, who had with infinite art manufactured such a dazzling apparatus; and each investigation into the incubation of tern-eggs or the mystery of sediment was but an ear pressed to the mechanism, the better to hear the click of gears, the swiveling of stars on cog and ambulating cam.

I was taught not merely the arts and knowledge of the physical world, but was given the strictest instruction in ethics, schooled in those virtues that must ever enflame each Christian heart: kindness, filial duty, piety, obedience, and humility.

Above all, brought up among the experiments and assays of these artists and philosophers, I was taught the importance of observation. They showed me how to be precise in notation, acute in investigation, and rational in inference. After I watched them pet a dog for some days, then drown it, and time its drowning; or after I watched them feed alley-cats to lure them so they could toss them off a scaffold and judge the height from which cats no longer catch themselves, but shatter; or, yea, after I saw the philosophers of this college acquire a docile child deprived of reason and speech, and, when she could not master the use of verbs, beat her to the point of gagging and swooning; after such experiments as these, I became most wondrous observant, and often stared unmoving at a wall for some hours together.

They quizzed me on what I had observed staring at these walls.

Once, at dinner, seated at the table, 03-01 asked me what I had noted in my hours spent immobile. I said, "Nothing, sir."

He said that one could not observe *nothing*.

The girl deprived of reason — who had just been beaten — began to sob. The servants were weighing and recording my dinner.

I ventured that I had watched a daddy longlegs. He asked what hypotheses I had made in that time. The girl sobbed and beat the table. I looked down at my dinner, which was before me, now. I said that I wondered whether the daddy longlegs was a spider.

Mr. 03-01 said to me, "Prove that it is so. Through the exercise of logic. Is the daddy longlegs a spider?"

I hesitated. He nodded to his manservant, who came to my side and picked up my food, not yet touched, and passed it to 03-01, who held it suspended across the table and waited for my reply. I could not think, with the moaning of the unfortunate speechless girl. I was hungry.

"Come along," said 03-01. "State your proposition as a three-part proof. A syllogism."

My mother urged me, "Octavian? 'One. Spiders have eight legs.'"

"Please observe silence, Your Majesty," said 03-01 to her. "You shall not give him help."

I repeated, "One. Spiders have eight legs." Considering it, I continued: "Two. Daddy longlegs have eight legs. Therefore, three, daddy longlegs must be spiders." I felt great relief. I looked covetously at my meal.

"I am afraid not," said 03-01. "That is a faulty proof." As he lowered my plate and fed my dinner to the dog, he explained kindly, "You exhibit an illicit process of the minor term. Your proof is invalid. The first phrase, supplied by your mother, was not suitable to your purposes." The dog was lapping my dinner off the plate. "You might as well retire to your bedchamber," he said to me. "You will get no food tonight at this table."

I turned to my mother. "Mother?" I said. "Mater?"

She sat staring imperiously across the table at no one — at a portrait, perhaps, on the wall. Her hands were poised near her fork and knife, but she did not raise them to eat.

03-01 said, "Your mother advised you poorly. This is not to deny her considerable charms; but in future, you would be well advised to attend less carefully to her every word."

She protested, "He is my son."

"Let us say rather," said 03-01, "that he belongs to all of us."

Thus, having observed, I retired; and I began to wonder who held power in that house, and who had none.

Still do I struggle to remember the moral precepts I was taught in that place. Kindness, humility, piety, respect for other human creatures—these are the great *desiderata* of all who pursue virtuous action, and it matters not whether those who preach them heed their own advice. Right thinking is ever a battle, and often I cast my mind back to these early lessons and pursue these early ideals, though now the ghastly purpose of that dim college has been made clear to me; and he who ran it appears to me not like a man but some monster who instructed me, some beast endued with the speech of a man, as the centaur Chiron wrote out lessons for young Achilles with his human hands, and spake his lectures with his human mouth, while his glossy hindquarters dropped fæces upon the Senate lawn.

It boots us nothing to feel rage for things that long ago transpired. We must curb our fury, and allow sadness to diminish, and speak our stories with coolness and deliberation. *"Animum rege, qui nisi paret, imperat,"* quoth the poet Horace. "Rule thy passion, for unless it obeys, it rules you." I ask the Lord God Jehovah for strength to forgive. Whatever I have felt about those men, I have much to thank them for. They lavished luxuries upon me. They supported my every interest and encouraged my curiosity. They instructed me in the Christian religion. They taught me the tongues of the Greeks and the Romans and opened for me the colonnaded vistas of those long-forgotten empires, in this, the dawning of a new empire. They schooled me in music, which is my greatest delight. These are not little things.

I do not believe they ever meant unkindness.

In another early recollection, I remember taking the food Mr. 03-01 had prepared for my dog down to the woodshed, that I might delight the creature and enjoy his company for some minutes before my lessons. The dog was a stray, though sweet enough in disposition once fed, and for two weeks it had been my constant care and practice to nurse him as a special pet. I was perhaps five or six years of age; the dog was named Cloud. I entered the woodshed to find him unmoving.

I rearranged his legs, but still he would not stir.

I recall no emotion on this occasion; nor do I recall emotion from many of the circumstances that formed the early passages of my life, for which nullity I have no explanation; for I know that such instances as this melted my heart and battered my sensibilities;

but I have no memory of those inward commotions. I was trained in observation, not in reaction.

It is indicative of the rigors of scrutiny to which I have always subjected myself that though I can recall none of the tremors of my breast, none of the calamity of spirit this must have occasioned, I do recall the floods of tears I shed as I ran through the house—the scolding I received from a footman—and at last the complaint I made to Mr. 03-01.

Mr. 03-01 swore and followed me to the woodshed to examine the body; there, I stood by the body of the dog as he examined it, and I gave myself over to silent weeping.

It was not for many years that I read an article he penned on that occasion, and found that Cloud had been memorialized; and, furthermore, grew to understand through this brief chemical treatise, frank in its disclosure of experimental methodology, that I had murdered my dog by my own hand; for that excellent and affectionate creature had been poisoned by the same food I gave him daily, Mr. 03-01 admixing an experimental mercurious compound into the meat and rice to determine whether it was fatal to mammals.

This I did not know when I was five; I merely knew a hollowness, as best I can recall it, so windy and sharp I could not stop weeping. Mr. 03-01, noting my sorrow, took me into the experimental chamber and sat me upon his knee. "Octavian," he said, "why do you feel sorrow?"

I could not formulate an answer.

"Do you think that Cloud hath passed to another world?" he asked.

I nodded, and he asked me what that place might resemble;

and in my answer I described a paradise of dogs; upon which he inquired whether dogs have a soul, and this, too, I answered.

So I sat on his lap and told him what he wished to know; and carefully, nodding, he transcribed my answers for study, comment, and future publication.

At the head of the stairs in that gaunt house there was a painting of a pleasant woodland in the Golden Age of Man, that sweet epoch when nude nymphs and youths would meet on the greensward in the cool of the morning to discuss architecture, the affections, or trigonometry. The painting was executed by one of our guests, Mr. 07-03, a young man with wild, unkempt hair, a passionate disposition, and prodigious talents: He had engraved a series of plates depicting the flora of the New World, and had, as well, published articles on the pursuits of the woodpecker, the musk of the bear, and the motion of electricity through water, the last of which experiments left him with a permanent jitter and no sense of smell. He painted the picture to represent Mr. 03-01's dream of a perfect world, one where all men and women, united in rationality, pursued knowledge together beneath the green leaves of summer and the distant blue of sacred mountains. Such, said the men who raised me, was their hope for our nation.

This was 03-01's ideal, and he pursued it with all those men who came to our academy.

I recall, as an example of this pursuit, an occasion when he arranged that we should go out into the countryside and take our supper beneath the summer sun. It was not an event of much moment; but my memory of it is clear, and it will act as a serviceable specimen of the conversations among our academicians.

We went out in several carriages and an open cart full of scholars. A few had brought their own carriages, attended by their own wives, who had organized the collation. All of those virtuosos still unwed, however, young or old, wished to be seated next to my mother in Mr. 03-01's carriage, and it took some time, us standing in the stable-yard while they each put in their bid, before we could even embark.

One wished to sit with her and Mr. 03-01 so he could speak about the appropriation of funds for a refracting telescope and octant; another had committed to memory a passage of Lucretius and wished to recite it with gestures; the music-master would sing; the botanist would speak on stamens; Mr. 07-03, the painter, wished to sketch while we drove, and said the cart would bounce too much for his already palsied hands.

Amidst this chaos of demand, 03-01 raised his finger, and pointed at the one man who had remained silent—an elderly *philosophe* named Dr. Trefusis, 09-01—and said, "Yes—09-01 shall go with us."

07-03 protested, "09-01 made no request, sir."

03-01 replied sharply, "Precisely. He is withered and his seminal vesicles eaten away entirely by the clap. He is the only one of you who will not succumb to love and spend the next hour ogling the Princess's bosom. Come!"

"I might still love her," 09-01 pointed out. "Hm? Who is to say that love must move through the loins to stir the heart?"

"He might," agreed 07-03.

"Indeed, sirs," mused another, "is love grounded in the body or in the intellect?"

"Or in the spirit?" added yet another.

"Is the spirit also the intellect?"

"And in truth, could we but—"

"Horsewhip!" 03-01 sang out gaily, holding one aloft, and the company silenced itself. He ordered, "Princess Cass—Octavian—Dr. 09-01, sir—into the carriage. We are off."

The ride was pleasant, though the road was wet in some places and rutted. My heart dilated at the prospect of travel through the streets of the town. The floating lights and miraculous gasses of our house did not intrigue me, being so familiar; but the trains of servants running through the streets with baskets of leeks, or the poles strung with dead hares, the ladies in their finery walking arm-in-arm—these filled my mind with questions, as if they were the most recondite of earthly tableaux.

There was little that did not excite my interest in these urban scenes: the broad avenues animated with the clamor of sales and traffic; the narrow alleys; the horses and fine equipages; the ladies carried through the streets in their chaises, their wigs high and as ornamental as shrubberies; the fishermen on the wharves; the persons of all races that milled upon the teeming docks; and even the urchins who, smeared with dirt and salt, played coachman in the gutters, a frolic that seemed to me, in my naïveté, delightful in the highest measure.

I fairly hung out the window, so eager was I to see the world that passed outside our walls; 03-01 indulgently did not scold my curiosity.

We made our way down Orange Street and through the city gates, across the marshy Neck to the mainland. We soon had left behind us the warehouses and the reeking tanneries, and traversed pastureland on muddy tracks.

There is no refreshment more gratifying to the soul than the sight of Nature in her summer finery, before the heat is at its most intense. She is soothing, but not soporific; intoxicating without inebriation.

We made our way through the fields. Laborers were cocking the hay for the first harvest. 03-01 and 09-01 watched them with some interest and exchanged views on haymaking and the weather.

When we reached the spot 03-01 had designated for our supper — a spreading oak that would afford us all shade from the afternoon sun — we stopped, and the footman helped us step down. The master's valet, 24-06, made good the preparations for the feast on blankets lain on the grass.

It was an afternoon that I shall long remember, not due to any incident remarkable for change and calamity, but rather because in the regularity of its pulse it suggested health and good humor, in a way that so many of my days, spent stammering out Latin in dark rooms, did not.

The supper was served. We ate, and the men reclined around my mother, with scarcely a look at the several wives who were present — 11-02, for example — notwithstanding, I reflected as I ate my slice of ham, it was they had planned the menu and organized its transportation. The other women gathered a ways off, their faces blank beneath their masks, and watched the squirrels play.

My mother did not speak, but sat smiling on all of the academicians as they addressed their remarks to her.

"This is most pleasant, is it not, Mademoiselle?"

"Like unto the first age of man, before we fell."

She smiled, and her arm was by 03-01's side, as he was holding her wrist, making note of her pulse.

Dr. 09-01, who had rid in the carriage with us, explained, "In the original state of man, we were happy — when we were animals. But when we rose from four feet to two, we became precarious. Now we hold ourselves away from Nature. Bipedal, we teeter always on the brink of collapse, and worry about balance. Gentlemen, it is a great pity that, knowing of our previous felicity and our current distresses, we do not return to our four-footed posture and feel the soil again beneath our hands. 'Tis a damned shame that we do not choose to revert to the blissful state of mammalian repose."

There were general cries of yea and indeed. 07-03 heaved himself up on all fours. He came to my side, and said, "You are so silent and solemn. Perhaps you too would like to crawl? As our ancestors did? What say to a race in the Blissful State of Mammalian Repose? First one to the cow?"

I looked at 03-01, who nodded indulgently, and at my mother, whose face did not change, and I got on all fours and raced with the others, waddling, our fundaments pointed at the heavens.

As we rushed the cow, that ponderous beast—uneasy still in spite of its four-legged stance—fled; and we gave up our race for aimless crawling and darting.

The academicians watched my mother as they played with me, to see how she took their games, their dandling of her beloved son, their demonstration of amiable paternity; and her smile warmed us all.

So we spent that day in the cheery grove, with the vivid light of later afternoon falling on the grasses; we spent it bumbling about in the Blissful State of Mammalian Repose.

I may have laughed.

My mother did, certainly, to see those philosophers grubbing as they did before her in the dirt. 03-01 clapped, and smoked his pipe. The three wives of academicians went for a walk up the lane, haughty and masked, unimpressed by the spectacle.

Evening fell, as it falls always on the entertainments of man, foretelling the solemnity of night and end.

I recall this day for the sake of Mr. Gitney, at that time called 03-01, as an homage to his desires for a world that cannot be.

He spake that evening of America, saying: "My friends—this is a continent that beckons with its mighty crags, its thunderous rivers, its gloomy forests, so filled with unknown life. Yes? God has spread here a mighty canvas, stretched and ready for the artist's hand. Everywhere there is bounty, demanding to be plucked from the tree; and trees, that, in their ancient beauty, beg to be felled and made into ships and houses on the illimitable hills of this land, offered so freely to civilized man. I believe fully, gentlemen, that the Golden Age shall come again in this new Eden."

In the gloaming, we rode back into Boston. I asked to sit up atop the carriage with 24-06, the valet. Though in the normal course of events such a request would have been refused due to the pernicious night airs, 03-01 was feeling indulgent after our idyll, and gave me license to sit there and watch the moon come out above the steeples of the city.

24-06 was but ten years older than me, and but a few years younger than my mother.

"24-06," I said, "why does the moon show its face sometimes before the sun is gone?"

"My name is not 24-06," he said.

I hazarded, "05?"

"I am called Bono," he said, "and I will change that name, too, before I die."

"Bono," I said, "why does the moon show its face sometimes—"

"Keep silent, Prince," he said, "or I shall kick you right off the carriage with my boot. You will lie in the bulrushes, weeping, and no one will come for you."

I did not move.

He said, "Do not weep. You must become accustomed to not weeping." With that, he reached to my upper arm, took ahold of the flesh, and pinched without cease.

At this, I became Observant. I ceased to move, but watched the world being gathered into night. I did not want to twitch, and compel 24-06 to further fury.

The carriage made its way through the city gates, where the felons hung on their nooses, the crows upon the scaffold, and we rolled past the Common.

He let go.

We came to the gates of 03-01's house. We went into the stable-yard.

The carriage came to a halt.

24-06 whispered to me, "You must learn fear. I do this for your own sake. Fear is like happiness, but the smile is wider."

And with that, he threw himself down off the box, and assisted the coachman in preparing the steps for the ladies' disembarkation.

In such episodes as these, I began to ponder the mystery of who I was, and what that might mean.

There was no field into which the men of the College of Lucidity did not make their inquiries. They watched the motions of the heavens and judged the composition of the earth. They corresponded with botanists throughout the Colonies, sending them bulbs and shoots when illustrations would not do. The banister of the rear staircase was hung with drying leaves and stalks sent from the frontier.

These specimens were delivered by a fellow named Druggett, who traveled the western forests, trading and purchasing furs from the savages of the Iroquois Nations. He was a shrewd naturalist in his own right, and often brought back samples of flora or fauna for pay. He had seen many wonders in the forests, and was responsible for many of the passing freaks of my academicians: their scheme to domesticate the moose for transport and milk, their commitment to edible lichen.

As Pliny the Naturalist saith, *"No man is wise in every hour."*

Druggett was a frightening man to me, his clothes always covered in burns and smears, his head wound in a bandage that, he claimed, fastened his brain. He had in his pocket a collection of broken clay pipes, being unwilling to purchase new ones, and he would stand in our parlor with his hands in his pockets, smoking and telling us tales of narrow escapes that even I, in my infancy, could tell were embroidered for our pleasure.

When I was four, he and six other men brought a dragon's skull which had been found far to the west. It was brown, and its teeth were terrible.

I gazed at it in wonder (I am told), and fingered its nostrils.

"Guaranteed before the flood," said Druggett. "Guaranteed old. Ancienter than Noah's lips and beard."

"In what situation was it discovered?" asked Mr. 03-01.

Druggett answered, "By a soap-boiler. He was jumping off a cliff in despair."

"In what attitude was it found? What layer of the sediment?"

Druggett nodded knowledgeably and closed one eye. "Aye. The sentiment was love. Had a young maiden he was fond of, or a baboon, and it run off."

I hardly recall their words. I remember my first sight of the dragon, though, its vacant sockets and knuckled teeth, and the murmur of their conversation; and I have been told by my mother that when they looked down, after some minutes speaking of the skull, they found my body lain out behind it, and my head within the monster's flat head, my arms against my sides, my chin on the floor, my eyes glaring out at 03-01 as if my tiny body belonged to the beast and I had always inhabited it.

And though I never spoke except when bidden to speak, in this one instance I cried and sobbed until they allowed me to sleep in the room with the monster, my head in its long-rotted cranium, my body curled behind it as if it and I were some nightmare tadpole waiting to burst from the murk and reinstate its reign upon the genteel fields of Earth.

When I was young, before I could tell numbers and operate a scales and so record the weight of my own excrement, the men of the house daily performed this calculation for me. They weighed what I ate when it went in, and daily took the measure of its transformation when it came out.

When the need came upon me, I would bashfully refer the matter to them, and they would fetch the golden platter made for the purpose, and I would straddle it while one of them held it near my knees.

Mr. 03-01, the master of the house, watching the process, would nod and declare some pronouncement: "Sallow in color . . . watery in consistency; altogether a dispirited, morose ejection" or "Solid and stippled with corn . . . brave and manly; a matter for some pride."

The other would take down his words in a column for that purpose.

Across the room, my mother would be learning her lessons on the harpsichord. The music-master counted out measures while I endeavored to deliver what was asked of me.

The gold of which the platter was made, I now descry, was necessary so that the metal should remain inert, and the composition of my fæces more firmly be established. As with so many elements of my upbringing, it took me some time to appreciate what thought had gone into the regulations by which I was raised, and the extreme purity and inviolability of their conception.

When I was five and was taught subtraction, 03-01 showed me how to weigh the golden chamber-pot and subtract its weight to determine more easily how much I had passed in the day. By such lessons did I become acclimated to scientific calculation in even the meanest function, so learning the secrets of tare and gross. When, at about that time, I perceived that others did not have their leavings weighed so, it made a great impression upon me; and I had an even greater sense of my mysterious importance in this murky scheme, the unaccountable preciousness of everything I did to those who strove to watch over me.

Of my origins, I know only the stories my mother told me; and she did not speak often of the past. When I was small, she would, when allowed to come to my bedside, tell me softly of her nation; but when I was seven or eight years of age, she spake no more of it, and if I asked, told me that I was fast becoming a man, and men have no need of mothers' tales.

My mother was a princess of the Egba people in the Empire of Oyo, in western Africa. She told me of the royal throne where she sate, crowned, while her father dispensed law to the people of that country: her throne a single orchid, grown vast through the influence of the tropical heat and rain. Enthralled by her description, I saw her issue forth from the palace in panoply, trumpets crying fanfares, she being drawn upon a chariot by the exertions of panthers, her serene features shaded by umbrellas of bright damask. There, in Oyo, she lived in blissful state with her brothers and sisters, the royal family; and there, in the palace of orchids, she fell in love with a prince from a neighboring state when he came to pay respects to her father.

The marriage of princess and prince, both struck with love, would have proceeded unhindered—for my grandfather the King approved the match—had a prince of another kingdom not jealously desired my mother. He—a cocksure brute much given to womanizing and the lion-hunt—nursed a grievance in his heart, and would not let it go. He went in to the King, my grandfather, and demanded that my mother break off the engagement with her paramour. The King laughed him to scorn, and told him to leave the court immediately.

Leave the court, the criminal brute did—and removed home to his warrior-kingdom, and rallied his army, and returned to assault the palace of orchids, which swiftly fell, knowing only the fruits of peace before this time.

My mother was snatched from my father; they were parted amidst smoke and the weeping of women; and she was dragged away. My father was slain. The rival brought her before him, and demanded she offer her hand in marriage. She refused, and said she would sooner die than submit to his loathsome caresses. He kept her for some weeks, and then, seeing that she would not capitulate, sent her off to the coast in exile.

She was conducted by her captors to the kingdom of Dahomey, and embarked from the quays of Whydah; thereafter being held for some months at the fortress of B——, off the coast, with no hope for communication with her grieving people. When

I asked her what that castle was like, she told me that it smelled always of spices, and the salt of the wind. It was full of flowers always—flowers in the garden, in the windows, on the tables. She walked there in the round courtyard with the Governor's wife, who used her with great kindness, knowing the nobility of her blood.

Once, when she heard me play the violin, she said she reckoned that I was musical because I grew in the womb while she sate in the courtyard on the Isle of B——, listening to the Governor's daughters play the harpsichord. He greatly missed the salons of Paris, and would ask them to play the music of Couperin, Rameau, and Royer in memory of his homeland. Weakly did the court tunes tinkle out above the crashing of surf on the basalt rocks at the castle's foundations.

It happened at about this time that the English took the Isle of B——, and my mother was taken on an English ship—the *Incontrovertible,* Captain Julian McFergus, Master—and brought to the shore of America. It was not an easy passage, for she was pregnant; and notwithstanding her state, the sailors clamored to commit the most indecent and inhuman violence upon her person; in which design they were only halted by the sword of Captain McFergus. For which, each night when I said my prayers, my mother always asked that I remember this same McFergus, and pray that he was well, and still walked in the ways of righteousness.

Having arrived in America, she found she did not fancy the southern ports to which she was taken—Savannah, Charleston, and New-York—and so, finally, she reached Boston. Mr. Gitney—that is, 03-01—reading of her arrival in the papers, went to the dock to greet her, and being impressed with her bearing and mental acuity, offered her a place in his home. He asked only, as a special favor, that I be brought up according to various philosophical principles, chief among which was the need for thorough tutelage in the Classics and in all the achievements of Europe.

My mother was, at this time, some thirteen years of age, big with child, and in little state to refuse.

So began our curious life in the College of Lucidity.

My mother was surrounded always by admirers: scholars, poets, painters, bucks, and blades. She let them all pay homage; for though she was now in low estate, she had been bred for the court, and was accustomed to the crush of supplicants. She hearkened little to the insinuations of flattery or the curtseys of obsequiousness, but returned all idle, pretty chatter in its own coin.

If she sought to leave a room, to guide me, perhaps, up to my bed, one of the scholars would cry, "But Mademoiselle, you are the bright center of our system. How may the sun, around which we all revolve, leave its planets spinning?"

And she would reply, "Sirs—you have gravity enough without me. And when I return, comet-like, to your orbit, you will welcome me all the more for my rarity and dazzle."

They applauded her understanding and the deep science of her counter-flattery.

She would rush me up the stairs and sit on my bed. She would tap her fingers while I prayed, and seemed vexed by the number of animals for whom I asked safety. No sooner had my "Amen" flown out my mouth, drifted its way to the ceiling, and popped — she would rise swiftly, and bid me good night, rub my chin once, and rush back to the salon below.

Increasingly, I was in awe of her majesty, and did not know what I might say to please her. I fear now that I failed to engage her; that I was too sallow a character. Indeed, as time went on and I reached my seventh, and then my eighth, year, I became aware of how dull my wit was when confronted with her beauty, how drab my bearing; and so, gradually, I came to stand in relation to her as another admirer, seeking a few words, a kiss, a sign of favor. I vied for her attention only as one man of many.

She smiled upon me to chasten the others, to spurn their envious glances at me when I was taken by her up to bed.

Her spirit was so light, so luminous, so gay, that I feared how leaden was my solemnity and silence. I assayed to try my own hand at *bons mots*, saying to her in the morning, "You are — you are come down to the breakfast room as the — some dew on the flowers. Falling."

She would say, "A few more years, Octavian."

But this is the grossest filial ingratitude; there is no object in the world that should inspire greater affection and enchain the heart of man more than that wellspring of all that is sweetest, that dear first progenitor, a mother; and if I speak now in a way that makes her seem the coquette, I do so only because there is no preserving a spirit in lying about them; a portrait that improves upon its subject, that removes the moles, undrops the double-chin, suspends the sagging cheeks—that is no portrait at all, and preserves nothing for all time but a fancy. In the painting of such a likeness, the subject has slipped away, evaporated; and after death, all that is left is a canvas of someone else, a likeness of a smiling fiction, and the spirit does not hover near, and cannot speak its comfortable words.

So here, in limning her portrait, must I paint her as she was, a girl of little more than my own age now. I do not know what she felt, nor what fires burned in her bosom, what memories she entertained, what plains she saw when she dreamed, what grasses, what beasts, what faces of mother, father, sister, lover.

I know but what I saw, and that was her glittering accomplishments; and then, on some nights, some very few nights, she would come to me, and sit by my bed and watch me sleep (or attempt to sleep, as sleep was impossible with her gaze so fiery upon me). She would betray no sign of emotion; but she read my prone form like a pamphlet that contained words to save her.

Often, if I moved uneasily beneath her gaze, she would bark that I should remain still; but once, me waking to find her near, she instead begged me: "Touch my hair."

She laid her head down upon my lap, burying her face in my chest, and I patted her head; and after a time, lying there as she clutched, I felt that I was become her mother, and she my son.

A man in a topiary maze cannot judge of the twistings and turnings, and which avenue might lead him to the heart; while one who stands above, on some pleasant prospect, looking down upon the labyrinth, is reduced to watching the bewildered circumnavigations of the tiny victim through obvious coils — as the gods, perhaps, looked down on besieged and blood-sprayed Troy from the safety of their couches, and thought mortals weak and foolish while they themselves reclined in comfort, and had only to snap to call Ganymede to their side with nectar decanted.

So I, now, with the vantage of years, am sensible of my foolishness, my blindness, as a child. I cannot think of my blunders without a shriveling of the inward parts — not merely the desiccation attendant on shame, but also the aggravation of remorse that

I did not demand more explanation, that I did not sooner take my mother by the hand, and—

I do not know what I regret. I sit with my pen, and cannot find an end to that sentence.

I do not know what we may do, to know another better.

Some days after our jaunt in the country, when we had all crawled in the Blissful State of Mammalian Repose, I was alone with Bono (for so I thought of him now, and not by his number). I watched him cleaning his master's woolen coat; he was wrapping wet scraps of brown paper about hot coals, and, with a tongs, dousing grease spots with the steaming paper.

I asked him, "Why do you wish to change your name from Bono?"

"It was give me as a jest," he said.

I said, "I do not understand the jest."

He lay down his tongs, and soaked another piece of paper.

"What jest?" I asked him.

"I understood you was a silent boy," he said.

I knew it was of importance that I pursue my inquiry.

I waited while he soaked another spot. The paper was tearing. He swore as the coal streaked black on the lapel. He cast aside the tongs.

I asked, "May I assist you?"

He fixed me with a look.

I offered, "I could hold the tongs and coal."

"I been plenty of things," he said, "but I never been on fire."

He stretched his arms out, and turned his head one way and the other to make his neck crack. He noted that I still watched him, and said, "You want to know?"

I nodded.

He seemed to be considering. He sucked in his cheeks. Then he released them.

At length, he said, "I was in my mother's womb when she was bought. My master purchased me and her, one price. My name's Pro Bono. For free. They got two, my mother and me, for the price of one."

I did not know what to say.

He put his hands on my shoulders, and said, in tones facetious, "See, Prince O., we're alike in more than just our skin."

I watched him carefully.

He said, "You and your mama were a single lot. See? The girls, they're cheaper when they're pregnant. Masters lose some months with her coming to bed, and the baby suckling. . . ."

He smiled at me. "You didn't know this," he said. It was a question, but I had no answer, for perhaps I had known it.

I said, "My mother is a princess."

He pulled forth another piece of brown paper and wrapped it round a coal. "Your mother *was* a princess," he amended.

I started; I stared.

Cautiously, I asked, "Where is your mother?"

"Cook," he answered. "At one of Mr. 03-01's nephew's houses. Can't remember which number nephew. Maybe 03-17."

"You were sold to us?" I asked.

He fixed me with a solemn and ironical gaze. "To you?" he repeated.

"My mother," I said, "chose to come here because she had heard such things about the town of Boston while on the Isle of B— that she wished to visit it."

I was surprised when this magisterial explanation met only with a look of pity and impatience.

He said, "Surely it don't have anything to do with them selling the sickliest slaves up New England way after no one buys them down South." He shook his head. "No," he said, "she walked down the gangplank with page boys and trumpets."

I struggled to understand his jest; and when I recognized what he imputed, my mother's low condition, I knew not what to say. I wished it to be a lie.

I put my arms about myself and spake no more. I desired no more explanations from Pro Bono.

He looked at me. "You didn't know," he said again. "You did not know?"

I watched him. He did not move, but held the steaming coal in the tongs and stared at me.

He said, "You can—this once—start crying."

I moved not a hair.

He said, "That will be the last time in your life when you're free."

[*From* The Boston Gazette, *June 12, 1759*]

. . . of *Tremont Street* announces that he will keep the famed RICHELIEU at stud this season. The horse is renowned for his strength and valour, and sires acrobatic colts. For all seminal endeavors, he may be engaged for 5s. the *single leap* or by seasonal subscription for £2 4s. Mares shall not complain of the performance. Enquire with owner.

For AUCTION! For AUCTION!

A boat-load of healthy, likely N E G R O E S

of all ages, both male & female,

brought hence by Capt. Julian McFergus

of the *INCONTROVERTIBLE*

available for bid SATURDAY next at noon

at the Arbuthnot Wharf off Essex Street

in the TOWN of BOSTON.

— *Do not doubt that these are fine specimens!* —

NEWLY IMPORTED from *LONDON*: linens, cambricks, buckrams, lawns, duffles, drabs, deroys, calicos, nankeens, serges and shalloons, camlets and grosgrams, East India cotton, Russia duck, crapes, callimancoes, huckabuck, ticking . . .

In the days that followed this conversation with Bono, I began to look about me with new eyes—that is to say, with eyes from which the scales had new-fallen, where bedazzlement was harsh and all about me; and I saw for the first time and understood that in our house and the houses we visited, there were black and white, bonded, freed, free-born, indentured, enslaved, and hired.

Perhaps I may be pardoned my naïveté; I was but eight, and had given little thought to service and recompense.

Knowing, now, that my mother and I had been purchased, I began to revolve the question, *For what purpose?*

And though the solution to this mystery was, to my young mind, occulted, yet did I know where it lay: behind the forbidden door. Thither—in spite of my fears—would I have to repair for answers.

No words can tell the agitation of my spirits occasioned by merely the thought of throwing open that portal and beholding the secrets of the gloomy closet within. Consider that on the door itself was pasted my visage, open-mouthed, above crossed bones. I fancied that, should I be discovered, I should be caged and tortured like the animals in the experimental chambers, burning compounds applied to my skin, incisions made near my eyes.

When I would pass the door in the morning, I would hesitate before it and regard its latch and its lock. I considered furtively when I might find occasion to slip into the room without detection. 03-01 and some of the other academicians repaired there with some frequency, and it was of utmost importance that they not discover me dabbling in their mysteries.

I found my opportunity one night when I knew them to be holding a dinner and entertainment for other wealthy men of the colony who protested Britain's yoke; that evening Mr. 03-01 and his brethren were to open their doors to a large company of prosperous merchants, doctors, lawyers, smugglers of Dutch tea and Madeira wine, owners of slave-ships, speculators in real estate, and colonial gentry who wished to give voice to their outrage and resist, as they said, the oppression of royal ministers and the bondage imposed upon them by Parliament. Well did I know that I would spend my evening in bed, from whence I could slip out, once they had begun their discussion in earnest and all ears were fixed upon the transports of incendiary disputation.

The chambers set aside for experiment were not lit at that hour. Though there were blankets over the cages, I could hear the animals stir as I passed by them, the floor creaking beneath my bare and chilled feet.

I stopped to watch the antics of the squirrels. They observed me in return. Their eyes were black as obsidian in the night. They stood upon their haunches.

"Play," I whispered, but they would not; their attentions were absorbed in my endeavor, as if they knew what was to come, and wished particularly to witness it.

I passed by them to the forbidden door. Over the lintel was affixed the ancient dragon's skull, its browning sockets gazing down the corridor.

On the door itself was the sketch of my own face.

I regarded it with that giddiness that comes of sin. I raised my hand and touched the metal latch, pressed it with my thumb, and found it, as I had suspected, locked; all the while hearing voices two rooms away which complained that Parliament would reduce honest men of business to the status of slaves.

In the days previous, I had observed the key used to open the door. It was a simple thing with but one tang. It was a matter of moments, then, for me to bend a wire so that I might motivate the tumblers of the lock and spring it open.

I lifted the elbow of the lock from the door's hasp. Face to face with the cartoon of my own infant anxiety, I lifted the latch, and opened the door, and beheld the secret chamber.

Perhaps I had expected masks and robes and all the imagined gimcrackery of cultism: bibs of animal teeth, screws for boring into the head, phials and plungers to extract and titrate the soul; perhaps, merely, I had wished for these things, knowing too well what I would find instead.

It was a small room, taken up mostly with a wide plank desk and three stools. On bookshelves were bound volumes with my name and my mother's embossed upon the spine beside a date; the dates stretching back to the time of my birth. Upon the wall, writ large, was a chart labeled "MAMMALIA—or, Beasts that Give Suck." And first upon it:

I. PRIMATES

MAN.	*HOMO.*
Sapient Man.	1. Homo Sapiens.
a. Wild Men.	a. Homo Feri.
b. American savages.	b. Homo Americani.
c. Europeans.	c. Homo Europæi.
d. Asiatics.	d. Homo Asiatici.
e. African savages.	e. Homo Afri.
f. Monsters.	f. Homo Monstrosi.
1. Dwarfish.	1. Alpini.
2. Gigantic.	2. Patagonici.
3. Mutilated.	3. Monorchides.
4. Beardless.	4. Imberbes.
5. Sharp-headed.	5. Macrocephali.
6. Flat-headed.	6. Plagiocephali.

HOMO SAPIENS—*KNOW THYSELF*

Below that, the primates continued in their course, each one named—the ape and the orangutan, the monkey—and then, the brutes, the *feræ,* the *glires,* all the beasts from sloth to pigmy shrew, arrayed silently in ordered cavalcade as if waiting admission to the Ark.

There was nothing, thus far, to affright. I had just leaned over to examine a print hung upon the wall, the figure of a woman unclothed, when I heard my name called. The painter, 07-03, was calling to the company, "He is not above-stairs!"

There was a cry of, "Music! We must have music!"

I ascertained that they wished me to perform, and it behove me to comply, that I might avoid detection. I backed out of the room, and had almost shut the door when my eyes fell again upon the engraving of the naked woman on the wall; and I saw that it was my mother.

"Octavian!" called 03-01. "Octavian? Your presence is cordially requested in the audience room! We have your violin!"

I stepped back into the forbidden chamber. I pulled the door shut behind me, and held my candle toward the print, viewing now more clearly than before her face, still and impassive, the close-cropped hair I rarely saw except concealed by wig or cap. I thought it strange that they should have a portrait of her here, especially in such a state of *dishabille*. Her portrait was entitled, "PLATE XVII. PUBESCENT FEMALE OF THE OYO COUNTRY IN AFRICA." I squinted, and edged my gaze down to her breasts, her stomach, the lines that marked her; which extended out from her prone form to letters worn like mechanical bouquets in the blank space where her image floated. She hung there corpse-like; her hands turned outwards, as, in paintings of Christ, he stands when with gentility he reveals to Thomas the holes torn in his side and palms.

"A puff of breath would have extinguished your candle," 03-01 chided, standing in the door—which now was wide open—behind me. I turned. He said, "A mere whisper across the flame. There could be no strategy simpler to pursue, nor so effective in delaying the punishment which is, as you are aware, contingent on your passing through this door."

I could not speak for awe of him.

He leaned back and shouted to the others, "I have found him! Proceed without us!" He stepped back into the chamber and shut the door behind him. "Set the candle down upon the desk," he said. "Sit upon a stool."

He sat beside me. He smiled faintly and watched my face. He said, "You have seen your mother." I did not reply. He offered, "In the illustration."

I could not look at him anymore. My spirits were so disarranged, my nerves so clamorous in their confusion, that no course of thought, speech, or action presented itself.

His breeches were satin. It was a fancy evening.

He sighed, and offered nothing. The candle guttered between us. From a far chamber, I could hear the conversation of vital men, men on whom depended the colony's well-being.

At length, he demanded, "Why have you trespassed here?"

"I wished . . . to know . . ."

"You know," he said, nodding. "You have already divined our purpose." He smiled. "In these volumes are recorded each bit of data that we have collected in the years since your mother came to live with us. Your height . . . your weight . . . your diseases . . . your sustenance both in its ingress and egress. Through the collection of such details, we hope to establish, in the broadest sense, the means by which children grow, the astounding systems of ingestion, decoction, and waste, the development of skills and the reception of ideas and language by the infant brain."

The embossed names on the volumes glowed faintly in the candlelight, the mother, the son, twinned in each passing month, and I thought of those months — playing at her knees; or her telling me tales of the Governor's wife and lap-dog, the barking, the stains, the hullabaloo of servants; I considered the nights of my childhood when she sat by my side and stared down upon me; and I recalled that earliest image, standing with her while men burned bubbles in the orchard like the ignition of cherubim. Such scenes as these, I had no doubt, were not extant in the volumes there, slipped between the quantification of my appetites; thus, I might read of the weight of peach cobbler I had eaten on a certain night when I was five, but not recall the blush of evening as I walked with her a half an hour later among the garden herbs.

I did not speak; instead, I meditated on the passage of time, and how it may be found in both a dry and a wet or gaseous state; how, though lush, it might be desiccated for storage.

"So you understand the experiment, then," said 03-01.

I grasped the edges of my stool. 03-01 had crossed his legs.

"That is not all, sir," I said.

"No," said 03-01. "That . . . is not all."

"Would you tell me, sir?"

"You know, Octavian."

I shook my head.

Mr. 03-01 frowned. "What did you revolve in your thoughts, during the long silence?"

"I was thinking of time, sir."

"I do not follow."

"How time has different states, like unto the elements."

"This is novel," said 03-01.

"And how it is become dried."

"You are a clever boy, though somewhat too obscure."

"Sir, you have not answered my question."

"Regarding?"

"Your work, sir," I said, "with me."

"True, I have not. You know what I shall say."

"Still, I am . . ." I spake no more.

He asked, "What would you know?"

"Why are we called by names, when all others have numbers?"

"For the reason that you are the experiment, and all the rest of this . . . the house, the guests, the servants . . . all are in service of that pursuit of truth. You are central to the work; we, but the disembodied observers of your progress."

"What do you propose to do with me?"

"You know the answer."

"Tell me, please, sir," I said.

He gave me a canny look, and explained slowly, "We are providing you with an education equal to any of the princes of Europe . . . We wish to divine whether you are a separate and distinct species. Thus, we wish to determine your capacity, as an African prince, for the acquisition of the noble arts and sciences."

"You wish to prove that I am the equal of any other?"

"We *wish* to prove nothing," said 03-01. "We simply aim at discovering the truth." He rose from his stool.

"Sir —"

"Stand," he said; which I did. "Put out your arms at your sides, straight," said he; which I did.

"Sir—," I said, "you shall be glad of my success?"

He smiled. "Of course I shall," he said. "You are a good boy."

I asked, "Shall I someday be called by a number?"

He looked fondly upon me. He said, "That, Octavian, is something to aspire to." He turned away from me, and began perusing the volumes upon the shelf, selecting some, drawing them out, and laying them in the crook of his arm.

I waited, my arms outstretched at either side, until he turned again, and began to stack them, volume after volume, on my hands.

"When I was a boy," said he, "this was my punishment. Standing with Milton weighing upon one hand and Shakespeare the other. But you . . . you shall be encumbered with your own past, hm?"

My hands bobbed beneath the weight.

"Drop one," he said, "and you shall be caned." He stepped out into the experimental chamber and shouted for Bono.

Turning back to me, he said, "Here, my boy, was the miraculous aspect of this little torture, as I found. When twenty minutes had passed, and I was permitted to set down the volumes, or they were taken from my hands—when I was relieved of the weight of the books—I marked that as I dropped my empty arms, they rose again of their own accord. . . . They drifted upwards. They felt as light as air. I could not keep them down. 'Twas an ecstatic sensation. . . . My arms yearned for the stance of punishment; and when they lifted thus, I could have been flying. This, you must understand, Octavian, is the true and sublime end of discipline: that you may rise into a new and glorious buoyancy."

And so the answer to my perplexities, which must appear in all its clarity to those who look from above, was finally clear to me: that I too was the subject of a zoological experiment.

I took new interest in the torpedo-fish with their crackling shocks; in the turtles that paced beside yardsticks; in the mice sliced end to end, that their gestation might be viewed.

They were my brethren.

As I parsed Latin sentences, I noted 03-01's interest in my progress. I knew that behind the forbidden door, he kept his records of what I did. There would be, someday, an article about me in the *Philosophical Ephemera of the Novanglian College of Lucidity*. My life, now, tended toward that moment.

Revolving my thoughts upon this curious state, I resolved thus: I would not fail 03-01. I would not fail my mother. I would prove the superior excellence of my faculties.

From that day, my studies took on a new intensity.

And I played the violin like a very devil.

Boston

March 10th, 1768

My dear Joan—

The packet-boat from New-York hath deposited me at long last upon *Boston* wharves; and now, being arrived at Mr. *Gitney's* establishment, I am like to remain for some weeks before I take my passage to *Calais*.

Heartily do I wish thou couldst see this household—its freaks and pranks and glories. The knowledge enshrined here is most luminous; but the extravagance is wearying, an outrage to God and man, especially when set amidst so pious a town, where the most finical youth buys his fopperies in brown and gray; and where, when a man whistles upon the street, it is a tune from Ainsworth's psalter.

Notwithstanding the noxious luxury of the College, I spent a most gratifying day in converse with the philosophers of this place before we set forth on a bold experiment: Inviting a gentleman to stand atop a platform of *rosin*, we electrified him, observing how pieces of gold-leaf he held upon a copper tray flew up to the fingertips of a man not yet imbricated by charge. Following this gratifying assay, we being shod in clogs of wax, a *battery* discharged shocks through wands we held and motivated metal filings, as

[*53*]

we sought to determine whether the particles of electro-ætherial flux were, in shape, triangular or lozenge.

In the evening, Mr. Gitney — who insists that we *enumerate* him 03-01 — held some fashion of *levee* for the Boston nobility, which hath lasted us near till dawn with music and a coati-mundi and another display of *electrical virtue* which tickled my palms and burnt my eyelashes to a frizzle. Chief among the pleasures was a most ravishing Negress, a Princess of *Africa,* who presided over the evening with a curious baton, like a Queen of the Djinns. Sigh not for jealousy, Mrs. Fruhling — she cast no eye upon me, and I made no overtures to that imperious individual, being of far too plain and low a stature for *Her Highness.*

Late in the evening, they arranged for her son, a solemn little article of eight or ten years old, to play the violin with his music-master and others in consort. He is a *beanpole* of a boy. Thou hast not heard fiddling, Joan, until thou hast heard this tiny *being,* legs thin as sumac twigs, produce such tones; which sweet music dazzled not merely in its display of speed and accuracy, but most in its gravity; the child being able to introduce an element of *melancholy* into even the liveliest of passages.

Of the glittering and outrageous train of that house, he was the least conspicuous; being dressed in dark, rich satins, and perpetually silent; and yet, among them all, amidst the revelry and the obscene antics of the poets and the coati-mundi, it was he who was the *wonder;* I would liefer speak to this boy for fifteen minutes than to some of their prating, babbling, atheistical horde for five hours together. I found an opportunity to exchange some words with him, the others rushing out into the yard, waxen clogs a-thumping, to place bets upon a battle royal between a mongoose and an asp.

I wish thou couldst have spoken to the child, as thou hadst drawn him out and set him at his ease; to me, he was civil, but so overwhelmed in humility he could barely converse. Howsoever humble he might be, a curious thing: When I looked upon him and spake with him, he would not meet my eyes with his; he stared fixedly at some point, and made his addresses as if to the air; but when no one looked upon him, he gazed upon us all with almost a *hungriness* in his assessment; as if memorizing the details of our dress and carriage and conversation; and chipping it unsmiling upon *tablets* so it might later be used to *damn* us at the end of Time, or at least *explain* us to some other Intelligence come after us.

I could not but think of Shadrach, Meshach, and Abed-nego, shortly to be consigned to the blast-furnaces of Nebuchadnezzar — captive *"children in whom was no blemish, but well favored, and skillful in all wisdom, and cunning in knowledge, and understanding science, and such as had ability to stand in the King's palace, and whom they might teach the learning and the tongue of the Chaldeans."*

Well might thou wonder how this vain household may continue in its expense and luxurious operations. I gained some little view of its financial arrangements when, late in the evening, Mr. *Gitney* asked me to consider a proposition; that he and his fellow Gitneys are joining with a consortium of Virginian gentlemen to purchase vast quantities of land from the *Indians;* which property they shall, once they own it, split up into smaller parcels and sell at profit to men of the middling sort wishing to head *West.*

I protested that making such purchases with the Indians, Parliament has disallowed in the strongest of *terms;* that we have been rebuked for annoying the Savages with our invasions and broken treaties; and to recall the heathen Pontiac, his terrible revenge; that we have late fought a war with the Savages over just such *encroachments;* and that the unfortunates who purchased said lots were likely, within two years, to succumb to *massacre* and retribution.

He rallied me upon my cowardice, and said that Parliament should never enforce their strictures against settling upon *Indian* territory; that property was property, and he was purchasing the land openly and without prejudice; that Americans should not be thwarted by the laws of ancient aristocracies, corrupt dukes, self-styled marquises and thanes; and that a friend in *Philadelphia* should be a great boon to the project, there being some *animosity* between Pennsylvania and Virginia in this matter.

Well canst thou imagine that I could not hazard our little portion on such a dangerous *business,* which venture can end only in financial ruin and the destruction of *Christians* by heathen tomahawk and the tricks of barbarous Deviltry. I should not be sorry, did the Lord sweep the savages further to the *west;* but I doubt His divine will shall ever be expressed through *Virginians.* They are not his especial people. Thus, Mrs. Fruhling, I joined no consortium, being content merely to observe the experiments here and engage in dispute about the nature of air.

I must retire from the scritoire; the frolic is over. It is now almost breakfast-time, the mongoose is being buried with full Catholic rites, and it appears Mrs. Ogilvy hath broken her jaw. She was, I fear, unaccustomed to waxen clogs.

I shall find a house of *prayer* as very soon as I can quit this place, so that I may remain

Thy devout and loving *husband*,

Matthias F.

Latin and Greek were taught me by Dr. Trefusis, 09-01, the aged *philosophe*. In his youth, he had been welcomed at the courts of Versailles and Sansouci. His knowledge was prodigious; his mastery of philosophic depths was total, though his notions were somewhat eccentric. He worked with me word by word, leaning over my shoulder as I parsed my way through Tacitus and Homer; which instruction must have seemed to him not unlike the sea-captain, who having braved the catastrophic blasts and giddy precipices of the mælstrom, and but skated to their side; having passed with expert haste through the clashing Simplegades; having sat in the sick green eye of the hurricane, surrounded by the hulking wrecks of other, less fortunate, fleets; now wades with a little nephew in the warm shallows, collecting trash and pretty bits of shell. He must have looked out to sea with his glass sometimes, and wished for the spray, and men with whom he could truly speak of the rigors of navigation.

With him did I read of the fall of empires and the rise of the gods from the darkness of eternal night. With him, I read Cicero's defense of murderers, and Suetonius's history of murderous kings; Plautus's comedies; Seneca's tragedies; Ovid on the art of love and Aristotle on the love of art.

I saw that emperors may have their day, but then, surrounded even by pomp and luxury, they may fall, and their cities be in ruin.

Dr. 09-01 had a kind, but gloomy, disposition. He only rarely cut my palms with his ferule for mistakes. He would, of an afternoon, smuggle up gingerbread from the kitchen, and would speak at length of Rome and Greece in their glory with his mouth full and spraying. He was exceeding lanky, and coiled himself in corners of the room, balled up silently and watching while I stuttered my construes.

Perhaps his gloom was due to his profession, that he lived among fallen empires, and in reading these languages that had not been spoken by the common man in centuries, he had all about him the ruins of language, evidence of toppled suburbs, grass growing among the mosaics, and voices that had been choked with poison, iron, age, or ash.

He was possessed of a belief that nothing existed, or to be more precise, that only when things were perceived could we be sure that they existed. He troubled himself in arguments, therefore, that when *he* was not in his chamber, and *no one else* was in his chamber, there was no one who could say *beyond a shadow of a doubt* that his desk still existed, no one to say that the candle still guttered by the bed; or that the bed had not simply frayed apart into atoms.

To combat this situation, he requested that one of the slaves periodically creep to his door when he was absent, and hurl it quickly open, to determine whether the desk remained, or whether, with no one to perceive it, it had simply given up and dissipated. When 03-01 protested that this was hardly worth the vigilance of busy servants, Dr. 09-01 took the task upon himself, and developed the habit of leaving company quite suddenly and charging above-stairs to his chamber, throwing the door open, and crying, "Ah ha!" He found, always, that matter had retained its dubious solidity in his absence; but this did not deter him.

Gradually, he developed the startling habit of entering rooms with a leap.

He maintained that we were surrounded by a vast shadow, a universal emptiness as wide and long as space, in which there were small molten bulbs of color and light, wheresoever there were beings to perceive them. He believed that as we walked, the world of objects unfurled before us like the painted scene for a play, turrets, and moats, and topiary aisles slapping down into place just before we would arrive.

Once, late at night, he roused me and took me to an empty room. I was somewhat afraid. The silence of the house was enormous.

He stood me with my back to the wall, one inch from the paneling. He stood next to me. We faced the same way.

"Sir," said I, "for what have you—," but he hissed, and I fell silent.

For a long while, we stared straight forwards, side by side, in

[60]

the empty room. It was a summer night, and the dogs of the town barked for a time, and then ceased. Still, we stood. Some ten minutes passed; then fifteen.

"Do you feel it, child?" he asked. "The wall is gone. Space is gone from behind us."

I could feel nothing.

He said, "All that is there now is the eye of God." He shivered. "The pupil is black, and as large as a world."

Dr. 09-01, among the academicians, stands above the rest in my recollection for his affection shown to myself and to my mother; also, in that regard, I remember fondly my music-master, 13-04.

The music-master was a young man, thin and clean, whose bright silk waistcoats belied the gravity of the rest of his vesture, which was black and brown. Now, upon reflection, I suspect that he did not have moneys sufficient to dress as he wished, and so settled for being but half-dandified. The effect was somewhat awkward—but I can say this only because my habiliments were paid for, and I was often dressed in silks; my frock-coats, as well as my waistcoats, tended to the florid before I had any choice in the matter. 03-01 chose such colors as he said offset the duskiness of my skin and tended towards picturesque effect.

13-04 had studied in Italy himself with the great masters. He taught my mother the art of playing the harpsichord, and, when I was four or five, began to tutor me on the violin. Together, we played not only the music of the moment, but music of the past, which I grew to love, though it was unfashionable. We played the sonatas of Mr. Handel and Dr. Boyce, of Locatelli, Tartini, and Gluck. My especial favorites were those autumnal sonatas of Signor Corelli, which had made such a stir in the century previous. We played them in the evenings as the sun set over the steeples of Boston, casting broad, brazen rectangles of light across the fraying rugs. We spun out the somber passages, our violins singing one to the other as my mother played upon the harpsichord, and perhaps this is as much of her sadness and joy as I shall know.

As I have been told, one evening when I was very young, Mr. 13-04 was lingering below-stairs, discussing harmonics and Pythagoras with 03-01 and 09-01, when he heard my mother singing me some lullaby from her homeland through an open door.

None of them spake. They sat, unmoving, while she sung, and then, without excusing himself, 13-04 rose and rushed above-stairs, and sought her out along the corridors.

He asked if she could recall other songs of her race. She had been gone then but two years, perhaps, and could. He asked her whether she would sing them for him, and allow him to write them down, so that they might not be lost. In this, she agreed.

I do not believe, had he asked her even a year later, she would have given her assent. As I have said, there was a reluctance in her to speak of the kingdom of her birth, or to allude in any way to knowledge of its practices; and this reluctance grew swiftly in the years of my childhood.

[63]

So, as I understand it, in exchange for his lessons on the harp-sichord, she sang him the songs of her homeland — my homeland, if my homeland were not these drab and rocky coasts, these marshes, these plains cut flat from forest for the growing of corn.

I cannot doubt that at first his interest in her songs was forensic, nothing but fodder for an article to be published in a forthcoming issue of the *Philosophical Ephemera of the Novanglian College of Lucidity*. As he listened to her Africk monodies, though, their unaccountable rhythms, their outbursts and their alien allusions, he grew passionate about them, and would often importune her to sing them again; which she did not, after she reached the age of sixteen or seventeen. She would always demur, saying, "You would not hear those olden, shrieking things."

"From your lips," he said, "even a shriek would be the very call of the nightingale."

"And a howl," she said, behind her fan, "like the song of the tit-mouse."

"You mock me, Mademoiselle."

"Don't tire me, sir. We'll sing something about cheeks, roses, and the garden swing."

On one occasion, 13-04 took me aside and requested that I try to coax her to sing the songs in private, and record them in my memory. I was perhaps eight.

That night, when I was brought into her presence before my bedtime, I asked her if she would sing for me. She said she would, one song, one aria for her darling son — which reply made the men in the sitting-room murmur, "Ah! Music!" and clap. She bowed her head before them graciously. She asked me for a request, and I said I would hear the royal songs of Oyo.

"You have been, I see, speaking to Mr. 13-04."

I remained silent.

"Have you not?"

I said not a word.

"Come along with me. To your bedchamber." She turned to the scholars, and said, "You must excuse my absence, sirs; if I favor this young gentleman above you, it is only because he wants manners you have already been taught. And he is prettier." She kissed me coyly upon the forehead. I was sensible of danger in the air. She was trembling with anger.

"Mademoiselle," said one, in the dry and oft-repeated jest, "to see you depart from our circle is to see the sun cast off its planets and roam. What shall we, massy bodies, do, left bereft?"

She pressed me towards the door. "You flatter me, sir. If there is any wayward *sun,* it is this boy here. Move along, Mungo." She snapped me at the base of my wig.

As we left, they clapped at her jest.

When we got to my bedchamber, her smile was gone. She helped me off with my frock-coat and sat me down. "Tonight," she said, "a reading from the Book of Psalms." And she drew down my Bible from the shelf, leafed through with her thin fingers, and began to recite:

> *"By the rivers of Babylon, we sat down and wept, when we remembered thee, O Zion. On the willows there, we hung up our harps, for they that carried us away captive required of us songs, saying, 'Sing us one of the songs of Zion.'*

[65]

How can we sing the songs of the Lord in a foreign land?"

She removed my wig, and laid her hand on my bare scalp. Then she continued:

"If I forget thee, O Jerusalem, let my right hand wither.

If I do not remember thee, let my tongue cleave to the roof of my mouth; if I prefer not Jerusalem above my chief joy.

O daughter of Babylon, you devastator! Happy shall be he who requites you with what you have done to us!

Happy shall be he who takes your little ones and dashes them against the stone."

Her hand was spread on my bald scalp like a compass rose; and I was astounded, and did not know what country lay there described.

Shed no tear for me; for I shed none for myself.

I should find it mortifying in the highest degree if those hearing of my childhood believed this record to be one of complaint; and if, swayed by some description of my circumstances, their hearts melted without cause, due more to the novelty of my situation than its rigors.

When I review this epoch, however it may seem to others, to me it appears a period of singular bounty; for having seen what I since have seen, I recognize how merciful Providence was in supplying me with luxuries: the sumptuous foods upon the table, the glory of music, the gift of literacy, the opportunities to survey the advancement of learning; but more than these, I look about me now — notwithstanding the terrors I have seen — and I declare it well befits me to thank our God for simpler pleasures than these, than teak or gold or India cloth. Daily, in my youth, should not I have fallen upon my knees and thanked Him who died for us upon the Cross for the warmth of kindled fires, for the freedom to swing my hands in the air? Should I not have praised Him for the liberty to open doors and pass through them, for the escape from drudgery, and most, my mother's hand to hold?

I consider those numberless of our race huddled beneath the rudest of roofs, lying amidst brackish water, skulls abuzz with sickness, knowing that tomorrow they shall rise and shall labor at some pitiless industry—those who have not had the blessings of warmth or liberty or family or friend—reduced to animal want and groans—and then I turn from my sufferings as mere trifles. I was fed and clothed in silks.

And know I did not weep then for myself; I did not know how one might. I looked upon my being as did those who raised me; I accounted myself an experimental subject to be observed and noted; and even within me, in my moments of sorrow or fear, there were two discourses: one which cried, and one which recorded that cry without compassion; one intelligence which wished warmly for an embrace; and the other which did not grant it and did not speak, but Observed, watchful, hands folded, inactive, and stylus at the ready.

If one massy Eye regarded me coldly from behind my back, it was my own.

O9-01 and 13-04, eager to show me things outside the compass of my poor experience, would of a time take me to an oyster house or the court-house or a drilling of the regiments, that I might see the commerce of the world.

It was Dr. 09-01's way to use all that we gazed upon as a lesson, and so demonstrate to me that knowledge and inquiry curled larval in all matter, awaiting release. As we passed the shipyard where the loftsmen raised the shape of a hull according to the measurements of a model, he taught me the secret of numerical proportions and scale. As we watched sailors and stevedores laboring up and down gangplanks, unloading cargo, or men and women smoking their pipes before shops that lined the wharf, or the haggling in the marketplace at Faneuil Hall, he posed me questions about expense, or told me of the trade of wood or molasses.

As we walked through the evening crowds, he was often distracted by activity, and countered my many holiday questions with enigmatical answers, as was often his wont. When I asked why time moved forward, he answered, "Because we have eyes on the front of our heads"; when I asked why we clung to the Earth, he answered, "Because the Earth tries so hard to hurl us off"; and when, my hand clinging to his cuff, I asked him why he was not a father, he answered, "Because there are many uses for sheeps' guts."

I asked him about color, and of what it consisted; and he told me that color—brown, black, white—resides in the eye of the beholder; that it does not inhere in the object itself, any more than pain dwells in the needle. So we spake as we walked amongst the servants purchasing their masters' dinners at the market.

Those were not easy times, in that city; the signs of disquiet were everywhere apparent. Soldiers were constantly among us, dispatched from far corners of the Empire to watch us; they did not stand easy upon the street corners, but stood in groups of two or three, their red coats bright in the bitter, falling snow, blowing upon their hands near hostile alleys; and they watched carefully those who passed, and they whispered jibes about the girth of fat men, the staleness of widows, and the bosoms of girls.

On some summer nights, when it was hot and the atmosphere itself seemed cut with anger—the buzzing of the cicadas in the trees of the avenue harsh with it, broiling—on those nights, we could hear mobs go by in the streets, issuing out from the docks. There were riots there, and men tumbled off the piers, pushed by crowds; wealth would not deign to pass through those quarters, for fear of what was yelled and what was thrown.

I gave little thought to the debates regarding taxation by our Parliament. When the King's ministers demanded that the Colonies pay the costs of the Indian and French wars, wherein the armies of our nation had fought with such abandon in my extreme youth to secure our borders from, as they said, the incursions of savagery, I had no memory of the conflicts, and no property with which to pay, and so taxation or no seemed all the same to me. I little could comprehend the ire these measures raised. I did not understand the complaints of Mr. 03-01 and his merchant brothers, uncles, nephews, and cousins, the others in the 03 series.

I did not understand the nonimportation compacts which my countrymen in their anger had raised against English products. I did not understand the measures some took against merchants who still carried British goods.

I did not understand the cries of "Liberty and Property!"

I did not understand when I saw a dry-goods store which had been besieged: the windows broken, the bolts of cloth lying half-unraveled out in the slush while rain fell upon them and the curtains blew out of the casements. The draper sat upon the cobbles of the street, his hair lank, and a daughter of perhaps my age wandered about through the wreckage, picking up silks and attempting to drag them back inside.

I did not understand when I saw boys urinating on the stone stoop of the store while men stood about and approved their micturation.

"Higher, boy," said one. "Write 'Tyranny' upon the door."

I did not understand these scenes of strife. I did not understand why men were hanged in effigy, or a boat dragged through town and burned on the Common, as if on grassy swells. I did not understand why a man dressed in a grinning mask rode through the streets publishing forth elegant threats—this last being a figure of our town's Pope's Day, who rode on an ass accompanied by imps, whistling high and eerie to draw rowdy boys from their sheds. I was told he was called Joyce Jr., and that he was a lord of chaos, possessed by the spirit of him who had cut off the crowned head of the King of England in the days of Cromwell. I understood none of these prodigious things.

I did not comprehend that my own domestic scene was threatened by these tumults; that Mr. 03-01 kept us in our finery and excellent foods through revenues from trade and speculation, and that these were suffering grievously. His young nephews and cousins—a brood of Gitneys he called "The Young Men"—would come to dine with grim faces. They brought word of ships waylaid for smuggling by Customs men, goods that could no longer be imported, and sundry losses.

The merchants of Boston had for some decades made some portion of their fortunes through smuggling, the Young Men of the Gitney family being, in this respect, no exception. In their circle, it was held to be no disgrace to import goods illegally, but rather sharp practice was accounted a sign of canny business acumen. They cursed Parliament roundly for interference in their business.

I did not understand that these interviews, so tedious to the young, did not simply regard numbers, but extended to the table we ate around, the excellent paneling on the walls, the paintings that looked down upon us.

Blithely, I believed business was not my business.

What I did understand was that there was a movement abroad

for liberty from oppression and from bondage; and that the promise of such a struggle could not but dilate the honest heart with hope and excite the spirits with the taste of future felicities; and in some hours, when I heard this discussed at table loudly or in whispers by the kitchen hearth, my frame trembled with the possibility that God worked His mighty will for all of us through these unrests, and that soon, the bondage I but little understood that encompassed Bono and my mother and so many others of my acquaintance should melt away, and kindness be found in the hearts of men; and that we should then have our own *soirées,* and tears be put behind us, and we should, if we wished, sail back to Africa to visit those I had never known, and we would work in our own fields, in our own shops, on our own wharves; and most, that we should have final proof that the human was made in love for the operations of magnanimity and fairness, reason and excellence, and that we all, unfettered by passions, could work together for the perfection of man.

One evening, Dr. 09-01 took me to walk up and down Long Wharf. We saw the schooners at rest in the Bay, and Castle William upon its island, the militia just visible as they made rounds upon the battlements.

We stood in the shadows of a ropewalk and observed the men dragging their cranked engines up and down the long corridor, twisting fibers into cord. He whispered, "They walk some ten miles a day along this track, half of it backwards. Note that man there. He is perhaps approaching my great antiquity. If he is, let us say, seventy, and has worked here since he was fifteen years of age, drawing rope six days a week, how many miles has he walked?"

I having little strength in calculation at that age, Dr. 09-01 led me through the steps to a solution, which was some one hundred and seventy thousand miles. While he spake, we walked outside into the dusk and made our way through the streets.

I asked Dr. 09-01 how far it was around the Earth.

He considered. "We have estimated some twenty-five thousand miles."

I tallied upon my fingers. "Then," ventured I, "in that man's life, he has walked backwards around the Earth three and a half times?"

Dr. 09-01 was very pleased with this, and laughed, tugging upon my lapel, saying, "Indeed! Or a third of the way to the moon!"

I delighted in the thought of the man plowing backwards through the seas, the cord stretched before him, or stalking the deserts of Cathay or the Indian jungles, oblivious to tigers, pausing for his tobacco in the shadow of some heathen shrine or suspended near a mountain peak.

At this time, our discourse was interrupted by the rattle and squeak of a cart upon the dirt of the alley; which conveyance rolled before us, a strange and distracting pageant: Pulled by two silent boys, their heads bowed, the wagon had in it a large, balled form of black char, heaving, furred patchily in white; an obscene form that lolled upon the cart; and amidst its cracked and gory surface, caked with feathers, I saw a reddened eye which seemed quick.

The cart came to rest before us; upon which, the boys raised their heads and to the closed, tight doors around us hollered, "Liberty cart!"

The mass shifted and moaned, and, my curiosity enflamed to no small degree, I asked my mentor, "What is it?" and he replied, "It is John Withers, a Customs Inspector."

I had no time to assemble the tortured frame into human organization—the cracked, tarred surface; the red, gaping mouth; the fingers that clutched and crawled across the stinking, feathered skin—before a door opened and a man came out with a length of wood, bowed before the boys, shook hands with them both, and moving to the side of the cart, began to beat the miserable creature where it lay.

The Customs Inspector made some enfeebled attempt to roll away from the blows, but was hindered in its retreat by the extreme pain of its burns from the tar and the utmost necessity of keeping its legs clenched and its hand across its privities, which were otherwise exposed, a mass of tar clumped about the pudendo and pubes.

The legs were so bruised beneath their integument that even the light blows served upon them made the man scream, at which his tormentor cried, "D'you sing 'Mercy,' royal nightingale?" to which the wretch howled inarticulate assent.

One of the boys raised his head and twittered, "Philomel. Philomel."

I was gone Observant, my body rigid; and Dr. 09-01 had his arm about me, and was with great effort trying to turn me away, though my gaze remained locked upon the awful spectacle.

I could say nought but, "What has he done, sir?"

My mentor murmured in Latin, "We Americans are not fond of the customs duties. We do not appreciate taxation."

"What," I asked, "are customs duties for?"

He answered almost too quickly for me to translate, "These? For the Crown's protection against the French and for the extermination and rout of the Indians so we might settle. We forget men must be paid to kill. Even an act as simple as leveling a village is costly; rapine is not cheap; and children, I am afraid, will not burn themselves."

The man stopped with his beating and turned. "What did ye say, sirrah?" The man stepped closer, brandishing his hickory. "Ye speak a pretty tongue."

"'Twas Greek, sir," Dr. 09-01 lied. "I was telling the boy that according to Plato, man is defined," he said, smiling affably and gesturing to the cart, "as a featherless biped with broad nails, receptive of political philosophy."

When I was eleven years of age, an event transpired that changed considerably the course of things at the College of Lucidity.

Lord Cheldthorpe, 02-01, who had for some years given graciously to 03-01 so that he might continue his studies and publish them forth to the world, had died. The effect of this death, though in a bedchamber some three thousand miles away, was great, beyond the natural depression of spirits produced in the breast of any human creature endowed with sympathy at the news of another slipping from daylight, from the realm of reason and the theater of motion, back into the obdurate chaos of uncreated night, into which we all eventually shall tumble.

The death of Lord Cheldthorpe came as a doubly heavy blow to the house of Gitney, the College of Lucidity, because on him did we all rely for a great many funds necessary for the continuance of our philosophical ventures. It was he who paid for various of the apparati, he who had overseen the publication of the findings of 03-01's society, he who had circulated those findings among the members of the Royal Society in London and, in Paris, the Académie Royale des Sciences.

Lord Cheldthorpe died without issue. His title would have lapsed, had His Highness the King not seen fit to name a nephew as the new Lord Cheldthorpe, and so create the title again anew.

03-01 did not know this nephew. He importuned the man, however, to visit the Province of Massachusetts Bay and see what his late uncle had funded. 03-01 promised the new Lord Cheldthorpe that, upon coming to our shores, he should not simply have an opportunity to inspect the experimental facilities at the Gitney house; but he should also be introduced to various schemes that would assure him income equal to that taken from his sugar plantations in the islands.

In writing his letter to this new Lord Cheldthorpe, 03-01 seemed most sanguine about the prospects of His Lordship's acquiescence and imminent financial gain. Privately, however, the impending visit of this nobleman, upon which hung so many of the house's fortunes, depressed 03-01's spirits as much as it agitated his nerves. When he heard that Lord Cheldthorpe would be arriving a few weeks hence, he spent days rushing from room to room, his gown sweeping behind him, waggling his hands rapidly before him.

He ordered that I be bought a new bag-wig, and my mother a whole series of costly dresses *à la mode du beau monde.*

At dinner, he instructed all of us, "You shall all show the greatest deference to His Lordship the Earl of Cheldthorpe. He is a young and energetic person, and shall be most interested in our endeavors. For those of you enthusiastic about my system of organizing human families metrically, he is numbered 02-06."

The house was cleaned meticulously against his arrival: Fittings were shined; the front path was repaved.

On the day that a runner finally came to the door to say that Lord Cheldthorpe had at last arrived in Boston-town, we were hurriedly dressed in our finery and brought down to the front hall to meet him.

He was a tall, loose-jointed man, perhaps thirty years of age, baronial in his stride, with a nose that spoke of Roman blood and eyebrows so blond they were almost white against the red of his skin. He looked a patrician and an adventurer.

When he entered, we all bowed low in courtesy.

"Welcome, My Lord," said 03-01, "to the Colonies."

"You are a man of deep science," said Lord Cheldthorpe. His voice was young and potent. "One puts a question before you: One had, as a kind of pet aboard the ship, a one-legged seagull. One was charmed by its sense of balance when the ship rocked. Would there be a way that one could attract it to this house? It, specifically?"

03-01 speculated, "Were we to ... spread garbage upon the roof, we would likely attract quite a number of ... seagulls ... but there is no guarantee ... My Lord ... that one should be your especial friend."

"We tried to knock it over by throwing lead-shot and failed." His Lordship made a hurling motion. "The bird was nimble."

"I see, My Lord."

"Could one attract it to one's side, one could keep it upon one's shoulder, and call it Hector, and it would be a fine, fine thing."

"Indeed, My Lord," said 03-01. "My very thought. . . . Perhaps you might give me some time to consider a solution? In the meantime, allow us to conduct you into our company, so you might meet our academicians."

We went into the parlor, and the men gathered about His Lordship. I remained near the door, standing, my hands folded before me.

He went immediately to my mother. He took her hand.

"Princess Cassiopeia," said 03-01, "may I present My Lord the Earl of Cheldthorpe?"

Cheldthorpe kissed my mother's hand. "Princess," he said, meeting her eyes, and then, to 03-01, corrected him, saying, "By the ancient and excellent rules of heraldry, having been newly created Lord Cheldthorpe in my late uncle's stead, I am to be referred to as Lord Cheldthorpe of the New Creation."

"My Lord of the New Creation, it is our pleasure to greet you," said my mother, spreading out her dress and sitting. "And we welcome you to Eden."

Thus it was that almost in the first instant of their meeting, my mother and Lord Cheldthorpe began some flirtation, which I greeted with the same admixture of acceptance and incomprehension with which I observed most of the familiarities and designs of adults.

My mother would play upon the harpsichord, and he would lie upon the sofa, tapping his hand out of time.

My mother, with colors and an elaborate quill, would be sketching some fantastical bird that even the adoring eyes of a son could see looked like nothing so much as a sirloin steak with a drill for a head.

Lord Cheldthorpe would stand by her, admiring over her shoulder. "Your Highness," he would say, "it breathes. Stop my vitals—I fear if you make it any more lifelike, it will flit off the page."

"You flatter me, sir."

"Hardly, Your Highness. I am startled at the number of your accomplishments."

"My Lord," she replied, "if, in your eyes, I seem accomplished, it is only because by your side, I reflect the luster of your own manifold achievements."

He laughed. "Oh—Princess."

"Milord?"

"Oh, Princess."

"Oh, Milord.... Octavian," said my mother, "stop breaking my crayons."

"I'm not breaking," said I. "I'm drawing."

"'Drawing' is not snapping crayons and hurling them across the room."

I said, "It's the volcano Vesuvius in the very height of its eruption. That's how you draw magma."

"Now that is a demme fine volcano," said Lord Cheldthorpe, squatting down by me.

I said, "It rained ash upon the living and the dead. And gasses came out that were killing."

"Indeed," said my mother, swatting my hand. "Killing my red."

"The Elder Pliny died of them."

Lord Cheldthorpe said, "Faugh! He is an astonishing child. The astonishing child of an astonishing mother."

"Oh," said my mother, "there is no true substitute for a Classical education."

After a few such sessions as these, Lord Cheldthorpe concluded that he should like to extend his stay before moving down the coast to see the Carolinas. He and Mr. 03-01 and several other of our academicians spake about possible endeavors.

They hit upon a plan. We saw that tents were purchased, and there was talk of provender, and transportation cases for the astronomical instruments. We did not know what these things signified.

One night, 03-01 called together several of the most select among the College, and outlined the venture further: "My friends, as many of you are doubtless sensible, this summer, a most remarkable celestial conjunction shall occur . . . the Transit of Venus. It is an astrological phenomenon we have long wished to observe . . . for it provides us an opportunity to calculate the Earth's distance from our sun. As Venus crosses the face of Sol, we may time its crossing and, by so doing, produce data for triangulation.

"At this moment, we are granted a unique opportunity to pursue this observation, My Lord Cheldthorpe agreeing to fund a voyage into the forests of northern New-York, that we might record a significant westerly account of the conjunction. Thus, first, we shall be able to observe clearly the Transit, which shall not occur again in our lifetimes. Second, My Lord 02-06, if I may call him so, is an avid sportsman, and in the wilds of New-York he shall find plenty of scope for unusual chases and kills. Finally, we may hope the charm and pleasure of such an excursion, in such excellent company, shall interest My Lord Cheldthorpe in our continuance.

"We hope to triumph upon three heads, therefore, introducing His Lordship to opportunities in the New World for profit, for pleasure, and for unparalleled scientific progress."

Thus we headed off into the wilderness, a company of philosophers, painters, and poets, with but a few servants to carry our tents and our supplies. 03-01, fathoming how interesting was my mother's presence to Lord Cheldthorpe of the New Creation, bade her come along as well; which invitation she was not at liberty to refuse, though the way would be rough for a gentlewoman and the provender indelicate.

After we had traveled a week, and some hundred miles, we met Druggett, Mr. 03-01's correspondent in the Indian territories; and he, with a few other guides drawn from his circle of acquaintance, led us onwards; halting the progress of the train only so that Mr. Druggett, who still wore the bandage wrapped around his skull, could endeavor to show Lord Cheldthorpe some sport with their fowling-pieces, bringing down ducks to be roasted by the company in the evenings.

Mr. Druggett acted also as our envoy to the Iroquois, requesting passage from them and explaining that we came but to view the sun and the planets. This perplexed them somewhat, as they said that the sun shone in all quarters, and could be as well observed in Boston; but it was no more nonsensical than most of what the white man did; and so they bid us to pass to the place staked out by Mr. Druggett for our exercises.

Two Iroquois rode with us to secure our safe passage. They did not speak much; the one, because he knew not our tongue; the other, because he did not have much he wished to convey.

He did, one night, question Bono, the other whispering to him in their language. "He asks," the man explained, "whether you know a valiant man of your hue named Cato Williams, who fought against us in the late war."

Bono shrugged his shoulders. He said, "Everyone is named Cato Williams."

The Iroquois nodded. "The likelihood was small."

Two mornings later, they were gone when we arose.

At length, we reached our proposed camp near Lake Champlain, not without some slight mishaps not worth recording.

The scene was such as could only inspire us with a greater sense of the remarkable majesty of Nature. The catalogue of trees alone was tremendous, lush in its variety: the white pine, the birch, the hemlock, the sumac, the elm . . . all of these situated on rocks and in hollows that, to a boy of my years, spake of great adventure — perhaps adventure executed while squinting and crawling on the belly. Down the slope from our encampment lay

Lake Champlain, where I vowed I should learn to swim before we finished our business with the planet Venus and returned to the city.

We erected our tents while Lord Cheldthorpe and Druggett rode about the paths through the wildwood, calling to one another and firing. Lord Cheldthorpe burst into the clearing and declared, "Mr. Gitney! Mark this, sir — mark this: I will down a bull moose for you and your academy before we strike camp."

Bono looked up from the tent stake we were driving into the ground. "Mercy in a jug," he swore. "I never seen a man so taken with aim and velocity."

Dr. 09-01 agreed. "It must be delightful to be so pleased simply to have one thing hit another thing."

"Off we go, Druggett!" called Cheldthorpe. "These forests shan't stay virgin for long!"

Bono said, "Good to see a man who don't need the Carnival in Venice, just so long as he's got a live squirrel and a pile of squash to huck."

Mr. 03-01 and his colleagues soon set to work unpacking the astronomical instruments, and, once they had, they busied themselves taking the latitude and longitude of our situation so that they might better calculate the parallax described by the Transit of Venus across the face of the sun, and, following that, might with more accuracy triangulate with others' observations of the same phenomenon, and arrive at last at a calculation of those awesome distances between our Earth and its roasting benefactor.

When I was not laboring with Dr. 09-01 over my lessons or observing the calculations made by Druggett and Mr. 03-01 for the purposes of surveying the site, I sat with my mother, who strove even in this mean setting to retain some semblance of her royal bearing, though all of us were hot and beset upon by mosquitoflies. Bono, Dr. 09-01, and I took to slapping them in rhythm, and

Bono, having slain one, ran about the tent, pinching it between his fingers and crying, "Mark this, Gitney! Mark this: Another trophy to hang in your academy! Post-haste, record the wingspan!"

My mother laughed at his jest, and seemed to agree that Cheldthorpe was a prancing fool; yet she did not shun any opportunity to converse with His Lordship; nor did she make an unfavorable impression upon that lively individual, having all the graces of intellect, as well as the beauties of her person, at her command. She did not avoid him when he returned, slicked with sweat, from the hunt; she did not excuse herself when over wine by the campfire His Lordship told his tales of what the day had brought. I saw by her gaze that she did not find his person unattractive.

I could well determine that Mr. 03-01, far from disapproving of this match — conducted though it was in a situation far removed from propriety — was desirous of its success, perhaps even more ardently than either of the actors in the drama.

One evening when I passed by Mr. Gitney's tent, I heard him speaking of this to my mother; and I paused, listening, as on the other side of the bare canvas, he said quietly, "I've been pleased to remark that you and His Lordship have struck up such a friendship." There was a silence while he waited for my mother to respond. She did not. He continued: "What is the . . . nature of your friendship?"

"It is a friendship, nothing more."

"Are the sentiments on your part genuine? Or do you entice him for gain?"

She laughed. "This interrogation is absolutely outrageous."

"I have no objection to Your Highness using your charms and wiles for your own private ends. I only ask that you do whatever you can to foster his continued involvement in our philosophical household."

My mother said lazily, "There is a professional title for what you are doing."

"Touch his hand. The back of the wrist. Breathe too closely to his face. All marks of desire. We have found that affection causes the pupil of the eye to dilate involuntarily."

"Sir —"

"I am not jesting. This flirtation is a boon, an unexpected gift. Foster it, Mademoiselle. Do you understand?"

Something was dropped within the tent. They moved on the grass. Startled from my reverie, I slipped onwards.

I wish she had spoke to me, and told me what it was that budded there in the clearing by the lake.

When I was not near the clamor and drollery of Bono and Dr. 09-01, I found myself Observant, like an eye, and could feel no more than that — was sensible only of my gaze upon my mother and His Lordship as they met and bandied about their pleasantries. Each night, I lay awake, waiting until I heard her retire to her mattress to sleep before I allowed myself slumber. I listened through the canvas as she whispered long hours with His Lordship, though words I could not divine, merely the hissing sibilants of collusion and intimacy.

I could not but note that Lord Cheldthorpe suffered my mother to address him not in the forms of humility, as a servant should, pleading, "Your Lordship"; rather she "My Lord"-ed him as might a princess. This was further mark of his regard.

So anxious was Mr. 03-01 to secure Lord Cheldthorpe's favor, that one evening, when the company had drunk a great deal, he invited the assembled to dance, looking particularly to my mother and His Lordship of the New Creation. The two of them dancing could not have presented a more charming scene, turning as they did upon the greensward, with the blue gloaming seeping through the pines behind them and the empty sky above, lit by the frisking fireflies against the black trunks; they could not have performed their steps more elegantly, or spun more sweetly, even when the music sped to a furious pace, skittering wildly, so that it could not have offered a reasonable beat to any but a raging Corybante dance-horde, drugged and frenzied before rending the flesh of fleeing men.

"Octavian," said my mother. "My dear? Might you observe the beat? You rush."

I stopped playing and set the violin down from my chin.

"You needn't cease, dearest," said my mother. "I merely request that you maintain an easier beat."

Lord Cheldthorpe took up her hands again. They waited. I played a few squawling fanfares. I said, "I fear the humidity has un-tuned me."

My mother turned to me. I watched to see the mask, and if it would lift. "Octavian," she said coldly, "don't be a child."

There was a silence.

"But," said 09-01, "he is a child."

"He has never been a child," my mother said, "and I see no reason he should begin now."

And yet—I malign her. O vain, treacherous, self-anguishing heart: Recall instead how, on other evenings, she and you chased fireflies, Lord Cheldthorpe clapping.

Recall her decorating cakes near the refracting telescope, her dress in the wind.

Recall how she could draw the birds to her with butter and song.

So we pursued our duties and pleasures while the end of May came. While in Boston, the Redcoats marched the streets and mustered on the Common; and washerwomen listened at doors for British plans; and boys bruited in the streets the names of those who consorted with the Crown officials; and merchants who sold British goods found their shops deserted of custom, or molested with rocks; while that hot summer first warmed the lakes and prompted the activities of flies, we reclined and disported ourselves by Lake Champlain.

It was a happy day when Lord Cheldthorpe, as if in answer to my unspoken wish, approached me and inquired whether I would like to learn how to swim. I agreed, and, as the days went on, delighted in the lessons. My mother watched, smiling, from shore.

I recall the thought: *He knows the way to her heart is through me.* And this, rather than causing me distress, that I might be used for the man's amorous ends, filled me with great pleasure and pride. *He knows well the way to her heart is through her son. Her son is the thing that makes her happier than any other thing.* I entertained the thought again and again; I broke the surface smiling, and gasped for air.

Bono watched the swimming lessons from on shore, too, and now there was no jest about him.

One night, as I prepared for bed, I said to him, "You wish to learn how to swim?"

He said nothing, but straightened the queue on my wig where it hung upon its stand.

"I have seen you watching," I said.

"You can't tell when a man will need to swim." He ceased with the wig; he looked at me, perplexed. "Do you understand none of this?"

Now it was I who did not respond.

He simply said, "D'you see? There are channels."

I did not see, for which I now sometimes curse myself.

I grew to find Lord Cheldthorpe's company more agreeable. His attentions elevated me to a position of unusual importance. I went with him on the hunt, even, and watched him bring down a doe. I lay by her body, sensible still of the shock of the gun's report. I remarked to him upon the prominence of the veins that crossed her cheeks, which I followed with a finger.

Sitting once on the rocks as we dried from swimming, he asked me, "Do you not find it somewhat strange to have your fæces weighed and recorded?"

"No, Your Lordship," I answered meekly.

He rolled his hand in the air. "Proceed," he invited.

I said, "It was stranger when I discovered others didn't have theirs weighed. I thought they must be very uncertain."

"Uncertain."

"They should never know how much they consumed, and how much they wasted."

"You are not the usual biscuit, are you?" he said, lying back and drawing his shirt across his loins.

Though day, the crickets called in the grass; my mother's singing rose from the camp. I lifted my arms; I could not help it. The breeze itself was warm; the islands soft with moss; the loons calling melancholy in forgotten bays; and Life in all its operations seemed unspeakably generous.

Shortly after two o'clock on June 3rd, 1769, Venus descended into the plane of the ecliptic and came between the Earth and sun. It is with awe that I treat of the event — so minute, so silent here upon the Earth — but there — one can scarce imagine the roaring of that vast orb through those frigid depths, tumbling, flung through the plane of our orbit; the glaring heat, the searing glare of Sol — and the gargantuan prodigality of that body, consuming its own substance ceaselessly while planets whirled like houris, veiled and ecstatic around the throne of some blast-turbaned, light-drunken king.

We lunched on a cold collation of duck and mutton shortly after noon; then betook ourselves to the instruments to observe the Transit. We had panes of smoked glass to peer through; and, for more precise accuracy, a refracting telescope trained upon a piece of paper, so that the image was cast down upon it. The day was not without its clouds, which Mr. 03-01 cursed; but though they passed over, they did not continually obscure the face of the sun, and so, when the fateful moment arrived and Venus made its first external contact, 03-01 could mark the moment with exactitude.

"Yes — first external contact," he said, and Dr. 09-01, standing near the pendulum clock, noted the time. "It should now be about eighteen minutes before the planet is fully within the sun's disk." Mr. 03-01 squinted through a piece of glass. "My boy — we are on the lap of history. . . . This Transit happens but twice in this century. . . . If we are to derive use from it, it must be now. . . ." He continued speaking while ducking his head, shifting his legs, looking always at the sun, which cast odd spidery reflections across his face. "The last Transit — *anno* 1761 — was observed the world over . . . men standing aloft and squinting at the sun . . . in Lapland . . . in Africa, your native land . . . in Petersburg, Russia . . . in . . . where else? . . . in the East Indies, by order of the East India Company . . . in Tobolsk, which is the capital of the country of Siberia. . . . Across the world, look you, right now, men are standing on promontories . . . raising their glasses to the heavens . . . writing down figures. . . . My boy — we are a tiny race . . . involved in a vast pursuit . . . amidst the cold stars . . . and all bound together by reason and amity."

We all were rapt at his distraction.

I write "we," and "all"; though Lord Cheldthorpe had not understood that the Transit would take a full five hours before it was completed, and, having demonstrated a brief, masculine interest in the pursuits of science, began to chafe.

"D'you see?" Mr. 03-01 was crying, some eight minutes later. "It has achieved its horns." And indeed it had — for Venus was now just perceptible by the spurs of light that crowned it to either side as it passed into the ring of the sun. "Some few minutes before total immersion. Dr. 09-01 — mark that Venus is half way to its first internal contact . . . half way . . . now."

"Anyone for a swim?" said Lord Cheldthorpe.

"I will go, Your Lordship," said Mr. Druggett. He was dabbling his hand in the duck grease and smearing it underneath his head-bandage.

My mother asked, "Octavian?"

"No, thank you, Mother."

"No one?" insisted Lord Cheldthorpe, looking at my mother. "Swim?"

"I said, Your Lordship, I would swim with you," offered Druggett again, applying more fat. "With this heat and the duck grease, I am prone to make gravy."

"My Lord," my mother murmured, low enough so that the others should not hear, "surely you are not suggesting that I should compromise my dignity so far as to disrobe and take the waters while you or any other man is in the vicinity?"

"Venus," said Lord Cheldthorpe, "is the planet of love."

"And, sir," she said with warning, "it is drooping in the descendent."

He laughed.

Mr. Druggett persisted, "I said I wished to swim with you, Your Lordship."

Lord Cheldthorpe nodded. "While I honor the leveling spirit in America that sees no distinction between classes," he admitted, "one draws the line at your gravy."

So my mother and Lord Cheldthorpe sat off from us a ways, her drawing him with her head tilted, him standing with a bow, in the person of Actæon about to set off on the hunt; and she summoned me to pronounce upon the picture, and offer my criticisms so she might improve the likeness. They laughed at my pronouncements.

Though my mother was at all times dazzling, I never saw her more fascinating than on this day, when her spirits were, as I imagine, in such a ferment at these tokens of regard, the amorous compliments and blandishments of His young Lordship; and indeed, to take up the inevitable jest, it did seem as if she were the sun at the center of our system, and the radiance she shed throughout our company was so brilliant that we feared that if it should cease, we should forever see her image in negative, blank where she was black, her color still wanted by the eye.

Venus passed, and we marked its progress. I swam, and the waters of Champlain were so cool that they warmed, so chill they were as coals. The loons began their crying. I rose from the soft lake dripping. Night fell, the sun eclipsed behind the trees before Venus emerged.

Once it was dark, we remained by the instruments and saw the stars in their vaster orbits above us. My head lay upon my mother's lap.

And I thought of the Transit of Venus: that though the bodies be vast and distant, and their motions occult, their hesitations retrograde, one could, I thought, with exceeding care and preparation, observe, and, in their distance, know them, triangulate to arrive at the ambits of their motivation; and that in this calculation alone, one might banish uncertainty, and know at last what constituted other bodies, and how small the gulf that lies between us all.

When we returned to Boston some few days later, and the time of Lord Cheldthorpe's visitation grew to its close, 03-01 appeared to be in ever more anxious a state. He fretted in the hallways and stood looking out windows, shaking his hands as if to restore circulation. He sat down in chairs and rose up again. From his agitation, I discerned that Lord Cheldthorpe had given no firm word on whether he would support our continued experiments and grace the arts of our house with his beneficence.

Two nights before His Lordship of the New Creation was to depart, the Royal Governor of the Province held a great levee to send Cheldthorpe off with pomp. There was to be a grand dinner, and then our music-master, Mr. 13-04, would lead a band and singers in a brief operatic divertissement, delectable to the taste of His Lordship.

My mother and I were told, before the event, that we should rest well and be prepared, for we might be called upon to play our instruments, and astound the assembled with our facility in music-making.

Mr. 03-01 used the occasion of the dinner to introduce his various suits to Lord Cheldthorpe: the need for another wing to the mansion, in which scholars could live; the desire for instruments which could be built only in Germany; and the hope that Lord Cheldthorpe would invest in a portion of Indian land west of Virginia, against the day when Parliament lifted its interdiction against settling there.

"I shall consider it," said Lord Cheldthorpe, dubiously.

"I beg you to," said Mr. 03-01.

"When shall we have opera?" asked Lord Cheldthorpe.

The opera that evening — sung, not acted, so as not to offend the sensibilites of the town — was a Peruvian love story, an entrée by Monsieur Rameau. An Incan princess felt the tenderest of passions for a Conquistador who had arrived with horses to subdue her nation. She ignored the warnings of a priest of her people who begged her to return to her gods; and she sang an aria of love for the Spaniard to the accompaniment of the flute.

My mother observed the plaint with gravity.

Come, Goddess of Wedlock, the Incan princess implored,
Come unite me to the conqueror, whom I adore!
Tie your knots, enchain me!
Tie your knots, she sang again and again, *enchain! — enchain! —*
  enchain me!

She clasped her hands in supplication to the heavens; she presented her wrists crossed, as if manacled. *"Enchaîne-moi, enchaîne-moi, enchaîne-moi,"* she sang, mingling her voice with the flute; and I looked at Mr. 03-01, and saw him smiling, and knew he had hit upon the clumsy symbolism of this bizarre pageant; and I turned to Cheldthorpe, and saw him nuzzling the air; and it occurred to me then that he heard this airy and liquid song and, within his fancy, was laying his head upon my mother's bare breast, and moving his hand down across her belly, and it was night in a bed dark with curtains and flowers, in a chamber where no sound could come from below of the mopping of stairs or the shoeing of horses. I knew not whether he had enjoyed her in flesh; regardless, he now enjoyed her in fantasy.

And my mother smiled at him.

So the Incan woman retired to a galleon arm-in-arm with her Spaniard, singing that the chains of slavery were sweet when bound with the chains of love, while her people were engulfed in magma.

Thus ended the grotesque entertainment.

No sooner had the applause begun than Mr. 13-04, the music-master, bounded out beside the band, held out his hands for silence, and begged the ladies and gentlemen that they should be still.

At this, I flew into a sweat, and knew the time of my performance had come.

He spake some words—I attended not to them—but one was my name. My mother and I, exotic princess and prince, were to play another selection from Monsieur Rameau's opera, the *"Air pour les Esclaves Africains,"* or Air for the African Slaves, which would give the assembled gentlemen and ladies much pleasure.

My mother rose and settled her dress about her. I went up before the assembly, and was given a violin that was not mine. I ran the bow across the strings, and listened for the tuning. My mother was perching herself before the harpsichord.

I had the music for the air before me. I began.

I played it through once; it was a simple tune. On the second time through, my mother was stumbling, having none but a parlor-training in the keyboard; but I grew bolder with each pass, and dressed up the simple tune with flourishes and descants, runs and arabesques. I looked at My Lord Cheldthorpe of the New Creation, and played the air and its ornaments to him, seeing the line of the tune in his loose, easy posture, and drawing all about his curved slouch in devilish profusion my extensions and diagrams, my lines and cross-hatching, my circles about his head and feet, until my eyes must have bulged with the sight of all the linearities and confusions in which I had engaged his sagging, rakish frame.

My bow stuttered across the strings; flew; landed; sung to my fingers; and thus, with a final thrust, a final parry, a final stab, I was done.

The sweat was on my nose.

There was silence, and then the applause was massive.

Mr. 13-04, returning to the front of the company, shook my hand. Below, Lord Cheldthorpe of the New Creation made his way to my mother's side to offer his congratulations.

All were jubilant as we rode back to the Gitneys' house. I alone did not speak. I watched my mother chatter with His Lordship.

At the house, there was more food laid out: oysters and duck, sweets, champagne. We ate abundantly, and the scholars took their final leave of Cheldthorpe. At last, the house was quiet.

My mother went alone to her closet and took off her wig. The maid came to loosen her stays.

Lord Cheldthorpe knocked upon the door. My mother sent the maid to answer it.

The maid said, "It's His Lordship of the New Creation."

"Indeed," said my mother. "It is past the hour when one habitually receives nobility." She sighed. "Franny, you may leave."

Cheldthorpe asked permission to enter, and my mother granted it to him. He closed the door behind him. He said, "I come to offer my respects."

"My son is a better musician than I," she said. "He and the music-master can play 'Stingo!' by rubbing wet goblets."

"Impressive."

"The effect is perhaps more quaint than awesome."

"How do we know he is not listening in?"

"To what?"

"To our present conversation. At a communicating door."

"Our doors do not communicate."

"He could have his ear pressed up against it."

"Be assured, My Lord, in this house, there is no communication. Is there any topic that you would broach that my son should not hear?"

"Conversation flows more freely when it is unobserved."

"Surely, My Lord, everything you say is observed, bandied about, and praised."

"Princess."

"For which reason, as you are a man of honor, you would not say or do anything that should be of discredit to your character in a sphere far more public than a lady's bedchamber at midnight."

"You know of my affection for you."

The talk stopped; and I shifted my posture near the communicating door.

"I have," she said, hesitating, "I have some inkling."

There was another silence.

He said, "I would like to offer that you return with me to England."

I could not crouch for much longer. My arms were around my knees. I hovered there, ready to sprint.

"In what capacity?" said my mother.

"You and your son. I may easily buy you from Gitney. We shall return to England. A woman of your accomplishments should not languish here in the Colonies. I shall buy you a flat in London. Your son shall be educated by Cambridge scholars."

"A flat."

"Apartments."

"Why are they called 'a flat'?"

"I have not the faintest idea."

"It makes it sound as if the ceiling is low."

"It is simply a term. The ceilings would be ten feet high and be adorned with moldings and bosses. Plaster swags."

"You would purchase me?"

"Of course."

"And Octavian?"

"Of course."

"And some of the others in the household, so they might act as our servants?"

"Yes."

"In our flat?"

"Indeed."

"As hired servants? Free men?"

"Mademoiselle . . ."

"Behind communicating doors?"

"Princess Cassiopeia, you can scarcely imagine — the passion that suffuses me — and the extremity of my need."

"Need?"

"The passion."

"Is that need, My Lord?"

"Want . . ."

"So you offer me what?"

"A flat. An annual allowance."

"Your hand?"

"To shake? Yes, is the deal to your liking?"

"In marriage. Your hand."

"Now, Mademoiselle —," he said, hedging.

"Wedlock?"

"You well know that —"

"What else follows love, sir?"

"I'll show you," said he.

"I will be wed in a church. With a Bishop."

"Mademoiselle —"

"The correct form is 'Your Royal Highness.'"

"Cassiopeia —"

"A Peer of the Realm addresses a princess as 'Your Royal Highness.'"

"Your Royal Highness —"

"Do you offer me freedom?"

"Any freedom you wish to take with my person."

"And the freedom of my person?"

"You misunderstand."

"Shall I be freed?"

"I shall call you my queen."

"The queen of your 'flat.'"

"The queen of my heart."

"A continent scarcely large enough for a round-dance."

"You shall rule there absolutely."

"Why do I suspect I would first have to visit the antipodes?"

"Mademoiselle, you are delightfully scurrilous."

"This is no banter, sir. This is no game." I could hear the fury in her voice. *"This is no jest, no frolic, no badinage. I was a princess, once; I am a princess still. Royal blood will mix only with other royal blood. Otherwise, it demeans the line. Tell me what nation you offer me, what alliance, what regal house — or leave."*

Still in a tone of play, he said, "My lady, you know what scepter I offer, and what orbs."

There was a stunned silence. And then she replied, "Then, sir, look out at the privy. There is my throne. Reach inside, sir, and you shall find the wedding feast. Eat well, My Lord. Eat abundantly."

I know not who attacked whom; but I heard the struggle, and burst in through the communicating door.

They both were standing, and I could not make out who was striking whom — though both, as I conceive it, had their violent intent — but I imagined that he was first aggressor, and I called out, "Murder! Murder!" as I dragged upon his coat and pummeled him.

I reached up and struck him on the side of the head, and for a moment, his fury with my mother relented, and he turned his attention to me, hissing, "If you touch me again, I'll see you hang—you and your mother both."

I backed away, and watched their difficult embrace.

My cries, however, had roused the house, and in no time, the door opened, and Mr. 03-01 was there, and there was confusion all about us.

My Lord Cheldthorpe of the New Creation dropped my mother, and she dropped him, and looked away demurely, and I fell upon a chair.

Lord Cheldthorpe said, "The slut and her bastard . . ." He ceased.

03-01 looked gravely around the chamber and discerned the struggle that had transacted there. He said, "Gone like a vapor. All of it. Nothing." He turned and walked out.

Lord Cheldthorpe followed. I heard him give an order.

My mother and I stirred not from where we stood.

Some minutes later, Bono came in with the footmen, and bound my mother and me, and took us outside, and we were lashed to the horse-post. The moon was gibbous that evening, and the air cold. There was a chill to the cobbles beneath my bare feet that made them arch.

My mother's back was bared. They pulled her shift from her shoulders, and for the first time I saw her exposed, as she had been in the engraved figure hung upon the wall.

For an hour, they left us there before coming to inflict their punishment. We were all but nude in the night's chill. We shivered tremendously, and did not look at one another.

I revolved in my head passages of ancient texts that recalled how Britons had been slaves. Horace, writing of their subjection; or the Venerable Bede, describing how Saint Gregory the Great, pope and punster, had come across some British slave-boys in the market, and had found them so fair he sent a mission to convert their race to the Christian faith.

The gates to the stable-yard where we were bound had been closed to exclude the gaze of the curious. It was early in the morning, perhaps three o'clock, and the city was quiet. The trees rattled in the wind, and then were still. I could hear my mother's respiration in the silence, and it was rushed, as if she sobbed or had fits, but when I looked, there were no tears upon her face. Perhaps it was the chill of night, which was considerable. We stood there for some time.

The seagulls called in the moonlight above the Charles River.

When the people of the house came out, they came in numbers. Guests and servants standing around us, silent as they witnessed these cruel solemnities, Lord Cheldthorpe's valet and his footman took turns whipping us with the rod.

We had not been told how many lashes we should receive. After each, we waited to see if there would be another; but they gave no sign.

We felt the eyes of all the house upon us.

The rod fell again. I was aware that, being silent habitually, I was expected to be silent now. I betrayed no grief, save wincing.

The rod fell again upon my mother. Following the stroke, she could not breathe, and gagged upon air.

The rod bit my back. I tried to stand, but could not, my hands were bound so low. I fell to the ground upon one knee.

Lord Cheldthorpe strolled around before us so that he could view our faces and judge the visage of punishment. My mother was vomiting; the issue was thin and yellow. She struggled for breath.

They ceased.

When, trembling, she regained her composure, and her breath came regularly again, Lord Cheldthorpe nodded, and they whipped her one last stroke.

She buckled and fell to her knees.

They came behind me. I would not grimace; I would not flinch; indeed, I would show nothing — considering, as the Stoic Phrygian slave, crippled by his master's blows, hath writ: *"Beyond the last inner tunic of my frail body, no one has authority over me. If I love too much this pitiful flesh, I have sold myself as a slave, for I have shown through pain what can be used to master me."*

So say I now, resolve standing tall in seclusion; but then, the rod cut; and, weakened by agony's chains, ambushed by astonishment, I could not forbear exclamations of torment.

I barked once, like a dog, then let forth a high whine.

I am ashamed of my weakness.

There is no need to rehearse the pain and the humiliation of spirit in such an act.

I gripped the post.

So we stood for some time. We could hear the household turning away, retiring back inside. Lord Cheldthorpe watched with some satisfaction. Mr. 03-01 liked the whole thing not a bit, and frowned.

We were untied and taken back into the orchard. I knew not what further retribution they should demand; death was not too grave a punishment for the assault of a Negro upon a nobleman, though I did not think that such extremity would be called for in this case, when trumpeting abroad the facts would invite the scrutiny of idleness and public censure, fascinated by the midnight transgressions of nobility.

We waited upon the grass. Crickets sang all about us, as they had in the glade beside Champlain. Figures were carrying a sofa.

Bono stood guard beside us; His Lordship's valet behind.

Bono reached up to wipe the slobber from my mother's chin. She turned her head away sharply, and when he seemed likely to persist, raised her bound hands to foil his assist.

He dropped his hand, and faced away from us.

Mr. 03-01 came out of the gloom, misery in his countenance. He gestured, and we were led into the ice-house. It was a door into a hill. We went in, and the cold surrounded us.

They had a lantern burning, so we could see. My mother's sofa had been deposited upon the stone floor. The ice was somewhat diminished, but still stood in blocks and shards all about the vault.

Lord Cheldthorpe was there. His arms were crossed.

Our shifts, which had been torn, were removed. We were naked in the room. We covered ourselves with our hands.

Lord Cheldthorpe said simply, "Here is your salon, Princess." He walked out; and the others followed him with lugubrious mien. The door shut, and locked.

There was no light when they were gone.

We sat upon the sofa. My back clamored with the lashes to so great an extent that well could I believe that, though my spine was wet with blood, it burned.

We each could hear the other's breath in the silence of the ice-house. Each motion across the embroidered stuff of the sofa sounded a great rasping.

I rested my elbows upon my knees, and my hands dangled. Casting about with my limbs, I could find no posture that did not scald, and returned, therefore, to my slump.

My mother's breathing had now fallen into rhythm.

For a long space of time, which may have been hours, we were silent.

Then, "I would embrace you," my mother said, "but for our nudity."

I nodded, which she could not hear.

She shifted her body upon the sofa; I felt the padding warp. She said, "When you were small, you grew affectionate for a dragon's skull. Do you recall?"

"Yes," I said.

"You played an infant game and crawled within it. Do you recall this? I, jesting, asked you whether you were not apprehensive that it might bite you. You answered me, 'Do not be afraid, Mother. Know you whose skull this is? Mine. I would not bite my own self.'"

Her voice echoed curiously around the chamber. The cold insinuated itself from every quarter; it unfurled itself throughout our skins.

I lifted my feet from the floor and jammed the heels into the cushion, teetering there upon the sofa.

My mother asked, "Do you understand why I acted as I did?"

I revolved the scene before me. At length, I answered, "No."

She ran her fingernail along a seam. I could hear the mutter of the stitch.

I asked, "Did you love him?"

"Or?" she asked.

"Did you play for gain?"

She considered my question. She answered: "When you wish to lay your head upon someone's breast . . . When . . . If one pictures a scene for oneself of sitting by a fire in one's own home, in a dress of the latest fashion, of the latest Parisian cut, and having someone enter the house and be announced; and before the maid can fetch him up . . . he runs into the room and catches you up in his arms to . . . I know not . . . vent wit about the day. . . . If one hushes him with a hand upon his lips . . . a hand asparkle with rings . . . lovely, for one is loved . . . and he laughs by one's hearth, which he has afforded one . . . and there one's son . . . is . . . Tell me . . . I have been most . . ."

I waited.

"What is love," she asked, "if not —," but said no more.

After a time, I glared into the gloom as if I could pierce it with my gaze, and felt it almost part into its constituent blacknesses, so that I could see the beetles there.

"Octavian?" she said.

I did not answer.

"If I had inclined my head some few degrees . . . ," she said. I did not know of what she spake, whether of that night or another night; whether of a kiss, a touch, or a blow.

"Mother?" I said, and she answered, "What?" We could barely speak, our jaws were so hardened with the cold and the pain of our backs. She reached out and found my hand and placed her wooden fingers around it.

Again, I said, "Mother. I . . ."

I had no insight; no sense of what to say; was sensible of nothing but the darkness, which was parted, which had resolved itself

[*113*]

so that objects there were defined, though they were not objects that could be seen by light, but properties of unbeing; the furniture of negation; and so I sat, perched upon the sofa in our frigid salon; I watched unbeing in the ebon room; and together, our teeth chattered; and outside in the city, the sun rose, and it was morning.

In the morning, we were taken inside, because it was known we would die of cold if exposed for any longer.

We were shivering. They left us tied in the kitchen, our wrists and ankles lashed together.

We sat against the wall while the cook stoked the welcome flames of the breakfast fire. We watched them make the morning meal for the house. The servants did not wish to look at us, and so regarded us not.

That morning, My Lord Cheldthorpe of the New Creation left for South Carolina upon the sloop *Rarity*. We were released from our bonds and bathed, and I do believe that if 03-01 was not preoccupied with his own ruination through this episode, he would have apologized for how cruelly we had been used.

But instead, he sat in his chair, undressed, in his robe and cap, and dug a compass into the table.

That week, the first of the philosophical apparati was sold.

With no hope of funds, an age was ended; the Novanglian College of Lucidity was to change forever.

[II.]

THE POX PARTY

taken from the
Manuscript Testimony of
Octavian Gitney

"Ipsa scientia potestas est." ("Knowledge itself is power.")
— Francis Bacon, *Meditationes Sacræ*

The day after my whipping, I sat upon my bed, half dressed; Bono stood by the window.

"We cannot put you in a shirt," he said. "You will ruin it."

I stared down at my knees. Bono cast a shirt upon the floor.

He said, "The blood will ruin it."

It was the rawness, the mess upon my back, its suppuration, more than simply the excruciation of the pain, which disturbed me; previous to this, all pain had been enveloped neatly within the confines of the human shell, as within a doctor's bag the spiny instruments, the gouges and tongs, are strapped compactly, an arrangement of agonies. These wounds, however—these stripes bit into the world, and spillt.

At every motion, I could feel the incisions chafe and the crawling of pus.

I began to cry.

Bono picked up the shirt and put it in my hands. "You can slip it on," he said. "You want, you can slip it on."

I shook my head. I cried. I could feel my teeth showing.

"Don't," he said. "Crying ain't something to do."

"In the ice-house," I sobbed, "in the ice-house, I defecated." I could not stop from crying. I said, holding up my hands and weeping, "I *had* to."

"That's fine," he said. He did not know what to do.

"It wasn't weighed. Tell Mr. 03-01. It's not accounted for."

Bono came and he put his hand upon my cheek. He pressed my cheek so my skull was against his palm; and he said, "Prince, he don't care today. There ain't any measuring happening today. No samples."

"What will happen to it?" I said.

He took the shirt from me and folded it over his arm. "Same thing as happens to the rest of us," he said. "After a while, it just goes into the ground."

My mother was found, later that day, down in the cellar of the main house. She had gone there alone. She had curled herself up tightly, her arms around her knees, and sat in the complete darkness, blood spangling the silk of her dress like the gloaming stars first bleeding into evening.

Following these dire scenes of correction, the house was grim. At meals, few spake; none came to dine; Mr. 03-01 surveyed the paintings on the walls, determining in what order they should be sold to discharge his debts.

My mother did not issue forth from her chamber for any but the most necessary engagements in the rest of the house. She chose, instead, to closet herself in her room, where she acted the tyrant with the servants.

The first few nights, heart moved with sympathy, the cook sent up in secret soothing delicates and stews, supplemented with heavy spirits to draw off the pain, and whispered comfortably things such as, "Tell the dear to rest well, and that we know her woes"; my mother returned the dishes peremptorily as being too cold, too liquid, too morose, too dry. She demanded other dishes, special preparations, sauces *glacées,* a blanquette of veal seasoned with oysters, *chapon Flandrois* in white wine, pluck and numbles rubbed with Ceylon herbs.

After two meals of this, the cook frowned and sent up half a loaf of salt bread, as instructed.

I did not return to my studies for several days following the altercation. I lurked around corners, and stood in the dark crevasses by the stairs, and could meet no one's eyes; this shrinking and secretive manner being the product not just of the extremity of my physical discomfort, which discouraged conversation, but also of the greater stinging and biting inwardly; for within me, the flagellation had not yet ceased.

I do not know that for four or five days I spake at all, after that first interview with Bono. My reserve was greater and more obdurate than ever before. Often, I was Observant for hours at a time, and would respond to none, but instead sat motionless and noted the minute stitching of brocade, or the ingenuity of wood.

When I was taken to Dr. 09-01's rooms upstairs for our lessons to be resumed, I dreaded the interview. He had, since the whipping, seemed in a perpetual irritation, glowering around the rooms, leaving company often, saying he wished to ascertain whether matter still subsisted in his chamber.

He was kind, however, when I went to him. He spake gently to me.

Still, surveying the page, I felt I knew no language. I would answer nothing. That day I did not speak.

Nor the next day. He returned me to my room.

On the third day when I went to him, he had a stack of books by his side.

"Sit down, Octavian," he said. "We begin a new lesson today."

I sat.

He handed me a book, open in the middle. It was some history I had never before read, written in the Latin tongue.

"One. Read the passage," he demanded. "Two. Construe."

I mumbled half a sentence of the Latin; he tapped his foot. "That is all?" he said. "Is it a day for *sotto voce?*"

I stared at him.

"Good God, boy, stop gawking." He snatched the book from me. He stood above me, held the book aloft, and in a loud, even piercing tenor, declaimed: *"Hoc anno, servus nomine Eunis qui a paucis esse magus dicebatur in dominos suos coortus est."* He looked down at me; and I began to translate—"In this year, a freeborn slave named Eunus, reputed a magician, rose against his masters . . ."—while he continued his bellowing over me—*"et, manu conservorum comitante, hos contra urbes in Siciliae finibus duxit"*—until my voice was as loud as his—". . . gathering a force of fellow slaves and leading them against cities in the region of Sicily . . ."—and together, we shouted of servitude, arms, and Rome.

One morning, we were summoned to the dining-room — the servants, the family, the dependents — and told that there the sole hope of our College awaited us. Thus it was with considerable anticipation that we gathered to see this most interesting individual.

We found before us a small, gray man in a gray silk coat who surveyed us as we entered, clearly assessing even the academicians among us for resale. We hung together — me at my mother's arm. He was a compact gentleman, and one could easily imagine that, in his earlier years, he had been adept at springing and vaulting.

Mr. 03-01 came before us, and said, "The Novanglian College of Lucidity has entered a new and even more astonishing chapter. Allow me to introduce Mr. Sharpe. He will address you. Mr. Sharpe, would you prefer to sit or stand?"

"I shall pace," said Mr. Sharpe. "Thank you, Mr. Gitney." Mr. Sharpe began his rounds. With Mr. Sharpe, I found in the years that followed, there was no facing a person, unless for assessment. Otherwise, he was turned always to the side, his hands clasped behind him or held before him, never at his sides; him choosing to subsist in the manner of those Ægyptian friezes where men, lateral with antiquity, tally their grain.

To us he said: "Point A: My friends, the question we must ask ourselves is this: Can a forest animal eat itself for sustenance? Have you seen a badger devour its own flanks? Indeed, good people, can any living thing feast upon its own flesh indefinitely, and yet remain whole? Outside of the menagerie of fancy, the answer is 'No.' A fox, let us say, that pursued this course should be involved in perpetual cartwheels." He paused and put his hands before his mouth, as if pondering.

We stared at him in bewilderment.

He swiveled to present his other profile, and continued: "I use this quaint illustration not only to put you at your ease by eliciting laughter at a risible scenario—for I am a man who appreciates a jest—and I found myself, last night at the inn, quite delighted by the thought of the fox, look you, the comical fox, his own white teeth bloodied with his own blood, gagging on his own pelt as he swallowed his legs—down the gullet!—but also to make a point. Point B. A point of great gravity: *No institution, like no fox, may long be sustained on its own flesh. We must devour elsewhere if we are not to devour ourselves, and so perish!*

"Point C: You gentlemen have done marvelous work here. Mr. Gitney has shown me your publications. Your scrutiny into the most obscure sciences has attracted the notice of the world. But you cannot simply pursue these ends without results that will aid the common man. This is a revolutionary age, my friends. You have been living in the turrets of a fairy-castle — which is a fine view — excellent prospect — until you realize that fairy-castles, my friends, consist in their architecture of tea-cake and icing. They are (a) frail; they are (b) sticky. And there are those below the battlements of this your confectionary keep who starve. It is time, sirs, madams, to become part of the world. It is time to enter the market, rather than feeding on your own stale flesh."

This all seemed excellent sense; an opportunity for renewal and usefulness.

Mr. Sharpe surveyed us. "Which one of you is the painter?"

07-03 raised his hand.

"Your name, sir?"

"07-03," he said.

"Eh —," interposed Mr. 03-01, rising. He explained to us, "Eh — I am afraid . . . I am afraid that our system of metric designation has come to an end. Mr. Sharpe, reviewing the practice, has determined that it contributes to hierarchy and rank. So we shall . . . cast aside our numbers, my friends . . . like shackles . . . and instead . . . names. Names for all."

"It is a glorious new day," said Mr. Sharpe.

Dr. 09-01 — now abruptly Trefusis — raised his hand. He remarked, "The alchemical worm Ouroboros that encircles the world devours itself."

"Pardon?" said Mr. Sharpe.

"The alchemical worm Ouroboros of ancient myth. Its teeth are sunk in its tail."

"Precisely," said Mr. Sharpe. "Precisely. This is the kind of bizarre academic interlude that profits absolutely no one." He turned back to the painter. "Sir, you, Mr. Painter. Do you see the spots where pictures lately hung, now sold off to pay the debts of your academy's intransigence? I would like a simple mural there depicting the sciences and arts allegorified, sitting on top of Utility."

The painter hesitated. "Sitting atop Utility? Are they . . . hurting him? What is Utility?"

"Perhaps an ox," said Mr. Sharpe. "With an humble countenance."

Over the course of the next several days, Mr. Sharpe met with each of the academicians to determine which philosophical projects should be pursued, and which put aside. In the end, they were each stinted various courses of inquiry that should in some measure produce more visible results than their previous studies: They now spent their days melting and rendering the subcutaneous fats of animals, or determining which birds ate which pests, or tracing the genealogy of the more amorous peaches.

The arts were not much marked in the new regime. Mr. Sharpe and the new investors made us sensible of how unprofitable were the products of crayon, quill, and fiddle. Our attention was directed at those pursuits which would yield clear benefit to ordinary men.

And is this, after all, not just? On this head, are not the afternoons spent playing Corelli with my mother — afternoons defunct, now that her harpsichord was sold — do these not seem like the arts of idleness? A galling, sweet example of privilege exercised?

I should say that chief among the peculiarities of the new regime was the use of surnames in address. So unaccustomed were we to appellations other than the numerical that we hesitated each time we spoke a name; we fumbled for words. So doth even the most absurd of habits, after a time, inscribe itself as law, and come to resonate as ineluctable truth.

Mr. Sharpe betrayed an early dislike for my mother, whose arts and airs excited in him nought but irritation. He spoke to her flatly, turned to the side; then swiveling to survey her heighth rapidly, he delivered his determinations respecting her inquiries, and was done with her. He engaged in no flirtation. He said he would not, at present, allow for expenditure on any dresses of fine stuffs, but rather recommended she brood on worsted and prunella twill. He would not brook special dishes being prepared for her at suppertime. He could not abide her luxuries; and when she wore the blood-speckled dress to shame him, he revealed no interest or consternation.

For some few weeks, I continued my studies as before, Dr. Trefusis guiding me without remark through stories of slaves who had achieved greatness. He prompted nothing; he betrayed by no comment that I should consider the courses described in these narratives. He simply supplied the texts, aided with the translations, and rapped my hand when I failed at declension or agreement.

This came to an end at the turn of the fourth week from the day I first laid eyes upon Mr. Sharpe. That individual requested to visit my tutorial with Dr. Trefusis. To this, we could do nothing but render assent.

He did not arrive punctually at the opening of the lesson. Dr. Trefusis and I sate awkwardly in silence, the pretense of tuition abandoned; knowing that the coming lesson would be but a simulation of learning; and being unwilling to begin this pretense without an audience.

After a time, Dr. Trefusis shrugged, went to the desk, and drew forth the text, and, he having set it before me, we began to read of the plebian revolution in Rome.

At this point, there was a rap on the door, and Mr. Sharpe sidestepped into the chamber and bowed. "Pray continue," he said. "Mind me not."

Continue we did. Dr. Trefusis had chosen Latin for the day, the better to show my excellence in the subject. The text was not a difficult one, and I encountered no obstacles in my translation. This gave me confidence, and when I saw Dr. Trefusis smile upon Mr. Sharpe after I had performed a particularly felicitous rendering, I was so bold as to smile upon the man too, as if to say: *We all pursue excellence together.*

"Yes, fine," said Mr. Sharpe.

"The boy is extraordinarily gifted," said Dr. Trefusis. "His grasp of sciences would be enough to recommend him as an excellent student; but his achievements in Classical literature and music suggest genius. He speaks Latin like a native of Augustus's Rome, he speaks French and Greek passably, and we are endeavoring to form him as an English prose stylist as well."

"I suppose I shall be the judge of all that," said Mr. Sharpe.

"Yes," said Dr. Trefusis.

"You misunderstand," said Mr. Sharpe. "I appreciate your efforts in training the child, but I feel that this experiment has been severely mismanaged." He pressed his hands, as if in prayer, against his nose. He said sadly, "I have read many of the boy's translation exercises. The course you have pursued is all wrong. You have engaged in entertainment rather than instruction. More to the point, you have prejudiced the results."

"Sir," said Dr. Trefusis, "I see no such thing."

"Precisely why I am afraid that you must retire from this experiment." He gestured carelessly towards me. "The subject's people are a story-telling people. Their converse is formed largely of tales of fallen heroes and the most absurd myths respecting talking jungle animals. Such propensities are hardly evidence of a rational society. And yet, you have been cultivating the same propensities in your lessons with the boy. You have nourished him on narrative. Narrative, sir, is precisely what we wish to wean him from.

"We wish to determine whether the subject is capable of growth in his rational faculties. That alone. This would constitute growth *away* from his hereditary savage nature. Do you see? What you have been doing is feeding him precisely the kind of story that he would have been receiving in his native land. It is to *this* that he has responded, not the abstract logic of the language. He evinces considerable enthusiasm at these stories — seems to be involved in them. You are, look ye, granting him an unfair advantage. You are training him, as a vine, upon a considerable armature, when we wish to see precisely whether he can flourish on his own.

"I, on the other hand, will teach him logic and grammar without narrative. We wish to judge his abstract thinking, not his commitment to tale-telling, which is, in any case, merely a relapse into the pagan stupor of his forebears."

He turned, at last, to me. "From this point out, you shall translate only fragments. You shall be debarred from literature and history. The history of a race fallen fifteen hundred years ago is, in any case, of little moment to us now. There is no utility in it."

Dr. Trefusis was aghast. "You will ruin the boy," he said.

"You have done that already," said Mr. Sharpe. And, turning to me: "Now. Let us begin."

For the next several hours of that day I labored over a Greek legal dispute regarding the ownership of twenty-five oxen ravaged by the mange. Following that, Mr. Sharpe set me to chopping firewood.

I did not complain, rather inclined to split timber than to labor at case and tense beneath his sallow eye; and having fled the lesson, I took some pleasure in the coolness of the air in the yard, the monotony of lifting, settling, appraising, and striking, throwing aside, and hauling up another limb for riving.

This chore being completed, I was sent upstairs with Bono to set out new candles in the bedroom sconces; and thereafter, set to shucking sweetcorn in the kitchen. This I did not find remarkable, it often being the case due to the illness or absence of one of the younger servants that some small duties had to be performed.

Over the next days, however, the roster of tasks grew longer; and I perceived that this was to be my lot. The permanency of the arrangement was confirmed two days later when Mr. Sharpe announced that he had sold the indentures of several of our servants to other households; that those same servants must gather their few possessions and remove themselves to their new homes.

It was Mr. Sharpe's intention that those of us who remained would do the work of those who had been sold; I was to be trained by Bono as a valet, and serve my master Mr. Sharpe at his pleasure. That gentleman believing that my education had been, up until that time, entirely lacking in any common-sensical preparation for the vocations established for men of my race, he averred that it would be a disservice to me to allow me to continue in scholarly pursuits save that of (a) Latin and (b) Greek (for these last were the substance of the experiment practiced upon me). He said it would be laughable for me to continue to study luxurious and abstract knowledge when a world of practical utility awaited my laboring hands.

Thus my studies altered forever in their essential nature as in their outward form. No longer did my teachers lay open for me the book of Nature and speak of botany and zoology; no longer was I given the works of Shakespeare and Pope to con. Instead, I spent some two hours a day in the translation of fragments from Greek and Latin; the texts being chosen for their convolution, recondite meaning, dryness, and insipidity.

I was disallowed the use of the house's library, for fear that liberty amongst the volumes there would allow me to study and so unfairly prejudice the results of the experiment. I was forbidden to read any of the Latin volumes of history and song to which I had turned; forbidden to read narratives in English; forbidden often even the practice of my violin.

It must be thought that such a deprivation would have deeply grieved me; but curiously, it did not, for many months; and this was due to the deep regard I had for Bono, who now was commanded to teach me the ways of service.

I looked to Bono with all the adulation of a younger brother, astonished always at his wisdom and his easy knowledge of solutions to the nice problems of household management; and I was not a little awestruck by his friendly disdain for me. I would willingly have followed him through any passageway to any laboring engine, up any staircase to any senseless task, any polishing or brushing or burnishing, just to spend time in his presence, who seemed so fearless and sure in the world.

Over the next months, he taught me how to remove stains, how to ensure that leather was supple. As we had but one footman left, he taught me the niceties of waiting on guests and receding motionless when nothing more was needed. He taught me how to bait the horses. He taught me how to offer my hand to a lady without offending with forwardness. He taught me that there are taxonomies in candlesticks as subtle and arcane as those of the *Lepidoptera* and arachnids: He taught me that some candlesticks are to be submerged in boiling water and rubbed dry with flannel to remove tallow; some are to be shined with rotten-stone; he taught me that the silver must be lifted from the water first, before the others, and rubbed with whiting; that steel candlesticks should not be submerged in water at all, but must be massaged with oil and emery. He taught me to serve; he taught me to hide.

I remember best one of the first lessons he gave me. I walked abroad with him through the city, learning the routes by which I would have to walk when I delivered messages.

"Down there's Mr. Byles. Up here's Mr. Sandson. He don't tip, even if you compliment his son's aim with blocks. If ever you has to take something to Mr. Pettit, he's down Foster Street. Don't you let him start talking about the Indian Wars and the fall of Louisberg. It'll last you 'til after the curfew, and the watchmen will snatch you for tardy and Negro."

I nodded.

He reached inside his frock-coat, and drew forth a letter. "You know to always carry this," he said. He handed the letter to me. It said,

> Sirs—
> My slave Pro Bono Gitney hath business abroad at the houses of Mr. Ogilvy and Mr. Trevor. I will thank you not to molest him in the course of his duties. This letter serving as a pass from
>
> Your respectful servant,
> *Mr. Josiah Gitney*

"Each time you walk alone in the city, best to have one of these. Otherwise, close to dark the watch'll assume you're off to explode the rum distillery or steal chickens from widows. Always—you always keep your papers on your poxy little person. Mr. Gitney, he'll let you write them yourself."

I nodded.

"You're a great one for nodding," he said. He jarred me with his elbow so I swerved and almost ran full into four slaves carrying a woman of distinction on a sedan-chair. "You got to stop nod-ding," he said. "That's what I'm telling you. Don't nod when there ain't a need to nod, see? You got to be blank."

He held out the written pass. "This is what they want us to be," he said. "They want us to be nothing but a bill of sale and a let-ter explaining where we is and instructions for where we go and what we do. They want us empty. They want us flat as paper. They want to be able to carry our souls in their hands, and read them out loud in court. All the time, they're on the exploration of themselves, going on the inner journey into their own breast. But us, they want there to be nothing inside of. They want us to be writ on. They want us to be a surface. Look at me; I'm mahogany."

I protested, "A man is known by his deeds."

"Oh, that's sure," said Bono. "Just like a house is known by its deeds. The deeds say who owns it, who sold it, and who'll be buy-ing a new one when it gets knocked down."

Day succeeded day, filled with fragments. Mr. Sharpe hardly spoke to me. I appeared at the appointed hour in the school room. He parlayed not, but simply handed me sheets of quotations, bowed briefly, and walked out. He pursued more stimulating projects, whilst I, alone in the chamber, labored through his Classical obscurities.

The languages swift became intractable. Whereas before, I had anticipated my lessons as the hour most gratifying in the day, now, in measure equal to my former pleasure, I dreaded their advent.

Whippings were the desert of failure.

These were not as harsh as the first I had received from Lord Cheldthorpe; they were transacted with a birch wand, rather than a whip, and were but a stroke or two; but they were more regular.

I still may bring to memory the smell of the varnish, my face smothered against the desk, my hands stretched before me in a gesture of offering and obeisance.

Mr. Sharpe did not seem sensible that these hands he cut with the ferule were the same which, an hour later, bleeding, bandaged, arranged his frock-coats according to his order. To mark the silk of his coats with blood would have merited the most grievous punishments, so Bono and I wrapped my hands tightly in cloth; but with my hands thus bandaged, I could not help but fumble. I received further reprimands for my labored and deliberate service, or, as he called it, my sloth. For this, he whipped my hands again.

I did not complain of my treatment; indeed, complaint may often make intolerable some circumstances which otherwise were swallowed, digested, and let pass. On some heads, this demotion from scholar to servant simplified my lot, for as I passed from childhood to youth, it would have been increasing awkward for me to act as a lordling in that house, merely reading and playing the violin while the others toiled around me; luxury would have pained me. I now saw their stares when I was favored, due to my experimental status; and so it was preferable to work alongside them; after a time, my lessons with Mr. Sharpe seeming to all—myself included—not so much like a privilege as a more peculiar and arcane chore, as we viewed the grooming of the silkworms or the supper of the asp.

It was curious to aid in my small ways with the preparation of the meal, turning the spit or shaving the sweet-potatoes, and then to run and dress for dining, when my presence was required at table; to sit amidst the chatter of those who never saw the yams skinned or the luncheon-fowl with its head on; Bono over my shoulder silently serving me morsels I had just cut into a bucket an hour before.

There were other lessons taught me by Bono, too.

He taught me where he hid when he did not wish to serve; most effective being the cellar, where, did Mr. Sharpe send a boy after him, he could claim he was inspecting the vintages or re-arranging tubers; or, in times of greater need, the kitchen of Mr. Gitney's nephew, some two streets away, where Bono's mother labored as a servant in the kitchen.

Once, when concocting a varnish with Mr. Gitney, Mr. Sharpe chanced to spill some of their new mixture on his cravat, which left a yellow stain. He entrusted it to the laundry-maid, who, being unable to remove the mark, entrusted it to Bono.

"This, Prince O.," said Bono, with some appreciation, "is a tearing fine cravat." He held it before his throat, wrapped once around his hand. "It makes a man look like a conqueror."

I asked, "Can you render the spot invisible?"

"Know what I'd do with this? Sheep's bones, burnt, beat all up into a powder, some vinegar maybe. You sift your powder onto the spot, press the cravat down with something heavy. Leave it lie for the night. In the morning, the powder, it all takes up the spot. You understand?"

"It leaches the oils of the spot."

"You catch on quick, when it's about leaching." He laid the cravat on Mr. Sharpe's bed and folded it carefully, running his thumbs over the creases. "You watch how this is done."

I followed him down to the parlor, where we kindled a fire for the ease of the academicians, who were retiring from the experimental chamber.

As Bono loaded the wood onto the andirons, Mr. Sharpe inquired, "Bono, I wonder whether you have removed that stain from my neck-kerchief. The girl did not think it within her power."

"Nancy."

Mr. Sharpe nodded. "She did not think it within her power. The blot was beyond her."

"That's some blot, sir." Bono shook his head. "That is some terrible blot."

"You doubt whether even your art can remove it."

"See, sir, that ain't your normal type of blot. It's some kind of novel, philosophical blot."

"It resists your efforts."

"Oh, it's fast." Bono again shook his head. "What you want I should do with the cravat?"

"You are certain there is no other recourse?"

"Can't be fixed, sir. But you could still wear it, Mr. Sharpe, sir, so long as you tuck it into your waistcoat, and so long as you don't turn too quick, with surprise or delight or some such."

Mr. Sharpe swore and turned away.

"Sir—," said Bono, "sir, if you don't have interest in it, would you object if I should wear it? I reckon I could wear it handsomely, if I keep my body held just right."

Mr. Sharpe waved his hand in reply.

That night, we burned and pulverized sheep's bones, doused the powder in a rendering of vinegar, and heaped the blot with the concoction. Two days later, Bono walked forth on errands with the cravat unspotted.

It looked, indeed, fit for a conqueror.

I aided in the pounding of boiled clothes; I translated dull tags; I daily ran my fingers through Mr. Sharpe's hair, greasing it and feeding his graying queue into a bag. So the days passed in Greek fragments and chores.

I missed my studies with Dr. Trefusis inveterately; for reading, once begun, quickly becomes home and circle and court and family; and indeed, without narrative, I felt exiled from my own country. By the transport of books, that which is most foreign becomes one's familiar walks and avenues; while that which is most familiar is removed to delightful strangeness; and unmoving, one travels infinite causeways; immobile and thus unfettered.

There being an intemperate storm one evening, I sat by the fire, recalling that just a few months before, such a night, the rain savage upon pane and sash, would have found me by the library fire reading ancient bestiaries: stories of the military endeavors of the crane, the violence of certain monkeys, and the peculiar blood of the hoopoe, who feeds on filth and whose gore, when spread on the human body, was said to cause visions of demons strangulating the dreamer with twine.

That evening, a small company, consisting of Bono; my mother; the cook, Aina; and Nancy, the laundry-maid, sate by the fire in my mother's room. There was a time when I would have cowered for fear that some adult should speak to me, that Mr. Gitney should badger me with questions, and so break my reverie, draw me back from Africa, Persia, or Muscovy; now, without books to leaven the evening, I sat listless.

"What's hypped the Prince?" asked Bono.

My mother answered, "He misses his books."

"Prince O.," said Bono. "Those books—you don't need them. They're madness without one lick of sense. Mr. Gitney told me I should read from the library. He tells me to read some romance; he wishes I should give him my opinion. I read it. Sweet Jesus. There was flying peoples and horses underground and trick swords and bosoms heaving. And there was battlements and the walking dead and oboes. It's a game for the idle. Forget the books. You han't need for children's stories anymore. Leave them for the rich, Little O."

In that moment, my spirits rallied against him—stifled—agitated—vexed and bound—and I discovered dislike even for he who commanded so much of my reverence; I could not brook his slander upon learning.

I must have glowered.

Bono took a bite of an apple. "That child," said he, through a mouth full of pulp, "could melt a liver with his eyes."

The next day the rain abated and commenced a silent drizzle. All the houses of the town were green in the mist. Figures in tricornes walked through the streets, gathering by carriages with curtains closed, and the smell of the docks hung over the squares.

That evening, chilled to the bone, I prepared for bed near our fire. Bono sat upon his pallet.

"O.," he whispered, "how would you fancy the *Something Fiddle-Faddle Histories* of Tacitus?"

I turned to him, smoothing my shirt.

"Lift up your mattress."

I did; the book was there: Tacitus's *Annals of Rome*.

"There's some good to be had in being a known cretin," said Bono. "I been granted full reign of the library."

I picked up the book. I held it in both hands, the leather boards pressed between my palms.

"Bono . . . ," said I, deprived almost of speech — eager already for the plumes, the charges, the palace intrigues.

"Don't let them find it, or we ain't walking straight for some days."

"Bono," I began again.

"You know there's a price," said he, reaching under his mattress and pulling forth another volume. "Before you read to yourself, you needs read to me." He handed it to me.

I looked through the book he had given me; it was a collection of old tales in English, so far as I could discern. "Why can you not read it yourself?" I asked.

"It ain't all in English," he said. He took it from me, turned the pages rapidly, and passed the volume back to me. He thumped upon the page. Bono explained, "They put some of those passages in Latin so the ladies couldn't read them. I got a most acute interest to know what they say."

I scanned the words, and, seeing their content, blushed.

I informed him, "It is regrettably impossible that I should render these lines into English. I am sorry, Bono, and I hope that this in no wise diminishes your sensibility of my gratitude for the hazard in which you have—"

"Octavian," he said, "you translate, or I take Mr. Tacitus back to his own bedroom." He tapped the cover of his fable-book. He said, "Miscreants got to hang together. Do wrong for me so I can do more wrong for you."

I watched him, burning with shame at my complicity; but there was no way out of this arrangement, should I wish to continue my education. And so I began reading—without joy—my tongue sunken in my mouth. "The monk . . . was of so great a girth . . . that the girl would have been crushed beneath him. . . . Thus she mounted atop him . . . and he penetrated her from beneath. . . ."

This became a feature of my evenings. I read in secret volumes from the library, and, in return, once a week perhaps would translate filth or chirurgical surveys of the womb and parts of reproduction; and so, through these crimes, my studies continued in secret.

Mr. Sharpe could not abide music; something in its vibrations agitated his animal spirits and contributed to his peevish disposition. When I practiced upon my violin, I did so in the top of the house, away from his apartments. In this secret music, I could tell those tales I was denied, and, there being no text, none could read whether I spake of docility or insubordination. I set myself tasks of description—thinking, *I shall play this passage indicating the burning of bread,* or, *the collapse of a chimney,* or, *the stealing of evening upon the linen of a girl's mob-cap in the alley as she whistles for her brother,* or—*This movement shall represent the march in triumph of a queen who sits upon a lily-throne.*

Thus, when Mr. Sharpe announced his visit to the garret where I played, I was deeply troubled, foreseeing that even this species of expression might be withdrawn. I knew that he had no liking for the violin, which instrument he called "the fiddle"; and that he had no liking for any but country dances, maintaining that the music of the concert hall, the chamber, and the chapel indulged nervous sophistication and confounded natural simplicity.

He heard me play for several days in a row, interrupting sonatas by Locatelli and Leclair to request "Cup o' Stingo" and "Cold and Raw." On the last day, he was accompanied by a man I did not know. They traded some whispered intelligence as I played, and the music-master, seated at our dilapidated spinet, closed his eyes.

The purpose of these visits quickly became clear. Mr. Sharpe, having heard reports of my success in years previous at our evening *soirées* and at the opera evening for Lord Cheldthorpe, had arranged for me to play as soloist for a subscription concert; the understanding being that, were my efforts received with the plaudits of the assembled, I should continue to appear in solo turns throughout the rest of the season.

In this way, he explained, I should pay back the College of Lucidity for the kindness shown in feeding and clothing me, and they should recoup the expense of maintaining me.

The uneasiness precipitated by the mere thought of such public performance disordered my nerves to a great degree, and I felt fearful of most everything. Sleep was impossible; study, too, suffered. My silence, at this point, was total; any scene which tended toward scrutiny, demonstration, and display was deeply repugnant to my current spirits.

The violinist Signor Tartini, it is said, dreamed one night that Satan, the Father of Lies, had appeared to him in sleep, crouching on his highboy, and instructed him on the art of the violin, playing in the course of the lesson a melody of astounding seduction. Waking from the dream, Tartini attempted to recollect the fugitive motives of this diabolic sonata, but could not—and wrote instead, from those fragments, his sonata, infamous for its difficulty, called "The Devil's Trill." It was this which was slated on the program for my first appearance—so I was informed by Mr. Sharpe.

The difficulties of execution were not insuperable; but I feared that there should be no vigor in my rendering when my senses were clogged with terror at crowds and a crippling imagination of imminent failure. I imagined the silence of the hall when I struck the last chord; my bow wavering in silence; and me standing alone before the faces of a mob unimpressed by my exertions.

It eased me not a bit to discover I was being fit with a new suit of clothes for the concert. I stood with my arms spread wide and let the tailors measure me. They lay various stuffs against my skin to determine hue. The principal item in the outfit was a frock-coat of black silk with crimson trim. It did not help to hear my mother carp about the colors.

"He will look," she said, "like a city parson at the racetrack. Someone who puts his money on horses named after the Patriarchs."

"No commentary from the mother," said Mr. Sharpe.

"It is barbaric to press the child into playing," said my mother. "Is not his fear evident? He will run distracted. He cannot sleep."

But Mr. Sharpe would listen to none of her importuning nor mine; and so the dreaded night approached.

From the steaming and corrosive blood of the Gorgon Medusa, most terrible to behold, she whose serpent-fringed visage incited petrifaction in all who gazed upon it, arose Pegasus, noblest of steeds, who alone could loft mortals to the heights of Mount Parnassus; in the same way, often that which most we fear births the resolve that spurs us on to altitudes we could not have achieved, had we continued walking on our customary paths.

On the evening of the concert, I was dressed with much fanfare. Bono stood behind me as I dressed. He laid his hands upon my shoulders, our two heads encompassed by the mirror; my ebon frock-coat glistening anew in the candlelight.

"Make them howl," he said.

In the coach, my mother took my hand. Mr. Gitney and Mr. Sharpe sat across from us, clearly disordered by an excitation of nerves almost as extreme as my own.

"One word," said Mr. Sharpe. "I have taken the liberty of informing the impresario that you acquired your astounding musical facility in one night through conversation with the Devil at a crossroads."

I gaped at him.

"Pardon?" demanded my mother.

"Do nothing to disabuse the public of this notion."

I said softly, "Sir, I labored for—"

"The common man likes a story," declared Sharpe. "As much as your Puritan Boston admires labor, there are times when the price of a commodity may be increased by concealing honest hard work. Work is not seductive. We wish to give the people some magic."

"This is outrageous," said my mother, turning to the window.

"Hence the garb," said Sharpe, betraying some pride. "The Devil is commonly supposed to be a black man in habiliments of black, playing the fiddle."

"Hence also," said my mother, "the 'Devil's Trill' sonata."

"Precisely," said Sharpe. "It is all one beautiful package."

"This does," said Mr. Gitney, "seem somewhat irregular, Dick."

"It is my hope," Mr. Sharpe said, "that it shall be weekly."

It was a warm night, wet, and all glistened from a recent rain. The windows of the houses we passed were lit, and I could snatch glimpses of quiet lives — a mother clearing a table, or men gesticulating with their pipes. Three children, arrayed in size, stood on their stoop in the spring air, eating cakes.

"Remember *beauty*," Mr. Sharpe instructed me. "Perhaps — know you what I like particularly? When notices in the newspapers describe a fiddler playing *like fire coursed from his fingertips*. Is that not inspiring? Your average concert enthusiast does not want to hear your melancholy perversities and pranks. Dazzle them, Octavian. Sweetness and light. Cheerful and gay. (A) Sweetness. (B) Light. See? This is the way to their hearts."

The carriage made its way through the streets of the town.

Cheerful and gay. Sweetness and light. These words stood before me like a rebuke of everything I loved in music. I held them before me as we pulled up by Faneuil Hall. I took my teeth around them as I sat behind a column at the theater, waiting to step out and play. I meditated upon them when I made my way out before the orchestra, before the silent multitude of Boston's finest citizens. I gazed before me, and, holding the bow aloft above the strings, envisioned Mr. Sharpe's gray face, turned to the side, as he instructed me, "Remember beauty. Sweetness and light. Cheerful and gay" — and I began the sonata.

I played the first movement like the lolling of a suicide's head in the tub, the corpse lukewarm, the roseate water lapping at the slackened lips. The melody was adorned in equal measure by the harshness of tone and a dismal, languorous mistuning with which I plagued all but the uneasy cadences. It is little marked upon how much skill must be exercised to produce the most piquant malformations.

The second movement, a more lively one as written by Signor Tartini, somewhat a dance, I played like the kicking of a turtle-headed spawn in a woman's womb.

Dissatisfaction marked the few attentive faces I could discern in the gloom.

The third movement contained the much-dreaded trill, rapid and triple-stopped, which gave the piece its name. My tone was dry and hoarse, a febrile scratching; the trill itself I began as an insect rattle, almost inaudible—a single fly that sups on the hand; then the rattle grew—swarming—grotesque—the air ateem with carrion-flies, swooping, crawling, rejoicing in Beelzebub their Master.

I gave them their Devil's Trill.

With a final, melancholic sawing, the piece was over.

The applause, perhaps, lacked something of the vigor, the generosity and celebratory ebullience it had in my previous performance. The clapping soon ended.

I felt a new bitterness in my heart; from whence, I knew not; and even as I retired to my seat, I assayed to address it through prayer to the most comfortable and equanimitous of Beings. Violinists from the orchestra shook my hand warmly, but my thoughts ran only to how I had, in anger, entertained the Serpent. I sent up hasty orisons, that the crabbed muscle within my breast be spread with balm by the hand divine, and so lose its present clogged flaccidity.

It little alleviated my disgust at the easy blasphemy I had entertained that the rest of the program consisted of excerpts from Handel's oratorios, selected on the theme of liberty, programmed so that the assembled might reflect upon the need for action in the present confrontation with the representatives of Parliament. Succeeded by the choir's acclamations and triumphal assurance, my grim melodic turns and bitterness showed themselves to be mere tantrums.

At the close of the program, Mr. Gitney greeted me warmly, telling me how deeply interesting had been my rendition; that it had chilled him quite pleasantly; my mother embraced me; and Mr. Sharpe took my arm, dug his fingers deeply into my flesh, and told me that I should sit back and recline in my chair while I could, for in a half an hour, my back would be too striped to admit of any respite whatsoever.

It is, however, with pleasure that I write—and at the time, with pleasure that I marked—that many in that convocation had found my rendition not without merit; though I cannot imagine that their compliments were not due in part to their pity for my obvious distress, rather than any sympathy for a performance distorted by pride and pique. Young men pressed my hand, vowing I had spoke more of the vile institution of slavery in my few moments of sonata than all the preachers in Boston in a year; I bowed my head and thanked them, though I little believed myself responsible for stirring their sympathies.

It was the memory of these compliments which I brought

before my eyes and held, engraved so deep and with so metallic a sheen, when that night Mr. Sharpe whipped me with the rod: a hand extended, a smiling youth— and then a blow upon my back —a lady with her fan— and then another blow— a child peering with wonder—the visions standing out in negative *intaglio* as the birch-wand hit and smarted.

"Now," said he, laying aside the rod, "prepare my hair."

He sitting, I tucked my shirt into my breeches and, trembling, moved to assist him. I untied the silk ribbons in his hair, and released his queue from its bag. It uncoiled sluggishly upon his back, and, with a shudder, I lifted it with my fingers so it might be combed out.

"You are not so grand now," he said. He did not face me.

My back stung; I prepared his hair for retiring.

Thereafter, Mr. Sharpe hired me out to play only simple dances, the impresario at Faneuil Hall disrelishing my acerbities; and several times I went, habited in my ebon frock-coat, and played country tunes and minuets while the gentry skipped it in a banquet hall. The country dances I found pleasant in the highest degree; the minuets too pretty for my taste, and dry.

Not infrequently, the others who played the British jigs and hornpipes with me on fiddle or pipe were of my Africk race. We were not permitted to speak much, there being little time for conversation; and so we were reduced to nods and watchful eyes. With each, I wondered, *Who hath taught thee these English tunes? Do you ask the same of me? We all have our tales. What music do you hear when you sleep?*

But most asked few questions, being content to play what the dancing-master demanded; and most, like me, found pleasure in the old tunes and their enlarging. And so the many turned, and bowed, and I played, and this was gratification enough.

Music hath its land of origin; and yet it is also its own country, its own sovereign power, and all may take refuge there, and all, once settled, may claim it as their own, and all may meet there in amity; and these instruments, as surely as instruments of torture, belong to all of us.

The tumults of the times are oft passed by in records of the private memoirist; for our days consist not of the Senatorial speech and the refracted solar beam cast through heroic cloud, but rather of bread eaten, and ink blotted, and talk of the sermon, and walks along the whiskery avenues in the garden.

And yet, in the town, in that year, there could be no avoidance of history, for the streets were full of her assaults and confusions. Many nights, bells were rung throughout the city, and we knew that somewhere, a mob had formed; a house was being stoned; on some street corner, malcontents hurled branches through shop windows with cries of "Liberty and Property!" Harvard men were standing amidst the crowds, inciting them to burn, to terrify, to beat, to batter.

We would hear the steeples ringing. Those who slept with windows on the front of the house would hear a small phalanx of apprentices run past on the cobbles, going to join the fracas, planning riot with verve.

The next morning, we would hear reports of a milliner's shop battered for importation, or an affray in a coffeehouse, gentlemen bruised, or a boy in a crowd shot mortally.

All the while, our gaunt house by the garden descended ever more into penury.

I am no believer in the fatal power of the stars; I do not hold with those ancient superstitions regarding the spiritual threads strung from the celestial bodies that tug us helpless as the spheres revolve; but nonetheless, I sometimes reflect that that most prodigious conjunction, the Transit of Venus, put a period to any simulation of happiness and ease amongst us. After Venus passed over the face of the sun, a new age began.

In the summer, we had stood on the shores of the lake, amidst the birch groves, and we had laughed like some new pantheon preparing for Creation. It seemed to me, bewildered as I was, that the world should go on unchanged in its course forever.

So little did I imagine, as I stood on the warm shores of that lake beside an English lord and heard the crickets sing, that only nine months hence, the Empire should receive its first blows; that I should hear bells rung all night, and cries of "Fire!" and lie awake in my frigid bed unable to warm myself; while outside, in the square near the Customs House, a crowd of hundreds would gather, shouting abuse at the Redcoats who stood on guard there; that this mob, full of false assurances that the King's soldiers could not fire upon citizens, would yell their spiteful taunts—"Fire! Fire at us, you cowards!"—"We ain't afraid!"—"Molly-boy! Bugger! Shoot for the heart!"—throwing fragments of ice and trying to knock the bearskin hats from the soldiers' heads. The crowd would surge forward; surround the Redcoats; one would raise a plank to beat in a soldier's head—whereupon a private stumbled, felled by thrown wood—and the soldiers, at long last, fired into the crowd.

Five citizens lay on the ice, their mouths open, their hands filled with slush.

The next day, two of them were on display, one in an apothecary shop, another lying on a table in a nearby tavern. Bono went to see the latter corpse, paying threepence.

"That ain't much," he said, "to pay to see history."

"*Worse than war,*" saith Seneca, "*is the dreadful waiting for war.*"

I have no desire to speak of the next several years, the years that conveyed me from childhood to youth. I take no pleasure in their memory.

The house was quieter — or, no, not quieter, for there were still shouts up and down the hallways — than what? I do not know. The very wood of the walls seemed darker, more worn and chipped.

Mr. Gitney was but rarely restored to his previous excitement about the pursuit of the sciences. He still directed philosophic operations, but it was clear to all that he was answerable to Mr. Sharpe, who lived in his house, apparently as a guest, but verily, as a master.

Mr. Sharpe, we divined, represented a consortium of investors. He had trained in the natural sciences himself, and so was considered fit to act as the under-writers' representative in the College. Some several of the new investors were merchant relatives of Mr. Gitney's, the Young Men whom I had seen about the house in earlier days, but whose presence had never amounted to much. Now they came by not only to dine and partake of the arts—of which there were fewer in evidence all the time—but rather to tour the facilities and pronounce upon progress. Most of the investors were *in absentia,* gentlemen from Philadelphia or the southern Colonies who corresponded regularly with Mr. Sharpe, but who never saw our Novanglian academy.

In those years, there was little pleasure of any kind in the house.

My mother, without her coterie, was often almost as silent as me. Her beauty did not fade, but she did not advertise it so in the passages and chambers. She read romances and slept much of the day. Mr. Sharpe employed her in sewing for the household.

When we attended the Meeting House of a Sunday—for we went no longer to King's Chapel, Mr. Sharpe finding the Anglican faith disgustful and near Papistical—my mother wore not the finery of former days, but sober garments of simple linsey-woolsey in sad colors. Seated in the Negro gallery amongst other servants, Indians, and white boys banished for whispering and tricks, she appeared no different, no more peculiar in her circumstances, than any lady's maid.

Her manner was languid, and her gestures without that gayety which had so marked her before. Some vital principle in her was compromised. She did not regain it, and, in truth, became almost immobile for some weeks after it was announced that the Chief Justice of the King's Bench had decreed (as we heard it then, conveyed by the mouth of rumor) that slavery was illegal on English soil; that any American slave there who sued in the British Isles for his or her freedom should be emancipated, for so long as they remained on those shores.

The day she heard of this determination, my mother walked as if in sleep to the room where Bono and I sate, shining boots.

"You have heard of the Somerset decision?" she said to Bono. "Freed. All of them, I suppose."

He nodded.

"Had I gone to London . . . and taken you all . . . Had I submitted to Lord Cheldthorpe's infamous . . ." She waved her hand. "Three years of bondage. Then release."

"Don't say this," said Bono. "I don't wish to hear any of this."

"Are you sensible of what I've done to my son?"

"Your Highness," said Bono, jerking a shoe towards me in a gesture of reminder. "Hold. Please."

I had stopped brushing a boot, and regarded her fixedly. She came to me and put aside the boot, and held on to me as though I were not a boy of some stature, but an infant, and she rocked me; singing me a crying song, again and again, that she was sorry; she was sorry; she was sorry that she had not—

But she couldn't find a verb which could describe with decency what had been demanded of her.

Bono himself became more quiet in those years. Always circumspect when addressing the white inhabitants of the house, he ceased to speak to them at all unless speech was demanded of him by his master. This was not defiance, but watchfulness. He would say nothing that gave them insight into his intelligences and stratagems. They, of course, did not notice.

Bono had been trained to read and write, as contributing to his usefulness as Mr. Gitney's valet. Shortly after the coming of Mr. Sharpe, Bono began to peruse the gazettes and papers when Mr. Gitney was quit of them; and he would tear out certain articles and paste them onto paper, making, after some six months, a sizeable book.

One day, Mr. Sharpe and I chanced to enter the kitchen while Bono pasted. Mr. Sharpe was sufficiently canny to see that Bono attempted to direct his attention elsewhere, towards the cook, who was laboring over beets. Mr. Sharpe would not be shaken.

"What are those papers?" asked Mr. Sharpe.

"I am a fashionable man," said Bono. "It's a catalogue of fashions."

Mr. Sharpe held out his hand.

Bono handed over the sheaf. "There ain't nothing illegal," he said, "about being devilish handsome."

Mr. Sharpe flipped through the pages. I stood behind him, but could not see Bono's miscellany. I could perceive, however, Mr. Sharpe's agitation. "For what purpose do you collect these?" he demanded.

"I'm part of the *bo mond*. I fancy seeing what your man on the street is wearing."

"Do you know where Mr. Gitney is?"

"I believe he is in the garden, sir."

"Let's go and fetch him."

"Yes, sir."

"To authorize your whipping. You," he said to me, "go call one of the grooms. Tell him to bring a riding crop and meet us in the garden."

Bono walked out of the kitchen, slamming the door behind him. Mr. Sharpe followed, saying, "Three more lashes for the slam."

I went to the table where the papers had been left. I lifted up the first, blank, page, and surveyed those beneath, to see, as Bono quoth, what the man on the street was wearing.

It was a catalogue of horrors. Page after page of Negroes in bridles, strapped to walls, advertisements for shackles, reports of hangings of slaves for theft or insubordination. He had, those many months, been collecting offers for children sold cheap, requests for aid in running down families who had fled their masters. For the first time, I saw masks of iron with metal mouth-bits for the slave to suck to enforce absolute silence. I saw razored necklaces, collars of spikes that supported the head. I saw women chained in coffles, bent over on the wharves.

Mr. Gitney burned Bono's fashion catalogue an hour later.

"Let us rid ourselves," he said, "of this noisome object."

But I could not rid myself of it. It was the common property of us all.

That night, after I had weighed my fæces and recorded their mass in the book which I had been given for that purpose, I paused; I set down the chamber-pot and replaced the lid.

I was sensible of a growing revolt of the spirit that suffused the whole of my frame, which would no longer be stifled or mollified. I saw again the instruments of torture before me.

I proceeded along the passage to my mother's chamber. She and one of the maids sat before the fire, sewing. She asked me what had brought me there at so unseasonable an hour. In response, I merely passed to her my record book, which with quizzical countenance, she turned through. Coming to the last page and finding it unremarkable, she looked at me for explanation.

I could not speak; and so merely shook my head. I shook it slowly and with finality.

She put a thread in her mouth and wet it with her lips. "Then go speak to him," she said. "For what little good it will do you."

I went out upon the landing. I went down the stairs. I sought out Mr. Gitney. I found him in the experimental chambers, burning hair.

"Sir," I said, "I am delivering my ingestion book."

He indicated that I should put it down on the table. He was absorbed in his calculations. "Is it full?" he said. "The book? That seems quick."

I did not answer.

He looked up, saw my face, and ceased his experiment. He drew the book to him across the slats of the table. He flipped through. "It is nearly half empty," he said.

I did not move. He watched me. He frowned, and he arranged his coat-tails around his thighs.

I could not look at him, so I cast my eyes down; but I shook my head as I had for my mother in clear refusal.

"That is not for you to say," he explained.

For a long time I revolved what I should next say. At long last, I hit upon, "Why are you doing this to me?"

"It is not *to* you, Octavian. It is *for* you."

"Sir—"

"We have noted that your attention lags. Your ability to comprehend Greek and Latin seems to have declined over the course of the last two years."

"I am given only fragments to read."

"Reading is but reading, Octavian. We are disappointed in you."

Our business was done. I wished heartily to withdraw. (O

turncoat heart, which in retirement speaks of great deeds, and then in the fray, whimpers for retreat and quiet!) Yearning for the door behind me, the passage, the darkness of my chamber and the assurances of Bono, I began almost to weep; but instead asked, voice husky with tears, "Why can I not study with Dr. Trefusis?"

"The investors have determined that he skewed the experimental results by introducing incentives. The material he had you study was deemed impractical."

"Who are the investors?"

"This is not relevant."

He waited for me to take my leave. I did not. I stood in that closet, before the books recording my defecation and the engraving of my mother naked, and I did not step from that space.

I said, "You wish me to fail."

"Octavian."

I did not move.

He said, "I wish no such thing. I have watched over your education with affection and benevolence." He leaned back in his chair. "In the formulary of Diocles the Physician, we are told that in the selfsame toad there are two livers—one poisonous, and one which brings instant health. We might consider: Is not this like unto—"

"Why does Mr. Sharpe interfere with my education?"

"He does no such thing."

I thought of the fragments he taught me and the whippings. I nodded without words; I would not stop; I could not while the lie still prospered.

"Octavian, I dislike this impertinence. Mr. Sharpe is impartial. He wishes neither your failure nor your success. That is the nature of an experiment. He is making a rational inquiry into your capacities."

"He wishes me to fail."

"That would counter the dictates of rationality."

"In Bono's catalogue, I saw devices . . . the ones which hobble the legs . . . so flight is impossible. . . ."

"I wish you had not seen that."

We stared at each other in the brown evening. Mr. Gitney could not hold my gaze. He looked away. "I could wish," he said, "that Mr. Sharpe had not instituted these regulations respecting your learning. I am sensible they do seem . . ."

I stepped closer to the table. "Sir," I demanded softly, "with the respect due to me as your student, tell me why Mr. Sharpe wishes me to fail."

Wearily, Mr. Gitney said, "Mr. Sharpe does not wish you to fail." He picked up strands of hair from before him and rolled them between his fingers. He wrapped the hairs around a thumb and tugged. At last, he admitted, "The nature . . . of the experiment . . . has changed."

"How?" I asked.

"We receive our funds now from a consortium of men of affairs who have some interest in proving the inequality of African capacities."

I had known the answer, and yet, to hear it stated so baldly was terrifying.

"Our investors took particular interest in your progress, but felt that the experiment was skewed by a certain favoritism towards the African subject. They requested that we institute new practices to ensure that the experiment was conducted with more complete impartiality."

"Who are they?" I whispered.

"They are drawn from several of the Colonies. They are, for the most part, merchants, the owners of some few plantations . . . rice, tobacco. . . . They have been most generous in their funding."

I stepped backwards. "Sir," I said, "how can this be supported?"

He looked careful in the candlelight. "I would be racked with guilt," he admitted, "were I not devoted to the belief that the results you will produce will more than outweigh their claim."

This was the comfort I received.

I left the book on the table.

Empedocles claims that *in utero,* our backbone is one long solid; and that through the constriction of the womb and the punishments of birth it must be snapped again and again to form our vertebræ; that for the child to have a spine, his back must first be broken.

Following this interview, I walked to the chamber I shared with Bono, and I recalled all the lessons in language Dr. Trefusis had set me in the last weeks I'd been permitted to study with him:

(A) In the reign of the Tarquins (so Livy tells us), a slave-boy was found sleeping in the palace with his head afire; it burned with a mystical flame as he slumbered, and yet was not consumed. When this boy, son of the captive Princess of Corniculum, awoke, the flames evaporated, leaving him unscarred; some years later, as this prodigious conflagration foretold, he was crowned King of Rome.

(B) I read of the slave revolt of the wizard called King Antiochus.

(C) I read of the Greek slaves who, endued with countless graces, taught their Roman masters' children philosophy, declamation, poetry, and all the arts.

(D) I read love-poems to bonded girls.

(E) I read in Plutarch of the rise of the gladiatorial slave Spartacus.

(F) I read of Diogenes the Cynic, who traveled the length and breadth of Greece in a bathtub, and who was captured by pirates and sold into slavery in Crete. When the slave-auctioneer inquired what skills Diogenes might offer, the philosopher replied, "Ruling men."

Some few months later, a mob assembled in Old South Meeting House; and, after a rousing word by Mr. Adams, some habited themselves as Mohawk Indians and repaired to the wharves, where they dumped tea.

I did not hear of this charade until the next day, and did not understand its purport; rather thinking it a pleasant interlude from the more brutal games of the Sons of Liberty. There was something almost gentlemanly about it, a hint of sport. Dr. Trefusis and I walked along the wharves and spake of disguise, color, substance, and the solidity of matter.

Far out in the harbor, tea clotted the brilliancy of sun upon the water. Men thin as insects rowed scows between the clumps, shepherding them with paddles, pressing down upon them, dousing them, drowning them, so that light might play unimpeded upon the winter sea.

The months went by; I read my fragments and powdered Mr. Sharpe's hair. I played dance-tunes at the convocations and entertainments of wealth. My mother sewed in the kitchen with the other slaves.

We heard the countryside was full of insurrection. In every town, Loyalists and rebels rose against each other. Men were beaten; some were shot at in jest. The spirit of Anarchy spread everywhere his light and agitated wings.

Merchants began to stock-pile for war, for siege. The Harbor was plied with barges and packets from all up and down the coast, delivering fuel and grain. There was, in all of the denizens of the town, an expectation of riot, famine, and sickness. In the countryside, rumors of smallpox spread like sedition. There was word that the pestilence crawled towards the city from the north shore, and that soon, in the alleys, we should be dying of it.

On June 1st of that year, the fatal blow fell: the Port of Boston was closed; the Assembly dismissed; the Governor rescinded to England; General Gage, newly come from London and an audience with the King, appointed in the Governor's place; the courts were in ruin; and it seemed all civil government was at an end.

Many families began to flee the town; while others fled into that last hive of the government for protection: being rural justices who cleaved to the Tory cause, and met with hard words and had their horses maimed or painted; journeymen who had spake too loudly of their loyalty to the King at taverns; men who had been belabored about the head with the butts of muskets; farmers who had been hoisted up Liberty poles and forced to recant; shop-keepers who had persisted in selling their English wares, despite the injunctions of the rebel Committees. Such made their way into the city, where transport ships seemed daily to arrive, disgorging regiments of soldiers who paraded through the streets and en-camped upon the Common.

Fasts were declared, and public prayer. We knelt in the Negro aisles of the Meeting House asking for deliverance from what was to come. Other cities, too, called for fasts to offer up their corporate orisons; and, sensible of our distress, they sent flour and rice. Carts came all day across Boston Neck.

We were among those who fled into the countryside.

At the Gitney house, we packed our things in trunks. We closed up the windows with shutters and laid sheets upon the furniture, the house being prepared for dormancy. We rushed through the uncarpeted chambers, candlesticks clutched to our breasts. On the streets, we heard the marching of soldiers.

Mr. Gitney hired wagons, and we were all employed in carrying out experimental apparati and stacking them behind the horses. Caged animals squabbled with us through the bars. We sent out wagon-load after wagon-load into the countryside.

We were retreating to the house of one of Mr. Gitney's brothers, one of the Young Men.

The house was a spacious one, new built, in the town of Canaan, Massachusetts. We set up experimental chambers there, and fed the raccoons and serpents. We constructed our curious machines.

We heard news — which word could not but quicken the blood — of common men rising in the thousands to empty the rural law courts of corruption and expel the un-elected favorites of government. We heard of troop movements in the countryside to seize powder and shot. We heard of free elections cancelled for fear of who would win.

And in the midst of it, Bono was given away as a Christmas gift to a trustee of the College.

Mr. Sharpe and Mr. Gitney both felt considerable trepidation at the onset of what promised to be the most mischievous of calamities. With the closure of the port, most of the College's income was stopped up and its investments nullified; and so to anxiety was added penury.

As a result, Mr. Sharpe and Mr. Gitney's remonstrances with the committee of investors were grown particularly groveling and obsequious. To this date, I know not what terms they discussed, what blasphemous deal they tried to strike, abhorrent to their humanity. I know only that, in the course of negotiations, they elected to deliver Pro Bono as a garnish to a gentleman donor in the Virginia Colony.

Bono and I sat in the country house's garden. A thin snow had fallen the night before and grimed the weeds.

"A new light of liberty appears in the land," I said, without hope.

"Aye," said Bono.

"It may be that we shall not long be slaves."

He nodded without reply.

We both surveyed the bedraggled stalks of dead things. The wind blew across us, over the brick walls. The sky was gray that day, and mobile.

I asked him, "What do you think of?"

"Coffles," he said.

"You will be a gentleman's valet."

"I'll be one skip closer to the West Indies," he said. "Where they don't bother to feed a man because they don't bother to keep him alive."

I could not think on it. I wished to embrace him.

O Lord of heaven—place Your hand upon him now, Your palm incised with age and suffering. The deeps of heat there in the Indies—he shall not go there—the ranks of chained men led out to the sugar-fields—the sun, buzzing in the heavens. O Lord— say that he shall not go there—decree it—the mud where men lie whitening as they die.

"Bono," I said, choking on my own panic—thinking thus then, as I pray devoutly now—"Bono, you have been like my—," and I held forth my hand to touch him, not knowing what word could supply his curious role—a brother? A father?

"Do not speak," he said, rising. He took my hand and pulled me to my feet. He yanked my arm, and dragged me through the desolate orchard. He said, "I ain't going anywhere I don't wish. You be sure." He led me through an arbor; we stood in a small grove of dead vines trailing purple across furniture of marble. There was a door there which led out into the pastures of Canaan. There were, as well, several terms, stone satyrs in the brambles.

Bono pushed my head down towards a flat rock, on which the snow lay.

"You see that?" he said. "Commit it to memory. It's a magic rock."

"I don't understand."

"You pray to that rock sometime, and it give you what you wish for. You see it now?"

"Is this some frenzied retreat into your native animism?" I asked.

"God damn, I'll retreat my boot up your arse. Do you see it?" He thrust my skull towards the stone.

"I see it."

I could hear him close to tears. "There's going to be some day when you need it, and you come out here, and you pray to it. And you hold it close to your belly. And it will give you everything you ask. Does His Highness understand?"

"I understand."

"Does His Highness remember?"

"His Highness does."

"Does His Highness, King of Nowhere, Monarch of Nothing, Lord of the Shit-hill Isles—"

"Bono," I said. "His Highness wishes to entertain a more decorous final image of you than being held over a rock and berated by some parcel of insanity."

He let loose his grip on me. I stood to my full height. I was of a height with him, though he was broader.

He looked out over the wall into the orchard, squinting. "First week I was at the College," he said, "they lit some kind of gas on fire. You recall that? Out in the orchard. You were little. A minikin."

"I recall it," I said.

"I thought they was gods. I thought, *Now I'm walking in heaven, and it won't ever matter what happens on Earth.*"

Together, we looked at the apple-trees against the winter sky.

"Fine, then," he said. "I'm going to go in now to put a bow in my hair. As befits a gift."

T he next day, they took him to Salem to dispatch him in a coaster bound for Virginia. Through Dr. Trefusis's kind intercession, I was permitted to ride with them, though atop the carriage, rather than within.

We reached the Salem wharves late in the day; I climbed down to open the carriage door and set in place the steps. As Mr. Gitney and Bono descended, I could see in the lineaments of their faces that the ride of hours had not been passed in idleness, but rather marked by contest of will.

Mr. Gitney having alerted the captain of the vessel to our arrival and arranged for two soldiers to conduct Bono to the ship, he returned to his charge.

He said to Bono, "You refuse still to tell me what you heard?"

Bono replied, "I don't know what you think I know, sir."

Mr. Gitney nodded and scowled. "Then I wish you enjoyment of the Southern Colonies," said he, and with that, turned and climbed back into the carriage.

Bono and I faced each other. We embraced — or I should say, I embraced him, as his hands were shackled behind him until such time as the ship made open water.

He looked at me; I looked at him.

"Next time we meet," he promised, "I'll have a different name."

They rowed him out to the ship. I stood upon the shore and waved.

He looked back once at us while they bundled him aboard; then he turned his face toward the sun.

Without Bono, my days were a brown drudgery. My mother seemed defeated too by his absence, as he had long supplied her with companionship; and she and I went about our tasks without pleasure, slept without release in dreams, and ate without satiety.

Canaan, where now we lodged, was full of Whigs and rebels. We watched at night by moonlight as they lugged cannon past our door on the way to Concord and Acton. They covered kegs of gunpowder with hay.

We heard reports from Boston. The body politic was so disordered that all government seemed suspended. Soldiers patrolled through the streets, apprehending Negroes out at unseasonable hours on suspect errands. Groups of rebels, communicating by eerie whistles, carried out a nighttime justice, descending on informants

silently. There was continual outcry against the troops by some —
soldiers scuffling with boys, their heel-marks in the slush; girls surrounded by lanky privates.

We went about our business in the countryside, in a town of
slow undulating fields and great clouds.

On the Canaan town green, the militia practiced loading and
firing their muskets. We sate inside, and jumped with the reports of
guns in the distance. Their officers claimed, with supercilious air,
that they practiced speed and marksmanship in case the French
should invade; but we all of us knew for what eventuality they
prepared.

And late in March, as we all awaited some imminent fatality,
Mr. Gitney sent out invitations for a pox party.

Canaan

March the 20th, 1775

Sir—Madam—

I would be most gratified by your attendance at a *Pox Party,* to be given beginning the 1st of April at my brother Lemuel Gitney's Lodgings—on which Day my Guests and their servants shall receive as it were the *Kiss of Life* upon the Arm—which shall prove your Immunity from the Plague of the Small Pox, according to the *most cur-rent Methods.* No one shall leave the Premises once the Inoculation is complete. The Party shall continue unabated, in full festival Mode, for some few weeks thereafter, or until the belittled Pestilence has run its course through the Assembled. Any inconvenience due to our seques-tration will be outweighed by the Protection afforded both against the Pox itself and against other Tumults of this Colony, of which we all must be sensible.

Commodious Quarters shall be erected for your Serving-People; the gayest and most gracious of Entertainments shall grace the Gathering throughout; and excellent Cuisine *the Like of which you shall not have again while these oppressive Measures last.* Contagion may well stalk these Fields, "his Eye-Sockets glaring Beams of frigid Light; his withered Weeds draped about the slats of his Emaciation"; *but can we not bask in those Rays? And can we not dress him instead in Raiment of Silk, and teach him to dance the Minuet—and, the dance over, bid him bow and be GONE?*

In short—if you must take the sickness—I beg that you share it with

Your most humble & affectionate,

Mr. Josiah Gitney

I have not been able to divine entirely why Mr. Gitney called for a pox party when he did. Certainly, the first and clearest motivation was that most obvious to view: that the smallpox circulated throughout the north shore at that time, and, in anticipation of its spread throughout the countryside—which, in a time of tumult, would be rapid and rapacious—he proposed that all who had not previously suffered from the disease should be exposed to it through a prescribed process which rendered it, in most cases, inoffensive. By submitting guests to a mild form of the distemper, which should last for some few weeks, he might greatly curtail the mortality of his acquaintance and their households.

And yet—at the time he announced the party, Boston was hearing only its first rumors of plague in the countryside. There was, as yet, no cause for alarm.

Mr. Gitney had other reasons for announcing this convocation; these darker purposes, I only happened upon as the party progressed. Suffice to say, it was not medical foresight which prompted him to arrange this gruesome fête.

Not foresight indeed—nor prognostication—for not except in nightmare could he have predicted what destruction this gathering would occasion; that even as my mother and I copied out the invitations at his command, the fates had bent their heads above our household, muttering, and were about to blast his College of Lucidity forever.

My mother and I, as I have said, wrote the invitations; and runners were hired to take them throughout the city and the countryside. It was not far advanced into the spring, and the narrow streets were thick with mud, puddles bright in ruts near heaves. Men on errands had to step dainty to avoid being spattered.

The guests, primarily, were the extended relations of Mr. Gitney, that sizeable clan of merchants known only as the Young Men, cheerful in demeanor, indeterminate in number. Some had fled the city; others, remaining, were sunk in an uncharacteristic despair, their trade irreparably harmed first by their investment in interdicted Indian lands, second by their participation in non-importation agreements, and thirdly, by the punitive closing of the Harbor by Parliamentary decree.

Warships drifted there now; none could slip past.

Taking good advantage of the bounty sent to the city's relief, Mr. Gitney and Mr. Sharpe ordered wines and spirits, fruits procured by special appointment, beeves and hams, flour and honey, game-birds and squash, and, from a pest-house in Salem, a glass jar full of contaminate matter from the pox-sores of the dead.

A harpsichord was rented for the festivities. We placed it in one of the experimental chambers and hauled the philosophic machines against the wall so there should be space for dancing. The day before the party, one of the grooms was employed to wax the floor.

He wore a slipper on one foot and a brush on the other. They required him to dance there alone for three hours.

I passed and watched.

In the silence, he skated.

The afternoon sun was cast across the floor. Where the bowing and leaping should soon commence, there the old man slid and spun by himself, his arms fluttering, making pretty courtesies to chairs; pausing for a *pas de Basque;* his heels thumping; executing secret glissades in beeswax.

Silence and sunlight were his partners.

On the first of April, we began our Pox Party. The handsome equipages of the wealthy delivered them up to our doorstep — the Young Men, their spouses, their children, their friends. There was, first, a reception in the parlor, animated with the same *frisson* of excitement that accompanies the tumbling of acrobats in high spaces.

Well do I recall the finery. Men of business wore waistcoats trimmed with silver galloon. Boston ladies, their skirts all passementarie and furbelow, India silk and jaconet, crowded the chambers, swiveling their hoops and panniers like dames on clocks to navigate the doors. The arrival of their trunks and their servants was advertised by the clamor of feet, heavy-laden, in the hall.

Following light refreshment, we were asked to form a queue leading back through the passage to the newly appointed philosophical apartments. The queue was fairly abuzz with gossip and greetings, the pleasantries of long acquaintance or new. I stood silently behind my mother, where we had been directed, waiting just behind the white denizens of the house, just before the other Negro servants; and we listened to the glad hubbub of the meandering line, the cries of "Ah, sir!" and "Your most affectionate . . ."; inquiries regarding the whereabouts of aunts; rapid intelligences between the ladies respecting flounces, petticoats, and stomachers, the quality of the civic mud.

At the front of the line waited Mr. Gitney by a birthing chair, his instruments laid out before him. As each guest sat and presented a bare arm, he spoke briefly with them of some small matter, asking them of the welfare of their hound or the qualities of the wine they had brought; and then gouged them with a scalpel and inserted into the wound a length of hair wet with pus from a victim in Salem.

Once the corruption was deep within them, Dr. Trefusis and Mr. Sharpe bound their arms with cloths.

Two little boys, dressed in identical gowns, were hopping in line, piping, "Now me! Next is me!"

"Octavian," said Mr. Gitney to me, full of cheer. "Know you that this remedy was first proposed by the inhabitants of Africa?" He rolled my sleeve to reveal my forearm. "It came hither by way of industrious slaves and Constantinople. As with so much medicine, the Arabs hath preceded us, know you . . . Averroës and Avicenna and such like. In Constantinople, too, they institute parties for the variolation against the pox. It is said that they—" He pierced me with the blade. I gasped.

I perceived a jolt—and trembled—as he laid the hair in my blood.

"Through corruption," he said, "you shall be healed."

Later that afternoon, servants unfurled great red silk flags from each window, on which were sewn, GOD HAVE MERCY UPON THIS HOUSE, as was statutory for a house infected with the pox; and as the banners snapped to their full extent, the company assembled all applauded with their fingers on their palms; for the pox party had begun.

It is generally held that any convocation of individuals im- mured is a *microcosm* of the wider world; and certainly, that was true of our pox party, if it is to be observed that misfortune fell upon the knaves and good alike.

In the foyer, tables had been assembled, and the Young Men were seated about them, playing at faro and whist. Servants stood against the wall, awaiting demands for port or biscuits. In the ex- perimental chambers, Mr. Gitney delivered addresses on our expe- dition to witness the Transit of Venus and the determination of natural law.

In the parlor, the women gathered, waiting for the contagion to enflame their chaste frames. My mother sat among them, speak- ing pleasantries, though some did not mark her speech; their disapproval being a curious mixture of awe at her beauty, suspicion for her capacities to charm, and repugnance at her frowardness in mingling.

Mr. Goff, once 07-03, had taken to executing portraits at the top of the stairs, with prospects out the window of the garden and the meadows of Canaan, advertising that he should limn the gentlemen and ladies in all their smooth and unruffled beauty before the pox descended, and, were they unlucky, curdled them forever. When he had not a sitter, he would circulate through the gaming tables and the women's parlor, quivering with his palsy, murmuring, "Madam? Insurance against the blight of your face? The blasting of hopes and future years?"

With such a street cry, he did not lack subjects.

Among the servants, too, there was some opportunity for social pleasantry, we being drawn from so many houses. Aina, the cook, was delighted to discover another of the Benin nation among the visiting maids, both of them being marked on the face with the scars of their kingdom. They spake to one another in a tongue Aina had not heard in long years; and I could tell that they related stories of places they had been as children. There was the quickening of the voice, the molten flurry of excitation, the motion of the hand — an affirmation, as if to say, "Yes! Yes!"—related to the appearance in their discourse, perhaps, of some citadel, or the cloth of some village, or the way the merchants of some certain city habitually treated boatmen.

Only a few days had passed when Intrigue in her shuttered gown was seen skulking through the corridors, as must be expected when numbers of the young, full of high animal spirits, are placed into confinement together.

[*193*]

I shall not dilate upon these intrigues; they were washed away by all that followed. Suffice it to say, there was a love triangle, and one who, to seek revenge, went spreading tales of having licked a breast. No further details were offered to me, and I requested to hear none of it.

Suffice it to say also that there were intrigues among the parental generation, as well—most mischievous, perhaps, to the peace of the gathering was the flirtation of the painter, Mr. Goff, with one of his lady sitters, who felt his queasy palpitations to be the thrumming of energies divine. Though there had been as yet no infidelity, her husband stormed about for some days, requesting the ejection of "that damned dauber," saying that such a one had no business in a gathering of respectable and successful men of the better sort; that painting was, after all, nought but deception one paid for dearly.

So our little intrigues played out while women whispered over the backs of the sofas and men, after supper, passed the port and listened to tales of the wars against the French and the Indians. An elderly veteran of the provincial forces in the late war recounted the peremptory cruelties and unmerited debaucheries of his officers in the King's Army, sparing no cruel details of the lash and noose. The company hung upon his every word.

In the evening, we held dances in the experimental chambers. Three of us among the servants made a little consort of music—I on the violin, an indentured Irishman who also played the fiddle, and a slave from another house who played the flageolet. The Irishman taught us jigs and country tunes, and it was one of the rare pleasures of that party, to learn from his divisions and variations upon those tunes, our strings speaking back and forth to each

other while the gentry did their contra-dances, skipping and turning in lines.

I watched them dance before me—the young and the
wealthy, their parents, full of knowledge of the ways of trade and
profit—delicate in the light of candles and fire—while behind
them, the metal orbs of Mercury, Jupiter, Venus, and Sol hung un-
used from their orrery gears, and in their cages, the raccoon and
serpent surveyed the hornpipe frisking with superstitious gaze; a
skeleton was hanging, face turned to the wall; and while those
dainty dancers skipped it on the polished floors, they brushed
against engines that could produce the sparks of electrical virtue
that brought thunder and lightning battering from the skies.

And this sublimity of danger around which we danced sug-
gests perhaps the final scene in our geography of the festivities: At
the top of the house, in the eaves, three of the Young Men were
posted at all hours in rotation, with the guns of many houses
stacked between them. I did not perceive why they were there,
nor why many who had survived the pox in its last visitation were
present, master and servant alike. When I trod to the top of the
stairs with their meals, I noted only the sentinels' air of watchfulness. They looked out at the windows; one smoked. They
watched the coming day; they watched the laborers turn in from
the fields.

They watched the servants in the yard.

M_{r.} Gitney, one night, called me away from my new duties serving refreshments in the parlor; he instructed that I was to come and see him in the forbidden chamber.

He sat sunk in green gloom. He gestured to a chair, and I sat. I observed that he had a pistol on the desk before him.

"Octavian," said he, "has anyone approached you with any request?"

"We are serving tea, sir, though calling it chocolate so as not to agitate the sensibilities of Patriots."

"Octavian," said he, "have any voices presented themselves to you—speaking in remote quarters—which you might not, in other seasons, hearken to?"

I sat in silence. His queries were insurmountably opaque.

"A slip of paper? Something you find in a basket of eggs?" He waited a space, then continued, "Behind the smithy, concealed in smoke? Handshakes by the brick-yard?" He reached to the desk and hefted the pistol. I watched it with awe. He said, "This is a matter of some interest to us all."

"I aver, sir, I have so little conception of the direction of this interview that I cannot offer any reply whatsoever."

"You swear solemnly that you have no conception of what I speak."

I raised my hand. "So do I swear."

"You swear to Christ in heaven that you have understood not a word of this interchange?"

"I do, sir."

"I have been in every way incomprehensible?"

"Your meaning as dark as night, sir."

"Very good then, Octavian." He placed the pistol on the desk and grasped my shoulder. "You know my affection for you."

I could not answer that either.

"You are sensible of the kindnesses which have been granted freely to you in this house."

I perceived that this interview would not conclude until I had given him assurance; and so I did, vowing that I was grateful, that I was not insensible of the considerable gifts lavished upon me; expatiating on the forthcoming dance that evening; and so, having made my lie, I bowed and made my exit.

When I returned to the kitchen to fetch a second urn of tea, I asked Aina, the cook, "Do you fathom what disaster Mr. Gitney and the Young Men anticipate?"

She looked back from the fire. "You tell me, Prince sir," she said, "what disaster don't they anticipate?"

After some days, the fevers began. In the parlor, the tea-cups rattled on their saucers. Women could not hold them steady. The children complained of head-ache, and their bones seemed to be thawing within them.

Mr. Gitney wandered amongst the guests, noting the progress of each. I accompanied him to the servants' quarters, where he squatted by our pallets and asked each of us to describe any symptoms we might feel. He touched the head of the sickly and felt their heat.

A little boy, the son of one of the Young Men, was the first to find a pock upon him. He insisted upon showing the company. It was on his lip. All praised him for his celerity in sickening.

By later in that day, there were empty seats at the dining table. Girls had seen their palms turning scarlet. A boy had a line of bumps upon his neck like a halter.

That night, we had one of our dances. I could feel the heat rising within me. My day had been uncommonly full of the duties of the servant, my throat felt dewy and raw, and I was in no little discomfort, standing before the remaining company, fevered, playing minuets.

After some twenty minutes, I begged reprieve for a dance, and sat by the wall, looking, I am afraid, much sunk in misery, one leg thrown out, the other against my chest, when Dr. Trefusis hunkered beside me.

"This is a bad business," he said. "They will start frowning if you remain seated. Shall I remove you to the servants' quarters?"

My mother was dancing. I watched her glide across the floor. I was drawn to observe the various manners in which men touched her, the grasp of their hands, the motions across the looped skirts and petticoats of her gown, the intricacies of her bodice.

"When my mother dances now, sir," said I, "men pull her more tightly to them than they do the other women . . . taking liberties . . . or they scarcely deign to touch her. Was it ever thus?" She passed from partner to partner out upon the floor. "I recall her dancing with utmost propriety and a singular beauty."

Dr. Trefusis swiveled on his heels to face the lines of dancers. He noted them for a while, not speaking; and finally, when he spake, he said, "I am sure that it is best you rely upon your memory."

Near us a boy owned loudly that this was a tearing fine collation; and a young maiden replied that she had not seen a more *belle assemblée* in all her years.

To Dr. Trefusis, I said, "None of this can last long."

Someone had slipped a dessert-plate between the ribs of the skeleton. On it sat a half-eaten pudding.

"Hesiod," said Dr. Trefusis, "believed that we were in the fifth declining Age of Man. First the Golden Age, when mankind was in its infancy, and the animals were paired in perfection, and the rivers ran with milk that never soured in the reeds; then from that state, when time began, we fell; and then we had the Silver Age, then the Bronze, followed by the Heroic Age; and now, finally, the base Age of Iron, when men, children of blood, ply the waves and kill for gain. But I fear that some new and even more dismal metal is upon us."

I said, "They fear a revolt, do they not?

"If you mean Mr. Sharpe and the Young Men, indeed, they fear a revolt, though they incite one."

"Mr. Gitney interviewed me. I did not understand his queries."

"Octavian, there is word up and down the coast that the British are attempting to convince slaves to take up arms against their American masters. The citizenry is terrified. You are lying here amongst us, your bodies too dark to see until it is too late." He smiled. "That is what they say. They fear you will all turn murderers." He fell silent, wary of the maids and youths who stood near us, bantering.

"Bono," said I. "Knew he something of this?"

"They suspected him of knowing," said Dr. Trefusis. "He had heard the rumor of an uprising, as had they; but I believe he knew no more."

With realization, I whispered, "They sent him away for this. Out of fear."

"Not simply for this," said Dr. Trefusis. "Bono was a valuable gift. A most excellent valet. Possessed of surprising arts."

At the revelation of this further indignity — Bono's life altered universally by mere rumor — I could not speak immediately. I could but hear the twittering of the music, and the badinage of the young persons to our side, who laughed about kisses; one girl exclaiming, "I will take the upper lip, Sarah, if you take the lower," another replying that the whole male race smellt of beef.

"You ladies are cruel," cried one of the youths, slapping his chest. "My heart is bursting in its rib-cage."

Lowering his head, Dr. Trefusis murmured, "The rebels cannot stand for this threat of insurrection. They look, and everywhere, up and down the coast, they see Africans. Their slaves sleep next to the family children. Their slaves touch their wives' necks in the mornings, as they lay out jewelry upon the breast. Their slaves," he said, "shave them with razors. The watch has been doubled. Mr. Sharpe and the Young Men have been discussing it when none of you are nearby. They say it is an outrage, that the British should so endeavor to turn a man's property against him. They fear that the British will stop at nothing to subdue them. It is yet another reason they prompt insurrection."

"This," I said sadly, "is why they have quarantined us here."

"One reason, indeed. They predict that within the month, something will come to pass; and it is best if they are out of it, with their slaves weak, and fearful of running. All shall be changed, Octavian. The rebels gather ammunition and gunpowder just outside the city. They are ready for an offensive, come it from the slave quarters or the barracks of the King's Army. The British will not abide this for long. Something, my Prince, shall come to pass."

Nearby us, the young pursued their flirtation. A boy declared, "I should like to see one of you ladies hung upside down by the ankles. Perhaps you would care to guess which one."

"Does anyone wish more Brie?" asked another youth. "I could eat Brie until I looked like soap."

"All shall be changed," I whispered.

"Except," said Dr. Trefusis, looking around the gathering, "that I fear one thing shall remain. When I peer into the reaches of the most distant futurity, I fear that even in some unseen epoch when there are colonies even upon the moon itself, there shall still be gatherings like this, where the young, blinded by privilege, shall dance and giggle and compare their poxy lesions." He balanced himself with his fingertips. "We are a young country, a country of the young," he said bitterly. "The young must have their little entertainments."

"I am young," I said.

"I did not mean you."

"I would—could I do it—I would wish to dance with them."

He winced.

My mother fell.

Dr. Trefusis rose instantly to his feet. I could not rise with such swiftness.

Others were gathered around her. I stumbled to my feet; my leg dragged, deficient in its circulation.

Already, she sat up. Her eyes were wide. She whispered to herself. Inquiries were made as to her strength; she responded that she had a turtle's shell upon her, would not let her vault as she wished. She attempted to swat at something—the shell—upon her back, crying with the frustration.

"She is distempered," said Dr. Trefusis. He went to her side. "Will a gentleman assist me?"

I went and took her other arm, and we raised her up. Dr. Trefusis stumbled beneath her weight, before Mr. Gitney stepped in.

Together, we drew her out of the dance.

As the door shut behind us, the music struck up again, and the dancing carried on.

My mother being laid upon her mattress, I bowed and made to retire from the chamber.

"Octavian," said Mr. Gitney, "you sat."

I inclined my head and awaited reproach.

"You require no instruction in this matter ... to sit before guests ... it disrespects them and the house."

"I plead my fever, sir."

"You are a rational being. Your fever is but a state. ... The sole mitigation I can summon is that you did not sit in a chair which might have been occupied by a guest, but settled upon the floor."

My mother moaned from her pallet.

"There is no time for the wanted objurgation," said Mr. Gitney, frowning. I knew not his word, and hesitated; he, perceiving my fault, explained its meaning and derivation while my mother begged for water. He bade me return to the dance and take up my fiddle again, and so I stepped out of the chamber, he kneeling beside my mother to minister to her.

My spirits flagged with the exhaustion of illness; their mute disorder rendered more uncomfortable by awareness of hostile suspicion all around me, fear at my mother's state, and, finally, by a confused sense that Bono had been exiled groundlessly. Circumstanced thus, my thoughts were not of the most acute, but moved with a bewildered sluggishness; and for some moments I stood outside in the dark of the yard, engaged in attempts to collect my wits before returning to my task.

The voices of the younger of the Young Men burst into the night; and the laughter of damsels; a youth yelling, "There is the Negro boy."

They approached, pulling each other by sleeve and hand. "Search up and down the house," said the youth to me. "Find us blindfolds."

I did not move, but regarded him with astonishment.

"Now," said he.

"Six," said a girl.

"We will have hiding."

"And forfeits."

"And blunders."

"I like a game to grant favors."

"And kisses."

I nodded. My spirits were all in a ferment. I thought on Bono; I thought on his final scene with me.

I walked away from them into the night.

"Boy?" one of them called.

"Mr. Gitney has requested . . . I should . . . " I said to them, and bowed, too weak to complete the excuse; and so I continued my retreat.

I fled to the garden; I fled to the stone Bono had marked out for me to worship.

The night was filled with wind, the orchard with motion. Dimly I heard calling behind me.

I fell upon my knees and scrabbled at the dirt around the stone. He had bade me pray to it, and in hasty wise, I did: hollers for my mother's safety, for Bono's own, pled silently within.

He had told me to lift the stone, and so recalling, I drew it forth from its socket. The dirt beneath was rich and marbled with the white roots of those plants which grow in darkness.

There lay on the dirt a ring of keys.

I blinked and reached forth to touch them.

Bono had, I ascertained, connived to secrete them when we had removed to this house from the town; having no use for them upon his exile, he had left them for me.

I drew them forth.

Once the surge of excitation had passed from my frame—his gesture in leaving them as sure as a hand upon my shoulder from that most solicitous of mentors—I revolved plans in my head of some future escape. Now that I had in my possession these keys, I might slip from the house with my mother, when she was well, and together we might run for—

My fancy convolved places of flight.

But there, my plan suffered, and I recognized that this was why Bono had not himself fled, all regions being hostile, freedom being found nowhere. In a house such as this, in all events, no key was necessary for exit. The doors were not often locked, and we frequently were sent out by night to the shed or the yard, and might at such times slip away, and our absence remain unnoticed until the next morning.

He had, I supposed, used them to assure himself of the freedom of the house; even more, for the defiance of knowing he had the liberty of motion, unknown to his masters.

Still, it was a gift from he whom I worshipped most in this world; and I determined that my mother and I should benefit from it.

And so I slipped the keys within my waistcoat pocket and returned to the house to find blindfolds for the guests.

And then the poxy days began in earnest: men groaning on their beds for water; women groping their way along the corridors; a girl singing by the rented harpsichord until blood came from her nose and mouth; the linens I dragged down the steps, befouled with sickness; a child uncovering his back to display a mass of cheesy suppuration.

Much of the company was miserable, but not otherwise too incommoded; some a few pocks, but not many; and of course, those upon whom it had been visited before were immune, and could aid in the care for their loved ones, who now lay panting on their mattresses.

My case was benign. The worst of it was the expectation that I still fulfill my duties in ministering to the others who were laid low; so I was employed running ewers of water up the steps; bathing the foreheads of the little ones; and aiding the cook and maids with the management of the dirty crockery. I felt every minute like I should tumble into sleep precipitously. In some quiet moments, I folded myself in a corner and did sleep, and the cook did not wake me.

A few men, slow-witted and pale, played faro at the gaming-tables. Wives doddered through, clutching at chair-backs. There were dramatic readings of poetry in the parlor.

The sickness was heaviest upon three: the boy to first achieve a pock; and one of the love-triangle — the triumphant rival, who now tossed and turned in his fever, his face swiftly stippled with sores; and, last, my mother, whose head was exceeding hot, and whose palms were gathering into virulence. Her cheeks were ruddy and chapped in a way that presaged irruption.

She regained her senses after her collapse. A night's sleep re-called her to herself. She requested a gourd filled with wine be placed by her side. She lay on her flat pallet in the servants' quarters, exiled from her bedchamber, where several of the women of quality were sleeping. The maids moved softly around her, padding to and fro from their ticking.

"Octavian," she said, "must you work?"

"They will let me sleep soon."

She raised her arm and dabbled her fingers in the wine. Her hand was limp and covered in sores. They were on her elbows now, too. "I was foolish, to dance," she said. "They must be laughing about me now."

"They are laughing about nothing," I said. "The most healthy among them are lying abed, reading out fairy tales to one another."

"Will you read me fairy tales?"

"I do not have any books," I said.

She frowned and turned to the wall. "Thank you, Octavian."

"I will—I will tell you stories. Fairy stories from Ovid. As I remember them. When I am released from my duties."

I would not have been released from my duties at all—nor would have the other less-fevered servants—and we would have received few of the comforts of the sick, had Mr. Gitney not been conducting an experiment to determine the relative susceptibility of *Homo afri* and *Homo europæi* to the pox; which survey, as I demonstrated to him, should be invalidated, did we not receive the same treatment as our masters.

Then he agreed, and sent me to go sleep; which is a good thing; for my balance was growing poor, and my head hurt so prodigiously that I could but picture one of the torture devices I had seen in Bono's book, a helmet of metal over my skull, constricting, my eyes peering out, like an animal about to be struck.

The fevers for some were passing. Children now played in the yard. Women went on long, constitutional walks with their husbands and beaux through the fields of the house. Slaves went before them, carrying red banners to warn off field hands and poachers.

The child who had first contracted the pox died in the night. The pestilence had grown so thick within his throat in colonies and clusters that he could not even sip water without the most excruciating pain. Late one night, as his brothers lay beside him, something within him ruptured, and with spasms of asphyxiation, he choked, and, hanging off the bed, he quivered and ceased; taken to that place where, I trust, the waters are cool on the tongue and the sunlight eternal.

His body was carried out to the shed, where it corrupted.

I ministered to the Young Man who had caught the pox worst. His disfiguration was complete, his whole skin clotted with pustules. They bled upon the linens, and every position was agony. We could not rearrange his limbs so that his nerves might quiet their shrill attack; he desperately sought, but could not find, sleep's oblivion.

Waking was a torment to him.

My mother's hands and face had burst forth in sores. I sat by her side when I could.

The darkness in the slaves' quarters was cut only by rushlights. In that ruddy light, I could not see the full bloody blush of the pustules. They ran across the ridges of her cheeks.

She reached up with her hand, already encrusted, and touched the excrudescencies gingerly.

"I won't scratch them," she said. "They will not scar if they don't burst."

Mr. Gitney had given me a lotion to spread over her sores. I put some upon my fingers and rubbed her face gently.

She wept. Her mouth was an horrible shape; a lamentatory shape.

At other times, she did not weep, but stared at the rafters and repeated, "I will not scratch, Octavian. Although I itch. I have never known an itch like this one. It fills the room."

I fetched her some water from the ewer.

"Can you feel it?" she asked. "You must. It is like a god. All-knowing."

At other times, blessedly, she slept.

The calamity which cast the world into flame occurred early on an April morning, when all was still black night. We awakened to the ringing of the Meeting House bell, the firing of warning muskets. We heard shouting in the main house.

My mother moaned and rustled her sheets. I told her I would ascertain the situation.

I dressed quickly and crossed the yard. Two of the Young Men stood by the back door of the house, watching me approach. They each held a fowling gun at ready.

Inside, the ladies were in high panic. They all sought seats away from the windows. The men called up and down the stairs. A Young Man dashed down two flights, a musket clamped in each hand.

Dr. Trefusis sat amidst the tumult, sketching a snakeskin.

I stood against the wall, awaiting instructions.

"The King's Army have marched out of Boston," said Dr. Trefusis, without concern. "It appears they plan on seizing munitions from our militia."

"By God!" said Mr. Gitney, who was walking by. "We shall not be moved by this!"

"When Syracuse fell," Dr. Trefusis offered, "Archimedes the engineer did not flee, but even as he was run through with a sword, sat in his own house, working out geometric equations with a stick in the sand. His last words were, 'You may attack my head, but stay away from my circles.'"

"Precisely!" said Mr. Gitney. "We shall not be chased from our own house!"

"We have been already," Dr. Trefusis noted. "We live in Boston."

Mr. Gitney, however, was moved on to another room, shouting out commands and flapping the arms of his banyan-robe.

We heard the whistle of fifes on the green and the rattle of cheap drums.

Mr. Sharpe descended upon me and sent me to the kitchen. Two Young Men with guns were posted there to watch the slaves. We began cooking their breakfast, somewhat constrained for space, with so many in so small a chamber, and the fire burning large within the hearth.

During the day, people ran by upon the road that passed the house. Many were men with guns.

The Young Men shouted to them from the windows, but few stopped. We could get but confused accounts of the engagement.

A few men from Acton, the next town over, had been slain; the British were marching in the thousands. At one moment, the British were in retreat; an hour later, the word was that they were triumphant, that they were upon us.

There is no need to animadvert to the deeds of that day, which shall resound, for weal or woe, as long as this terrestrial globe has habitation.

Suffice it to say the British expedition met with resistance at Lexington, and fired upon the local militia. I have heard that a woman watching from her house saw her husband hit; that he crawled, dying, across the grass while Patriots stepped over him and fired at the regiment; that he made it to the door of his house, to the arms of his wife, where, liberty quickened, he expired.

Suffice it also to say that brave men faced each other across the bridge at Concord; that more blood was spillt; and that the British retreated then towards Boston, hounded all the way from behind stone wall and smokehouse, from the garret windows of great houses and the dooryards of small ones. The atrocities were countless: At Concord Bridge, a Patriot boy swollen with ire saw that a Redcoat had not died with sufficient haste, and as the man screamed, scalped him with an axe. Fearful of all windows, of any door, of walls and banks and gullies and wells, the grenadiers and light infantry shot indiscriminately as they ran for hours along the road, starving, parched, covered in mud from the waist down from having waded through swamp to reach the mainland. Muzzles were leveled at them from every side. A soldier paused to bind an old man's wound, and the old man, revived, shot him. Soldiers ran a bayonet through a woman in labor. The final casualty of this sanguine retreat was a little boy who paused by a window to see the brave coats and flashing gorgets of the army-men; glimpsing a head there by the glass, they shot him in the face.

Outside, the British Colonies of America detached themselves with infinite lumbering care, while within our enclave I thought on nothing that day but my mother. I did not mark the sobbing in the street, though I saw, when I passed by a window, that a hay-wagon laid with three corpses rolled past.

Her cries were a fine trickle. They leaked from her without cease, as the pox mobbed her face and ravaged her gullet. Her agony was continual.

I looked on the appalling irruptions that bubbled across her forehead now, her cheeks, her chin, her eyelids, and I knew that I should never see her again as once she was. She knew it, too, and in the silence when only her breath rasped, we regarded this fact, both of us, as if together admiring a portrait painted of her on the wall.

I could not hold her hand without causing her irritation so great that she writhed. I wished to comfort her, but there was no comfortable action I could take; I desired to console her, but there was no word that could be a consolation.

Her fever grew worse in the evening, as it did every evening. No one marked much my absence from the house. There was too much rushing about from window to window, too much stacking of arms in the bedrooms, too much muttering of strategic niceties as men smoked in the attic, for the presence or absence of one boy to be noted.

A silence and immobility came upon her in the evening-tide.

"A death-bed's a detector of the heart," the poet Young has written. *"Here tired dissimulation drops her mask."*

I sat by her side.

"I was born," she whispered, "half a world away."

I could not imagine what skies she saw, what men and women gathered about her, what childish scenes crowded in upon her. I could not imagine the face of my grandfather, my grandmother, whom I have never seen. Perhaps an image of my father, blank to me, beckoned in her fancy in a house where I might have grown. I drew my chair close upon the edge of the bed.

"Tell me," I said, "of your country."

"I have told you before."

"I do not wish to . . . I will not question you, but . . ." I stopped, unwilling to make my first foray into filial disobedience with one who faced her Maker—but could not refrain from saying, "I ask you not to tell me children's tales of panthers pulling chariots."

"I never spake of panthers."

"And there was no orchid throne. Tell me what you sat on."

"Octavian . . ."

"I beg of you," said I, "tell me of the Empire of Oyo."

"That would gain you nothing," she whispered. "It is all gone."

"Gone?"

"Not gone. Lost."

"When you sat, what did you sit upon?"

She sighed, and in a cracked voice, said, "This is no time . . . for telling stories. . . ."

"Tell me one true thing. I will know *one true thing*. Tell me what you sat on."

She did not speak to me.

"The ground?" I demanded. "Did you sit sometime upon the ground? A stool?" I pushed aside my chair and squatted, placing my palms upon the floorboards. "I want to touch something. Tell me of an object! Tell me something I could have touched!"

She did not respond. Her breath was heavy. There was a stench in the air. Her hands lay before her.

We stared at one another. Our heads were on a level.

Whether there is some transmission of knowledge through the ether, or whether physiognomy and expression have some linguistic virtue so subtle that we do not remark its operation, the eyes may indeed speak.

And so, for a while, for perhaps some ten minutes, I was not looking at my mother, but at a woman who knew me, and I was a man who knew her; she was a girl of thirteen, newly arrived in a frigid, alien country; a woman who had been that girl; who had given birth in bondage, while men with devices and pencils had observed. She had played the harpsichord and painted. She was a woman who had known desire, and who had danced upon the knolls by Lake Champlain. She had flirted with the New World's great virtuosi. We stared at one another, and in that moment, we knew each other for the first and last time.

And then, this she offered to me, my one truth: "Our language," she said, "is not spoken, but sung. . . . Not simply words . . . and grammar . . . but melody. It was hard . . . thus . . . to learn English . . . this language of wood. For the people of your nation, Octavian, all speech is song."

We watched each other's eyes. We were as strangers, in that moment—as intimate as strangers—for strangers know more of us, and can judge of us more without reproach than ever those we love.

[*219*]

Refugees streamed out of Boston; we saw them on the roads, carrying everything they owned. Many had no place to go. The plague banners still hung from the windows of our house.

Up and down the coast, we were to learn, there were preparations for war. Men-of-war patrolled the harbors. Soldiers dug ditches; they threw up redoubts and ravelins.

In the Colony of Virginia, as in Massachusetts, the Governor sent out forces to seize Patriot gunpowder, and so disarm revolution. As General Gage's, his maneuver occurred in the night, in darkest secrecy. The militia guards stationed at the Williamsburg armory having retired home to bed, a detachment of Royal Marines entered the powderhouse and removed fifteen barrels of powder, lifting them onto carts and disappearing with them before dawn. The Governor, Lord Dunmore, avowed that he had ordered the powder removed to deprive the slaves of possible armaments, should they rise; but the Virginia rebels, hearing that their stores had been confiscated, feared the opposite: that their Governor sought to deprive them of weaponry so that they should not be able to defend themselves against a Negro uprising of his own dire engineering. They feared that he had already called for the slaves to form into legions against their masters, so raising an African army to secure the British hold over the Colonies; they feared that slaves, enflamed with overheard talk of liberty, would assume that such freedom applied to them and take up arms, instituting murder in bedrooms and on balconies, sinking the region into impossible chaos and bloodshed.

Within our house, the only chaos was that of a dismal joy: the pleasure of girls at new-found health, the jubilation of children at the restoration of outdoor play; the relief of full convalescence after the long night of fever; the excitation of nerves amongst men eager to fight for a cause; the delight of the young in the spring's heartless arrival.

My mother's wounds were begun to smell. The reek was so great that the other servants slept on the floor in the house rather than endure the miasma near their pallets.

Mr. Gitney had begun to take a greater interest in the extremity of my mother's condition. He prepared several cures which he hoped should combat the disease, far-progressed as it was.

My mother did not move; the encrustation was complete. She could not speak any longer; nor could she swallow without pain. Her sheets were fastened to her with her exudations.

~~Knowing I knew that death could not be far, and I wished to have a final interview, where some word that~~
~~It is ever the burden of the living that they must~~

In the extremity of the disease, her features could not be recognized as hers. Her visage was an assemblage of holes, the nostrils flaring with each breath. There was no kindness, no gentleness to this departure; nothing human, but rather a degeneration into some demonic substratum of the body that had waited to lay waste to all the lineaments of grace.

~~When they removed her from her bed so that they might~~ but it was to no avail.

[Excerpted from The Philosophical Ephemera of the Novanglian College of Lucidity, *vol. v (1775), circulated in manuscript form]*

OBSERVATIONS UPON THE PROGRESSION OF THE SMALLPOX IN *HOMO AFRI.*

ꙮ

BY Mr. Josiah Gitney, M. Phil. Cantab.,
AND Mr. Richard Sharpe

THE PLAGUE of Smallpox being so great among us and so rapacious in its appetites, it is a most desirable article of knowledge, to establish how its hungers might best be combated, for the great comfort of Mankind. The question has arisen frequently among the planters of the South, whether the Negro suffer the affliction with the same degree of hardship as the European, with a practical view, on this head, of establishing whether inoculation of slaves will prove both effective and efficient.

TO THIS END, taking advantage of the current unrest, we arranged for the inoculation and sequestration of a number of subjects, both white and black; and, combining the data from this quarantined sample with mortality figures from two *Virginia* plantations, we have made certain physiological and forensic observations which may shed some practical light on the question of whether inoculation of bonded Africans should be undertaken by individuals fearful that such a course will hamper productivity and adversely affect profit.

THE *MASSACHUSETTS* SEQUESTRATION involved 49 individuals; of whom 11 had previously had the pox, and were thus

[225]

immune. Of the remaining 38, 20 were of African and 18 of European blood. The inoculation was administered on the arm of each subject.[1] Of those variolated, only three developed symptoms of any magnitude: a white male of seven years, the first to show pustules, died of internal rupture; a white male of sixteen years was enflamed in his entirety with the excrudescences, and yet survived, though disfigured significantly; and a black female of twenty-nine years demonstrated a severe cutaneous infection which eventually traveled inwards; of which she died.

SEVERAL HEROICAL ATTEMPTS at palliative intervention were attempted, especially to the last-mentioned subject. Initially desirous of maintaining the circulation of animal spirits and humoral percolation, we administered (a) venesection by fleam, and, having let her blood to no little degree, we instantly turned the subject over and (b) inserted a glyster of quinine. This occasioned the subject discomfort only; and we feared that the vital juices would cease circulation. Accordingly, we alternated draughts of (c) laudanum and (d) volatiles, trusting that where the former would soothe, the latter would excite; the first quelling the patient's disposition to dramatic phrenzy (such as was demonstrated at the application of the enema), the second restoring the patient to consciousness; but both relaxant and stimulant met with similar indifference, given the exhaustion attendant upon the disease. The subject's papules at this time—the third day since their first appearance—consolidated and gave rise to pustular vesicles, which no amount of

---

1. Did we repeat the experiment, we should instead inoculate in the *leg*, which, being further removed from the pneumatic, electrico-ætherial, and hydraulico-vascular machinery, is less likely to lead to internal corrosion and fatality, *viz.* Dr. Adam Thomson's *Discourse for the Preparation of the Body, &c.*

cauterization with poker or rupture with lancet could stem. We administered (e) an oral infusion of quinine; (f) a saline bath suggested by a celebrated balneologist; and (g) several cathartics (jalap, senna, sublimate of mercury, crab's claw); the extreme dose of which may have been what occasioned the loss of her hair and most of her teeth two days before her death.

These measures failing, we resorted to an *Indian* method of which we had heard no little report: We placed the subject in a small underground chamber which we had infused with a great quantity of steam; and after she had come to a prodigious sweat, removed her to the frigid, icy bath; alternating back and forth between them for some time. The results of this were inconclusive, beyond the extraordinary discomfort it apparently occasioned the subject, who protested weakly as we placed her in the steam chamber the first several times; eventually falling silent. She did not speak again before her death.

It would appear that, a day before the moment of demise, the subject was blind, and sufficiently fevered as to be insensate. It is unclear whether the blindness proceeded from the invasion of the disease in the ocular area or from an internal nervous disorganization attendant upon her distemper.

It was to scrutinize such questions as these that we undertook a dissection.

WE REMOVED the corpse to a chamber separate from the other subjects and prepared the body for disassembly. Of particular interest in our investigation was the disruption of the skin and its humoral balance by the sores; it being established that, in the African, the median layer of the skin, or *secondary lemulla*, is suffused with black bile released in the relaxation of the nervous system. It would be of particular interest to determine whether the torment of this tissue in any way interfered with the augmentation of bilious fluxion.

THUS, we began our investigation. A vertical incision was made along the abdomena of the subject from just below the breasts down almost as far as the pubis, terminating at the upper expression of the pelvic cavity. We prepared to make lateral incisions at the termini of this first; these being of no great depth, our interest in the first stage of the dissection being wholly cutaneous; which was to be followed by an inquiry into the progress of the corruption in the alimentary and pneumatic apparati.

WE SHOULD MARK an interruption in our proceedings at this point, which we would omit, were it not of behavioral interest. The son of the subject, an African male of sixteen years, demanded entrance to the experimental chamber; this being denied, he forced the door. Once within, he spied the body. He had not for some three days seen the subject, and had not been at liberty to be present at the subject's expiration; it being determined that her much-disfigured, impetiginous state and her insensibility would cause unnecessary anguish in a son and could potentially lead to the disordering of his reason.

He stood for some time unmoving, as did we; we, observing, he, oblivious.

Mr. Sharpe noted to the others that the boy was deprived of speech and reason, returned by the sight of the familial dead to his originary savage superstition and stupefaction.

At this, the youth turned to gaze upon Mr. Sharpe. Mr. Sharpe addressed him directly, asking if the boy were capable yet of ratiocination, or was become dumb.

At this, the child produced a scream of startling savagery and attempted to do violence to Mr. Sharpe. He was intercepted in his design by one of the young men who assisted with the procedure; they wrestled.

As their melee progressed, Mr. Sharpe, standing to the side, observed to the African youth that the boy fought for no good end, as no goal could be accomplished by him defeating his opponent; this being excellent proof of the boy's degeneration back into his natural state, the trappings of civilization having fallen from him.

At this, the boy ceased struggle. The young man who wrestled with him released him, and they both rose.

The African youth stood before us, a gawky and immobile spectacle.

He said, "I cannot fight — nor can I refrain — without imputations of savagery." And he finished, in a voice not of defiance, but suffused with realization: "I am no one. I am not a man. I am nothing."

He turned and absented himself from the chamber, his body betraying signs of considerable inward turmoil of spirits in his irregularity of movement.

We called for one of our number who had refrained from the dissection — Dr. John Trefusis — to attend the youth and ensure that he did not lay a hand of violence upon himself or any other. Dr. Trefusis sat with him for some hours; at which point the elder man unfortunately fell asleep, and the youth made his escape, having through some low guile procured a set of keys which he had kept about his person.

By the time we had been roused to his flight, he could not be found in the neighborhood, in spite of the best efforts of many to hunt him down through the night; his sable skin providing cover in the dusk.

We cite this vignette as an example of possible recidivism; it demonstrates not only the confusion but also the fractious and insubordinate natural inclination of the African subject.

WE RETURN to the dissection, as went on apace. Mr. Gitney excused himself from the procedure at this point, so all further notes were taken by Mr. Sharpe.

Making the lateral incisions on the abdomena, we were able to disclose to view both (a) the viscera and (b) the obverse leaf of the skin, which appeared much ravaged by . . .

Canaan — August 12th, 1775

Sir, dear friend —

Some two weeks ago, you received a manuscript copy of *The Philosophical Ephemera of the Novanglian College of Lucidity* which contained an article on the dissection of a subject afflicted with smallpox.

You have, I cannot doubt, read this excellent article and admired its formidable merits of proof and argumentation. Transparent in its prose; yet dense with the opacity of flesh; unflagging, even fleet, in its inquiries; yet never scrupling to linger sagely over the most minute of incisions; this most excellent of articles hath been purged of all speculation unacquainted with fact; and, a triumph of philosophy, hath been cleansed entirely of all the cloudings of passion, the confusions of humanity, the irritations of pity, the sorties of affection, indeed, anything which might mark the beating, breathing, humane breast.

However, I note that in a few regards its observations are incomplete, for which reason, I send this addendum to you, my ancient friend, so tender in your sensibilities, that you might circulate it as necessary at the American Philosophical Society and gratify them with further enlargement upon this interesting subject.

[*231*]

Of what does fact consist? This article—*cacata charta*[1]—omitted, so far as I can tell, in both text and footnote, to mention that one of its authors, Mr. Josiah Gitney of the Novanglian College of etc. spent the day previous to the said dissection bowed by the insensate corpse of the woman he would soon dissect, holding its hands, touching its face, weeping and whispering, "I love you. I loved you. I love you."

This, my colleague, is fact, true and empirical; yet Mr. Gitney saw fit to obscure it in his account. Why conceal it? In what way does it not merit scientific attention as well? When a man falls upon his knees and grieves, doth not his musculature contract and his ligaments distend? Doth the heart not dilate, the humors circulate? Do the animal liquors in the nerves not suffer agitation? Do the cortices not enter into lamentatory conversation, taking the impress of exteriorities?

Hath not his tears salinity, which might be measured, were they burnt away with flame?

Your humble & affectionate,
Dr. John Trefusis

1. "shitty paper." Dr. Trefusis draws the quotation from Catullus, *Poems, XXXVI.*—ed.

Not to have been born at all,

Never to have seen the light of the sun:

This is the best thing for mortals.

Or, if begotten, to have fallen from the womb

Straight into the grave,

And to be smothered, unknowing,

In the dirt of Hades.

— Theognis

[III.]

LIBERTY
& PROPERTY

drawn from Letters,
principally those of *Private Ev Goring,*
Reed's Regiment

Nature, in her Menagerie, preserves Animals in six different forms:

MAMMALIA,	covered with hair,	walk on the earth,	speaking.
BIRDS,	covered with feathers,	fly in the air,	singing.
AMPHIBIA,	covered with skin,	creep in warm places,	hissing.
FISHES,	covered with scales,	swim in the water,	smacking.
INSECTS,	covered with armour,	skip on dry ground,	buzzing.
WORMS,	without skin,	crawl in moist places,	silent.

—Charles Linnæus, *Systema Naturæ*

RUN AWAY from the Subscriber in *Canaan, Massachusetts,* at the close of April a tall NEGRO boy of sixteen who answers to the name of *OCTAVIAN* when he answers at all which is not frequent, being of a silent and melancholy disposition. He is of an handsome countenance; and is some six foot tall and exceeding lanky, last seen wearing a frock-coat and breeches of green satin and a waistcoat of pale silk with floral embroiderings. He plays excellently well upon the VIOLIN and speaks Latin, Greek, and French. He is the bonded property of *MR. JOSIAH GITNEY,* currently resident in Canaan at the house of *MR. LEMUEL GITNEY.* All masters of vessels who treat with this youth in any wise will be answerable to it in law. Whoever apprehends the said NEGRO and delivers him up to *MR. GITNEY* shall have £5 reward.

YIELD HIM UP – J.G.

May 3rd, 1775. Clouds all day and it was cold for the month. Got the stumps and the brackin out of the new field. There was a negroe boy presented himself for work and sd he wd work for food. Ast him had he halled out stumps before and he sd yes he could. After some time with us struggling with the lever and the ox was skittish I ast him had he realy ever halled stumps and he sd no sir. It hd begin to rain. We was all mud. He was shivering so bad he cdnt barely move and he just kept staring. I sd can you cut wood. He sd yes. I sd you cut wood before? He dnt answer, so I sd it agin, You cut wood before? He sd nothing, then sd Yes, lyeing. I give him the ax and sd so cut and he jus stood and helt the ax and the rain fell on him. I sd Tilly-vally!, you hant cut wood befor boy. what can you do? have you ever done any thing? and he dint anser. I sd I ast you what can you do can you do anything, can you cut wood, can you carry? and he sd nothing.

Get off of here I sd. I cd of whipt him, shoud of. I yellt at his worthless hide and told him did he stand around Id take the whip to him and then he dropt the ax and walked away. He dint run just walked, shivering, across the chopt down trees. I sd run but he walked, and good riddance.

John and I pullt out the rest of the stumps. Rain got harder in the afternoon. The Jerseys baby it is sick, and we could here it wailing thro the day. It wailed in their cottage, and the rain fell, but it loosened the mud and it was easier to pull out the stumps then. We got it all done before night.

. . . and Clarice spent the morning with the chickens.

Round about noon there was a Negro boy begging for work, slow-moving and most likely stupefied. I inquired after his papers to see if he was free, but he lied and said that he had lost them. "Then there is no work for you here," I said, but he was so gaping and simple-looking that my heart went out to him, and I gave him some Indian pudding to eat before sending him on his way.

There are many such vagrants now who have fled the city. Gen. Gage issues passes for those who wish to leave, but many more are fleeing without, as we all predict bombardment and flame. There is a constant expectation of some fatal event. . . .

Lincoln

May 6th, 1775

To Mr. Josiah Gitney —

This morning it was feed time and we was providing the fowls with their repast when my boy comes out to me and says *that there is a beast in the smokehouse.* I asked him, *What manner of beast,* and he said he had not seen it but heard it breathing and crying, as did one of the carcasses hanging there stir from the toils of death and make plaint.

I figured 'twas some personage and mayhap one of the King's soldiers so I repaired to the house and brought out my gun. We have slaughtered early and we are smoking now for to sell to the militia. We drew open the door to the shed, and at first our eyes were blinded by the smoke, and then we saw this uncanny sight: for it was a boy knelt upon the floor, regarding a hung swine stripped of skin as if it taught him a lesson, and his legs were curled under him. The plumes rose around him through the slats in the floor. He didn't move just regarded the swine.

'Twas a negro boy of maybe fifteen or seventeen years. He was covered in mud but dressed fancy in breeches and an old coat and I figured he must have been a gentleman's valet. I pointed the gun at him and said he should not move. He did not move a hair, but wiped his eyes which he couldn't barely hold open to witness the world. His face was covered with tears from the smoke and his eyes they were red. I told him he was caught. He got up and started walking towards me. Standing he was taller than sitting, and I grew apprehensive for my safety and wondered should I have to discharge the gun?

[240]

He walked to in front of the muzzle. He stood and waited to receive the shot.

I said, I will shoot you. He stood firm. I said again *that I would shoot him*. He pressed his chest to the gun and closed his eyes.

I stood amazed, and I didn't know how to threat, he offering himself.

I looked at him standing against the gun, and it was like he was dead already, there was—I known't how to give it expression—there was a flatness in this boy and a gray; he was already dead; and the mud which was upon him it was like *the integuments of the tomb*.

Come with me, I said.

He didn't move, so I drew the gun away.

His hand came out and he grabs the muzzle and points it at him again.

No, I say. That's a sin.

We didn't move. Fire, he says.

You come with me, I say.

He closes his eyes and pleads: Fire.

I went to hit him over the head with the gun and he attacked me and my boy he run at us to get by us. I tried to grab him and I did grab his coat but he fought me. We fought for some time but fear must have made him strong because I am no little wrestler and he threw me and run off. I said to my boy to call the neighbors and we would find him because he was escaped, but I didn't want to send the boy alone, so we went and got the horse and raised the alarm. The neighbors they searched for him but we could not find him.

We looked through the papers for advertisements and we thought it was most likely he was yourn. We tried our best to get him for you and we hope that you will remember us financially for giving you some hint of where he might be.

God help you on your search, because he is a silent and dangerous one.

Surely as I am

Your humble servant,
Elijah Tolley

May 11th, 1775

Fruition — Sis — Shun — bosom Friend —

*So saith the Lord from out his Shrub of Flame: Proclaim
LIBERTY, every one to his Brother, and every Man to his Neighbor!*
And I to my sister.

O Fruition, dear Sis, the Spirit of Liberty stirs the
Countryside like Sap, & everywhere I am sensible of the
Blossoms. I am in such Spirits I cannot describe the like. As we
march towards Boston, we meet every Mile upon the Way an-
other Column of Patriots bound for the Encampment at
Cambridge. There is much talk upon the Road of Boston & its
Captivity, for Parliament's Army hides within — silent — mum —
& its Citizens trapped, while without, our Numbers grow.

Among our Townspeople, you may report to Aunts &
Belles & Fathers — ALL WELL. Mr. Wheeler wishes I should
write to Mrs. Wheeler his Regards — nay (he stops me) — his
Love — which is a momentous Word, from him; & he further says,
to give his Regards to little Josephine and Aaron, *pat them on the
Head, hold Aaron by the Hair,* and tell them their Pa is marching
and thinks on them oft.

Mr. Bullock, he hath overheard Mr. Wheeler, & adds his
Sentiments of Affection for Mrs. B. and his Regard for her. Yea, &
the Rest, who will line up Tomorrow & belabor my Quill, tho'
they hear this Missive is already sent.

Shem and John, they is competing for Blisters. Though
warned by One and All, they still, around the Fire, will pick &
pick & pick — & bleed & bleed & bleed. You are welcome to

[243]

Shem, Shun, when he returns Home decorated — his feet like Hives a-weeping Honey.

I hope Ma is well. Tell her stop putting her Hand through the Window-Glass & that before she knows I'm gone, I'll be bounding up the Meadow to watch her burn the Cobbler & dry up Turkey as in days of yore. Give her a kiss on each Cheek & don't avoid the Mole for she is the sweetest Mamma a Man could have, or you, Sweetness, too.

The Company of Kedron hath a new Recruit who is somewhat extraordinary & it happened this Way. Yesterday Evening, we having some several Hours still to march before we reached the Encampment at Cambridge, we halted for the Night & pitched tents near an Inn in this town; and my Brother Soldiers retiring for Refreshment in the Tavern, I followed. There we all boughten our Cup of Flip & we raised a bumper Toast of Health to the King & Long Life, & Confusion to Parliament & the King's Ministers & the E. India Company that Own Them, & may they all die Penniless &c.

There was Music, & it was a Fiddler played an Irish Jig, and we would have thought no more on it, if he had not played it so slow, so doleful, that it set a perpetual Gloom over the Company. And it was not simply one Tune he played thus, for faith, every Dance he played thereafter was like to set us all a-weeping.

He was a Negro Youth, a Tall, Gawky Thing, and he played upon a Fiddle built, I would hazard, from two Gourds & a discarded Peg-Leg, but, Shun, he played like a Seraph — a *Disconsolate Seraph*. Capt. Draper, he opined it was sure the sweetest Music he had heard.

We was all somewhat Awed by his Solemnity & thinking of Home & our Danger but the Innkeeper did not hold that good for Custom & spake, "Oy, Mungo—you heard of Lilt? Or is it all yammer yammer yammer with you?" upon which the Boy stopped with his Bow, and waited for Instruction. Mine Host demanded *something we could dance to, if we would; & not gouge our Eyes out with the Cutlery.*

Upon which Witticism all the Patrons laughed; and the Boy, somewhat confused, blushed & placed the Bow on his Fiddle, & drew it across in a fine Shake; following which, he played a pleasant Song by one of the old Italians—or mayhap Germans—or some other People—which Song silenced the Crowds, for soon there was a Tear in all our Eyes.

Still, however, Mine Host expressed no Satisfaction, and said it was all too *Dolorous,* and that the Boy should get no Supper, at which the Boy looked with Supplication & Humility & said he had played all the Evening through. Capt. Draper could not countenance the Boy's Hunger & so he said, "Sir, I shall pay for the Boy's Supper," & requested the Boy to play the Song again, which the Boy did, & the Sound, even on so mean an Instrument, was delightful, full of curious Turns and hearty Lamentation.

And when we saw the Boy turned out of doors to sleep in the Stable, *coughing prodigiously from a Chill he had caughten,* his Head bowed as he went . . . When I shall tell you that from our Camp, we heard him coughing without Respite and went down to view him, & found him being chided by the Innkeeper for waking the Patrons (no more pathetic a Sight could be imagined) . . . When I shall tell you this, Shun, *your generous Heart shall not question* that we considered Means by which we might relieve him of his Suffering.

'Twas I came upon the Notion that he might serve us as Musician, our only Music being John upon the Drum, who keeps not so good Time. This Proposal being applauded by the Rest, excepting John, we petitioned Capt. Draper (Kindest of Men!) & he heard of the Indignity this Boy suffered and said *such should not happen in a Land roused for Liberty.*

This Morning Capt. Draper spake to the Innkeep of hiring away the Negro & then spake to the Boy himself, telling him of coming Liberty; of the Need to stand with his Brother Man & resist the Tyranny of *Those Who Own Us All, Slave & Free Alike;* that Parliament are Protectors of the *Slave-Trade,* having Interests in it; that, can we Sting Parliament, they shall no longer think so easily to rob us, & we shall have Government founded not on Piracy & Slavery, but the *Rights of Englishmen;* & other Fiery Words. Capt. Draper offered a small Sustenance & Pay for the Boy's excellent Music, *could he rally us upon the Fife.* We gave him the Fife for Trial & he said that though he had but little Training upon that Instrument, he would assay it yet; & his Tunes on it was fine & crisp & we applauded, if only for the Festival Air of these Times, when an Innkeeper's Boy shall be a Musician & a Peg-Leg be a Fiddle & a Cooper be a Soldier & a Slave a Free Man & *ALL SHALL BE CHANGED.* We having heard him play several Tunes, Capt. Draper clapped the Boy upon the Shoulder and said that *his services should be of indispensable Utility.*

"Utility," says the Innkeep. "He speaks Latin. I beg you to find the Utility in that."

But the Negro hath this Day as we marched provided us with much merry Music upon the Way.

Upon the Road, we passed a prodigious Number of Companies, & some went towards Cambridge & some away, & there seemed a great Confusion. When we was got to Menotomy, there was in the middle of the Road a Gentleman at a Desk. There was Papers on the Desk helt down with Rocks. The Gentleman asked us for Company and Regiment & marked them down on a Book & then clapped & a Boy came out of a Shed by the Side of the Road & took a Note from him & went into the Shed. Others came upon the Road & the Gentleman, knowing them, directed them to proceed, or to take some several Barrels which had been marked for them. There had been some Rain & the Earth of the Road was soft & his Desk was somewhat mired as he leaned upon it.

After perhaps a portion of an Hour, another Gentleman come out of the Shed and asked us, *was we the Kedron Company,* and Serj. Lammas replied we was, & this new Officer, who was some Muster-Master, directed us ride North to the Shore to a Town where we should find others of our New Hampshire Brethren and there await Orders.

So now we are come to the Shore and encamped & tomorrow after a short March shall gain our Goal, which is the Town of Dulwich.

'Tis now near time for Sleeping & so I shall end —

dreaming of my Home & my Sister,

who am her Heroical Brother,

Private Evidence Goring

One final Word, Shun, which is that if you see Liz when
the Girls gather to Clack, you might read her this Letter
(excepting this Note) & mention how Fine a Brother I am &
an excellent figure of a Man & invested in all Virtues &c. For this
great Kindness, Sis, thank thee (if I may "thou" you), thou most
Perfect of Sisters & thou most Sweet of Siblings & may Blessings
settle like a Mess of Doves all over thy Hair. — yr Ev.

Dulwich, Massachusetts
May 15th, 1775

My dear Fruition—

Earlier this Week, a Day of Marching in the Rain hath brought us
to Dulwich, where we is encamped upon the Green.

     Along the Road, we had a Prospect of Boston Town
across the River Charles, which Warren of Unfortunates shewed
no Activity—being mere Roofs & Steeples & Quays & the
Masts of Warships in the Bay. This blank Scene regarded,
productive of no Intelligence, we marched onward.

     We do not know what transpires within the Town, but
there is much Word among the assembled Regiments that it is
become a Prison & only those who obtains Passes from Gen.
Gage may leave. Many are the Women and Children held
therein by the King's Army, & they is held hostage so we will
not bomb. *I tremble for them.*

     Our Tents are pitched, 5 for 21 of us. Would that we were
encamped like unto the Israelites, *according to our own Tribes, every
Man by his own Camp, & every Man by his own Standard, throughout our Hosts.* But we are in close Quarters, there being 4 in my
Tent—Shem, John, the Negro, & me. The Others, they call us
The Wags for our Raillery though the Negro is hardly a Wag,
him never speaking. We may the rest of us be Wags, but I am
no Rascal, which John & your Beau Shem is, & they weary me.
They are always teazing the Negro on his Silence, in hopes of
drawing him out, saying, "The Negro stares at a Tree. Han't he
seen a Tree before?" & "The Negro stares at a House," & "Now

[249]

the Negro stares at Cattle," & "Now he gapes at his Feet. This the first time you seen your Own Feet?" They mean it in Jest, but I told them still to mum up or we shall all Beat them silly.

Our Tent is pitched beneath a spreading Oak, for Shem & John held that the Green of Leaves cooled their bleeding Stumps. I am not well pleased by the Arrangement since we is in some kind Culvert & I am in continual Fears of us all being washed away by Floods. I have told the Negro that I would sleep by the Flap because he is ill and the Water will come in & wet him. 'Twas a fine Piece of Chivalry when I spake it, but now it is but a few Moments until we sleep & I have little Relish for the Swamp which I shall cuddle to me Tonight.

Capt. Draper hath asked me to watch this Negro Fiddler & acquaint the Boy with the Ways of our Company. He is a curious Baggage, the Fiddler—odd—unspeaking, & there is a Jest that Capt. Draper hath asked me to be the Acquainter owing to me talking for 2 Men & he talking for None.

Your Heart would melt if you could see this Wretched, Silent Boy. When I waked at Night, I seen that he does not sleep, but sits staring at the Walls. Even when he curls beneath his Blanket, his Eyes are open. I can see them by the Candle before I snuff it—the Eyes peering.

His Name, he tells me, is Prince.

Your bro., your Prince—

Priv. Evidence Goring

[Written on the back of the letter, apparently the same day]

Prince's Catechism

At Capt. Draper's Request, I have asked the Negro boy Questions to prepare against we should be asked them by the Adjutant, should we ever find an Adjutant, and I have received the following answers for my satisfaction.

Where are you from?
Answered not.

Did you flee Boston?
Answered not.

Where learned you to play so skillful on the Violin?
Answered not.

Where learned you Latin?
Answered not.

Do you have Papers to show you is free?
Answered not.

Where, formerly, did you live?
Answered not.

Come, sir. Did you live in an House?
Answered not.

I see. Did you perhaps live outside, then?
To which he replied, "I have lived outside, sir."

Did you live recently in a House with a Family?
Countenance cast down—yet defying Answer—he
whispered: "I have never even dwellt inside myself."

I fear, Shun, faith—look ye, I fear he is fled from some tyrant
Master, which is Capt. Draper's Belief. I disclosed no such Suspicion, but said to him simply, "Slavery & Subjugation shall soon
enough fall away, sir."

And so they shall, in the coming Tumults, as Peter's
Chains slipped from off his Wrists when the Angel smote him
upon the Side; & the Gates shall be opened, & we shall issue
forth, & the Meadows shall lie before us all.

And God shall curse those who hold their fellow Men as
Slaves; and in the Last Day, they shall know Weeping, when
Christ comes striding from the Skies, Hands drizzling His Blood,
Eyes filled with a Sorrow at what He must do: For then they
who hold others in Bondage shall know the Lash & Shackle—
& shall remain enchained to this Flesh, hobbled with Bone,
when the Rest are released from their Gross Bodies into the
hallowed Air.

[From Mr. Richard Sharpe to Mr. Clepp Asquith of Virginia, a Trustee of the Novanglian College of Lucidity]

Canaan, Massachusetts

Sir—

Thank you for your letter of the 2nd *inst.* It is with regret that I confirm the report that has come to your ears: The experimental subject has indeed absconded from the property, and, at present, has not been located. It pains me to provide you with this intelligence, for truth should sit with comfort, falsehood with vexation; and yet, in such a case, verity—though discomfortable—is absolutely required. Your forbearance in this matter shall be a testimony to the equilibrium of your temperament, and provide us with yet another example of the amplitude of your generosity.

I may assure you that every pain is currently being taken to find the boy. We have reason to believe that he headed to the east, perhaps planning to join the militia encampments outside the city of Boston. As of this morning, I dispatched two riders to make inquiries in the towns of (a) Roxbury; (b) Charlestown; (c) Cambridge; (d) Salem; and (e) Newburyport, these last being ports of possible embarkation. If he is amongst the militia encampments outside the town, we shall locate him in the next few days—and you will receive full satisfaction from—

Your humble & affectionate servant,
Richard Sharpe, Esq.

[253]

Dulwich, Massachusetts
May 18th, 1775

My dear Fruition—

In my Fancy, you perch in the Cooperage & I smell the Peel of the
Wood, & the Staves are around you & the white Hogsheads newly
bound & the Shavings curled and looped upon the Floor, silver and
gold—& you are eating a fat Mushroom.

There is little Word from Boston. What have you heard
in Kedron? Some Men of this Village put out in Whaleboats
for to survey Boston's Streets from the Water—but Boats are
harassed by the Fleet strung across the Harbor & they could not
tarry long.

What can be seen in the City? Regiments of Redcoats
parading through the Streets & still encamped upon the
Common; Officers fishing off Balconies above the Water; Ladies
in wide Windows, applying Lineament to each other's Elbows;
&c; the Stuff of Nothing. No News.

Here, Drills & Drills & Drills. March & turn & march &
turn & affix Bayonets & present Bayonets & *Charge*. We want
Precision; we shall meet soon with the King's Regulars, & they
shall be precise enough, I trow.

In the evening, we retire to our Fly & mess. Those among
us with Whistle or Fiddle strikes up a Jig or Lilt—until Mr.
Gower complains of the wretched Ungodliness of it all & the
Coming of Flames & scorching Gouges & Tridents & Vats &c.
at which, to preserve Harmony, we all break out in Hymnody,
Prince playing like an Angel upon his wretched Fiddle. How

feeble our Voices, but how glorious is our Praise of the ALMIGHTY! And then, does no one stop him, Prince plays us some piece of European Confusion, more, says I, for his own ear than ours.

Prince—your Heart (tender Being) would melt to see this curious Fellow Prince.

He must have suffered some great Wrong. I worry at what secret Ill he hides. My Vigor cools to speak of him, so girt is he in Solemnity—Helm and Hauberk—with only the Eyes peering out through the gloomy Visor. His Motions are slow with Sadness's weight, forged Link on Link, a Vestment about his Chest.

Yesterday, at the Bidding of Capt. Draper, I took Prince to spend his small Sum for Enlistment on a new Shirt and Breeches. He wished none of it, & when I said to him *that we must purchase new Clothing for him,* his Looks were all of cast-down Resentment, as were I proposing to dandify him—so I remarked somewhat smartly to him that torn Satin Breeches, Silk Stockings a-bled on, and a lace Jabot smeared with Chicken-Cack whistle, *"Runaway Slave—fetch me and prosper!"* in a manner ill-befitting a long-time Freeman like himself. He thought my Observations on Fashion exceeding Seasonable & we retired some miles down the Road and purchased him a Shirt out of some Negro cloth & some Breeches, which we got at a very fine Price.

His Sadness is impenetrable. He speaks not.

In the Evening, we each do our Stint at cooking on the Fire. Mr. Wheeler and I have been forced to teach him how; he hath no skill in this.

Last night, we et Squab—which he left overlong on the Spit—we might as well have dined on Sandals—and I saw him cease chewing. He did not eat, though the Meat was in his Mouth.

"Prince," says I, "it will go down the easier if you Chew."

He did not respond; so I repeated my Instructions.

Said he, "We take in the Flesh of other Beasts. We pack ourselves full of them. We are their Burial Ground."

The Rest of us — his Mess — gaped.

He reached into his Mouth, & removed the Gobbet; & placed the Gobbet on his Plate. He regarded the Plate balanced upon his skinny Knees; & all life left him as he beheld that Mound of Flesh.

Poor, unspeaking, tormented Creature.

As says the Psalmist, *"When I kept Silence, my Bones waxed old through my Roaring all the Day long."*

From One who shall never keep Silence,
would he or no,

Ev. Goring

Dulwich, Massachusetts
May 21ˢᵗ, 1775

My dear Fruition—

The Waiting, it is terrible. I can't abide the Drills, but as I turn on
the Green & muster, this Point keeps me a-marching: *that we must
be in utmost Preparation for the Battle,* should it come.

Yesterday Evening, some Boys of the Village delivered
several Pails of Oysters for our Mess, which we set about preparing; following which Repast, we went out upon the Docks for to
smoke our Pipes & play Music with Men of other Companies.

You would hardly guess it, but Mr. Wheeler is no little
Flutist, and played us all Tunes while we rallied him on the droll
Faces he makes when he blows. You've seen a Cow with a Hand
up its Fundament; I speak of Surprize.

We had "Pea Straw" & "Dusty Miller." When we was
fallen quiet and some had fall asleep on the Dock and others
looked out into the Darkness, I asked Prince, who prepared more
Oysters with John, to play us a Song; to which Prince replied,
"What do you wish, sir?"—me answering, "Whatever gives you
Pleasure."

Says he, "I do not seek Pleasure."

Says I, "Then play what you will," and says he, *that he will
play what I wish,* & now I am in some dudgeon, & says I, "Then,
Prince, I wish to hear your Favorite."

Says he, "You will find the Effusions of Europe too stiff
and dainty after the Delights of such pleasant Jigs."

"Prince, cast aside these Foreign Airs, which don't speak,

'cept to the Head," said I (without Thought, but only Combustion of the Tongue), crying, "Poor timid Creature, cast them aside, and instead play the Simple Things in your HEART!"

He replied, "What is in my Heart is not simple."

& I says, "Then you han't listened."

& He says, "I listen, & cannot understand its Speech."

& I says, "Then it ain't your Heart you hear."

"The Human Heart," recited he bitterly as if from some damp Lesson, "is a Muscle that operates through Constriction." His Work on the Oysters grew defiant. "I have seen a Heart lying on a Plate, jolted with Electricity. It had as much to say *dead* as *alive*."

Now I was terrified at his Past & his Secrets & I asked for no more Music.

Later I awoke in the Dark to hear a Shuffling & saw he was crawling over me & out of the Tent & I feigned Sleep until he was gone; but fearing that he had determined to absent himself from our Company and spare us the Hazard & Gloom of his Presence, I followed.

He made his Way down to the Docks where the Smoke-House was & the Flakes was & the Herring-Horses. I held up for some Moments & then when a little Time had passed, I went down after him & was surrounded by the Fish in their Barrels and on their Racks, with their Eyes stark staring, and Fin & Tail unfurled for an Acre around. There, midst their thousand Eyes, their black, open Eyes, he sate slumped — him looking out to Sea at the Moon.

I went to him & put my Hand upon his Shoulder.

Said he to me, "God forgive me. Her Name—I never knew her Name."

Which meant not a Jot to me—and yet my Heart was the Thing that broke.

Your brother,

Ev.

Shaft of Light

Chelsea

Your Klerical Brother

To Salem

Hog Isle

Dulwich

To Sudbury
Concord
Canaan &c.

Mystic River

Noddle's Isle

Cambridge,
Head Quarters
of the
free

charlestown

Boston
The Enemy

Boston
Harbor

Apple
Isle

Charles
River

Fortifications

The
Castle

N

Boston
Neck

Roxbury

Dulwich, Massachusetts
May 25th, 1775
Dear Sister — & Mother —

We shall in some Minutes go *Drilling*, but this Letter must inform you that Today a Captain is arrived with several more Companies & Word from the Quartermaster-Serjeant that we are to aid in providing Forage & Bat. I reckon on the Morrow we shall be seizing Stores from the Islands.

    Nothing amiss, my Dears, but still just I say that I am your Ev & shall always be your Ev & I shall always love you. That is all.

    Shun, I can little credit that but three Months hence, Mr. Porringer & I sat in the Cooperage discussing the Battles of yore: Damsels & Standards & Turrets & Trumpets & Jerusalem Delivered & Joshua sun-burnt before the Gates of Jericho & Christian, huddled with his Pack of Woe, ducking before Apollyon's fiery Darts, &c. — and now we await Battle, & shall know how the Flesh feels when rent.

    There are Times, Shun, when I think real hard on the Fireside & you & Ma & a Volume to mull. I just wished to write you that.

    Remember — standing or falling, I am

your humble & affect. Son & Brother,

Ev.

Burn Acre, Virginia

May 27th, 1775

Mr. Sharpe — sir —

I can't scarcely credit the report that you have allowed the Negro boy to make good his escape. This word couldn't fill us with more displeasure. What signifies your years of inquiry — and — frankly, sir — our years of investment — *if the subject has slipped away through your ineptitude?*

I expect regular intelligence on this. Spend what resources you will to apprehend him.

Perhaps it will be of no little interest for you to hear that Pro Bono the serving-man you sent me has fled similar. These are a wicked lot you work with. The Negro took some silver spoons and a sauce boat when he ran, and left our household in circumstances the most outrageous. We presume he has fled to Governor Dunmore. There ain't no getting him back right now. Rumor swells daily that the Governor will proclaim the freedom of the Africans from bondage. He will involve us all in calamity and chaos without measure. The thing is intolerable. That flagitious dog Dunmore has confiscated powder and public muskets; the word being, that he does so, that Patriots shall be defenseless when he bids our own slaves rise up against us and slit our throats. The Negro-Watch have been doubled to apprehend them. We expect hourly some plot to hatch. I cannot look at the face of my Negro woodchopper without fancying that he sharpens the axe for my daughter. Have you seen my daughter for the last some years? I think not, and she is a sweet and agreeable thing with a lick of a curl over her forehead. I cannot bear any of this. The Governor's palace is guarded by brutes—Negroes and Shawnee Indians—patrolling the grounds—frowning out at the people. I have sent to Gov. Dunmore to inquire after the boy you sent me as a gift, to see if he fled there—but Dunmore will yield no reply. He don't care a thing for our property any more and I fear the worst kind of tyranny to come.

'Tis time to shake off the yoke of oppression. 'Tis not enough that the royal tyrants reduce us to slavery—they raise up our slaves to lord it over us.

We shall break all their backs. We shall show them chaos and rebellion. There shall be retribution. Watch and ward—reporting with regularity to—

Clepp Asquith, Esq.

Dulwich, Massachusetts

May 28th, 1775

Fruition—

    Sis—

We have engaged with the Parliamentary Army.

    We rose early & assembled on the Green, & met there with the rest of the victualing Party. Here we heard detail of our Commission: The Parliamentary Army, it was known, graze a great Bustle of Livestock on the Grasses of Hog & Noddle's Islands. We was to assemble on the Shore of Boston Harbor & meet Others shortly before Low Tide & then together we cross to Hog Island & from there, to the farther Island, Noddle's. When the Channel between Hog Island & the Mainland was at its lowest, we was to drive the Livestock off the Islands over to Chelsea, with the squatter Animals poled over to the mainland on Scows.

    Little by little we hope to deprive the Army of their Meat & Hay, and with them trapped in the Town they will Feel the Pinch & mayhap then, once their Troops are Starving, mayhap Parliament will take Notice that we are in Earnest.

    We commended ourselves to God & marched to the Shore in no even Formation. Shem & John was lagging behind, striking each other on the Shoulders, & Prince was before us, playing upon the Fife. He had nothing with to fight save an old Saber someone had granted him, but we did not expect Engagement, our Detachment being instructed to fetch home the Livestock while Others from the Company shewed forth Arms, if such a display should become Requisite.

Farmers came from out their Houses to watch us pass; as did their pretty Daughters, & we waved & called that we should be back in the Evening.

When Prince put aside the Fife his Face was a Thing to see, for he walked without Words — as he does always — but with a Smolder not his usual Custom, & there was about him a Skeleton Air, the Eyes staring & fiery, & I saw finally the Sadness had Left Him, & now instead there was a Hunger which he would *slake at all Costs.*

He would seize his Freedom by any Means.

Seeing him, now my Vitals were Boiling by Knowledge of what we was to do, facing the strongest Army in the World; & my Spirits were in a Ferment; & my Heart beating quick in my Breast as I saw the Faces of those who marched with me, the Fine Men of our Town, that we had come here to fight & perhaps to die.

For two Miles we marched & then came to the Shore of Boston Harbor, & there, across a little Channel, largely gray with Mud, stood Hog Island, & its Hills were soft with Grass like unto the Hills of *Judah.*

There was assembled there flat Boats to take us across, and Oyster Boys to pole them along through the Rushes. Prince & I shared one with Shem & John, which giddy Pair near capsized the Boat playing a Slapping Game, until Mr. Gower called out to them, "My Friends, we are about to cross the profound Flood into open Rebellion. These are not Waters for Laughter."

There burnt the Sun of Massachusetts Bay above us, the

Eye of God too, & the Kelp was around us, & the grassy heaped Hills was before us, where grazed dumb Beasts. 'Twas a rustic Scene, and yet, *so must the River Rubicon have looked to the great Cæsar when he forded it, and so declared himself the Enemy of Rome.*

When we was disembarked, we marched along the eastern Shore of Hog Island, making for its far End, where we would ford a few feet of Water to Noddle's. We could see—at some half mile's Distance—other Patriot bands similarly headed.

We forded over to Noddle's Island across the low Channel, climbing up the Rocks in double File, crouched like Crabs for Footing. Having gained this second Island, we proceeded to cross to its other Side to advance, we fearing the Tory Mansions at the far end, which should be able to spy us, did we keep to the eastern Shore. We marched another mile or so Silent, with the dire Expectation of Grapeshot & Cannonade. Still, no Missile interrupted the Scene, which was only the Grasses & the Cattle & Swallows above a few gray Trees.

Then heard we on the Sea Wind the Whicker of Sheep; & there burst over the Crest of a Hill a powerful Load of them with Patriots behind them whooping & swinging Switches, driving them to the Channel. Parliament's Sheep were thick about us & so was their cries, too, & we raised our Hands and Muskets & laughed as they passed, to feel the Running & Bumbling of these Beasts all about us, scampering on the Clods.

Near Silence fell after they was passed, the Silence of the Grass & the Sky; & in that Silence, there was a distant Crackle.

Nought to it. A distant *Popping.* The Sjt. ordered Shem mount the Hilltop & survey. Shem come running back down & told us that the Enemy was alerted up & that Smoke arose from the far End of the Island & that *they was on the Move.*

We kept forward, though, moving *toward them,* and came upon a Valley with a Farm House of Stone, fallen to Bits, & a

Paddock of Horses. As you can reckon, I was full by now of Apprehension & everywhere in the Grass & Hollows saw Redcoats. Capt. Draper desired we Requisition the Horses for the Cause — most, to deprive the Enemy — but no one had the slightest Halter to lead the Horses with, & they appeared greatly skittish from the Detonation of some few Minutes before. There was much Argument, & Mr. Wheeler saying to try to drive the Horses, & others saying leave them; finally Capt. Draper raising his Voice & saying *we could not leave, without we had completed our Commission* — and so he ordered we Shoot the poor Beasts.

It was no orderly Execution but rather a Rout; & it was Pitiable. In the first Volley, Mares spun, Legs broken, Skulls crushed, & the rest charged the far Wall of the Paddock & leaped it or crashed through it & coursed up the Hillside away from us. In the 2nd Volley more collapsed screaming & the Hollow was now filled with Smoke & at the 3rd Volley the wretched Brutes were dragged howling back down the Hill by their own dead Quarters & their Foals blasted & splayed. Mares cried for their own particular Young & struggled to drag their broken Limbs through the Grass.

Our gruesome Task complete, shattered Horses still screaming on the Hillside, we was ordered to Retreat & did so, around the Hill, and run — i'faith, I have never run so swift — over the Fields. We passed other Corrals, now emptied. Smoke was thick & black & gray & white against the Grasses.

The Corporal was in a pet with Capt. Draper, saying that slaying the Horses had been an infernal Waste of Powder & Shot; to which Capt. Draper replied sharply, "You shall be another."

We passed through Valleys & over Hillocks of Grass & saw Smoke ahead of us.

We came to a Barn that burned full of Hay. Patriots were ringed about it, devastating the Fields with their Torches. The Meadow was a-fire. Flames snapped all around them & the Smoke was great & the Men skipped backwards through the Grass like Morris-dancers, trailing their flaming Pickets.

We fled onwards.

Now we came to the north-western Shore of the Isle. We could see the wide Channel & even Boston-Town, & — my God, I do not jest — there, drawing up, was a Sloop & a Schooner, discharged Boats with Parliament's Marines to protect their seized Animals.

We still had a Mile, we reckoned, before we reached the Channel to Hog Island & from thence back to Land.

We was sore afraid & wished only to get off these infernal Islands alive, & Sis, well can ye see the Boundary-stone of my Valor here — that it is set too close to the comfortable Dooryard, the Garden-Gate, the Pipe & Can of Flip.

Now, the Fires having greatly advanced, Livestock was pouring out of the Folds of the Hills down towards Hog Island without any Human Encouragement. Drovers were already there, ushering them across the Current between the Isles.

We reached the Stream & begun to Ford the Sheep, John & Shem butting Heads with Rams. For some Half an Hour we splashed in the Sea Water between the Isles.

Another Detachment of Militia broke from the Hillside & beat their way towards us. They hollered that the Marines came on apace & that we had best flee. Oh, Shun, you scarce can think of the Panic this Word occasioned.

We hurled ourselves across the Ford, waist-deep, & the Current running thick and strong with the Tide — & I slipped & almost dropped my Musket — had not Prince been standing by & seized my Arm & guided me. (May he be similarly *propped by Hands Angelical.*)

The Ships now fired upon the Shore. We was terrified of the Grapeshot, which we could hear Strike the Sand — so when we gained Hog Island Shore, we hurled ourselves into a Ditch quivering & there remained.

Twelve of us lay there without Speech, sensible always of the Crack of Gunshots & the Blast of the Cannon. Bewildered dumb Beasts wandered by, bleating.

Shun — as I lied there, devoid of *Motion*, besieged by Greenhead Flies, which Insects took no Mercy, but charged from the Sand & bit us like Voluptuaries — I thought only of you & Ma & *how all I did must tend towards your Protection.* I cast us already in a Time after this War, when I shall be Home & we shall work together in the Garden & jest — and I shall tell these Tales — & I beat at Heaven's Gates, demanding that such a Time should come, and me ALIVE.

We lay there for some Hours. We heard constant Conflict, which was often Distant (the tapping of Bullets & Blast of the Guns). With our Eyes we saw only the most Gentle Scene: the Grass waving on the Silver Hills & the Driftwood on the Beach.

We could not have known — but have since learned — that on Noddle's Island, our Militia lay in Ambush for the Royal Marines & eventually sprung up, firing upon them from the Hill-side, & they made no small Havoc among Parliament's Rowdy-Boys, but drove them back towards the Bay.

While this transpired, *the Ditch was ours*. Others huddled in it, farther down, some watching, some weeping. We heard always the Shots in the clear Air.

Cows came & posed — blinked at the Fire that had over-taken one of the Hills on Noddle's Island — and continued their Progress.

When we rose once to move, we saw instanter a Boat not three hundred Feet off, in which Redcoat Guns were leveled at both Shores — and we sank again for Hours.

The Firing went on all around us, we lying, Belly down, all in a Row. The Marines drifted up & down through the Channel — & sometimes were but a few Rods from our Shivering-Place.

It is curious how quickly a Man forgets Alarm. After an hour, the Mind toiling with nothing but repeated Warnings & Desperate Strategies & Calculations of Escape — it resolves itself to distant Explosion & Danger.

Shem & John whispered to one another, lying side by side in the Dirt. Other Men amongst us began muttering. Mr. Wheeler spake of Miss Joan; Mr. Bullock of Mrs. B. We all wished in that Moment to be with those we loved & held most enshrined in our Hearts. I need not tell you I spake of you & Ma, which you may tell her. Mr. Wheeler spake of the Glories of Mothers, as we listened to the Firing in the Channel, and the Fathers in the Ditch, they grew solemn at the thought of their Little Ones, many Mountains away.

Mr. Symes, dreaming on the possibility of Mrs. S. fructifying, inquired of Mr. Wheeler of the conditions under which Joan was conceived, and whether the Moon's Visitations had favorably affected the Engendering; Mr. Wheeler— never the most loose-tongued, & dumb-founded by the Impertinence of the Question—replied not, glaring out of the Corner of his Eyes at Mr. Symes before shaking his Head.

"It is a mysterious Business, Conception," says Mr. S.

"And wonderful," says Shem, thinking clearly of some seaside Trollop.

"Birth," said Mr. Bullock, moved to Words, "is magical, my Boys."

"I have heard," said Mr. Symes, "that one of the old Emperors of Rome wondered so greatly about the mysteries of the Womb, that he cut his Mother's Belly open to view the Place he came from."

I remarked Prince then jolting like he been Burnt, & I said, "Prince, here to my Left, is our Classicist. Which Emperor was that, sir? Julius Cæsar? Cæsar Augustus?"

Prince spake not; his Eyes were large; his Breath perfectly even; something amiss.

"Agricola?" said John.

Prince lowered his Forehead so he gazed at the Sand.

"Nero," he whispered. "The Emperor Nero."

He turned away from us, and lay on his Side.

We spake no more.

Then—I was aware he was stood to his full height, *exposed,* and he stalked away from us, saying, "It is in Suetonius."

We histled he would attract the Enemy and I grabbed at his Ankles to fell him, & fall he did, & lay in the Sand without Sign of Life beneath the Glare of our Townsmen.

After that, there was no more Speaking.

In the early Evening, the Firing grew greater, which was General Putnam arrived with Reinforcements & engaging with Parliament's Schooner.

Oh, Shun, I cannot describe the Scene. The Air above us was burning, & we heard the Bursts of Fire, & it put me in mind of that terrible Day when

> *The Sea & Sky must perish too,*
> *And vast Destruction come;*
> *For all the Sea shall shrink away,*
> *And Flame melt down the Skies—*

We saw bursts of Light from the Shells & the Smoke from the ranked Volleys. The Detonations grew exceeding fierce as the Patriots brought forward their Cannon & began firing at the Schooner that had been discharging at the Islands & there was fighting even in the Channel near our Hiding-Spot.

We lay huddled in a Line, & well wot we that at any Moment a Shell might fall upon us & our Ditch and leave us maimed or buried.

Now there was a continual *BLASTING* —

the Shouting of Commands —

—and no moment to think —

but A CLAP OF THUNDER —

too close —

which made the spongy Earth shudder —

And I saw a Motion: that John was risen, deranged with fear, & confronted the Battle Screaming.

I raised my Head & saw two ranks of Redcoats standing at attention across the Channel, & their Scouts darting before them, crouched & scurrying like Jackals, with their white Gaiters flashing in the grasses.

John screamed & begun to run down the Length of the Beach towards the Enemy; & though we wished to call to him, we could not, though Shem started up before someone grabbed him & yanked him back to the Sand while he gasped —

& then we heard the shouted Order from the Enemy & their Muskets tumbled to the Fore: DEATH PRESENTED TO VIEW.

& John — without Musket — still run down the Beach towards the Line of Fire; & he moaned & wailed like an Infant Baby as he run towards them —

& there was cried a sharp Order; the Redcoats fired off a small Volley, & the Sand whickered with Shot —

& half-way down the Beach, John spun & fell; struck in the Hip.

He moaned & rolled upon the Dirt, grasping at himself as if he believed he should soon slip away; he tore at his Side.

I raised my Head again to survey. The Redcoats, they

stood with their Muskets in a line & they was motionless & silent—

John lay near the Water—pained on the Strand—his Blood smearing on the gray Beach in the Evening.

The Redcoat officer called out a Command—

& with a SCREAM—which froze the very Blood—the Ranks began to advance towards the Channel—stiff-legged & unstoppable & Muskets ready & Bayonets pronged. IT WAS ALL THE MORE TERRIFYING FOR BEING SLOW—& John watched them come on towards him— O ghastly *Inevitability*.

& then I saw that on my other Side, PRINCE was risen to his Feet & walked towards John; walking with an Air of *Defiance*; with no simple intent of Heroism; but we could see he WISHED TO DIE.

Another *Blast*, then—& though I am sure it was but one or two Muskets discharged upon us, it sounded as a Volley of a Thousand.

Prince had Tears running down his Face; he walked for-wards in utter Regularity; & Shun, it was as if he had no Body & no Substance to slay.

Prince stood before them, Saber drawn but not raised.

He presented a Target so they would not fire upon John.

'Twas time for us to rise & fire—but we could not, Prince impeding our Shot—he standing between us & the Enemy—& still John lay upon the Sand, crying out & still they advanced.

Capt. Draper gave out the Command that we should charge our Muskets and prepare to rise & surprise the Enemy, & I saw he would have us fire despite Prince—& I could not abide it—my Spirits in such Confusions.

I would not otherwise have risen—knowing that I might leave Life behind. I would not otherwise have risen as I did & run forwards, tripping on the clods, expecting at every second the Bite of Lead—every second—to be torn asunder—

So when I reached Prince, I threw us both into the Mud & Brine.

"Life," said I, "is worth at least Threepence."

A Volley was fired—I know not who—and whether directed at us or at Capt. Draper or from Capt. Draper at the Enemy.

I know only that my Back, mounded, felt as huge as a Knoll—

& that Prince sobbed beneath me—

& that I was deaf with Shot—

& that I heard Capt. Draper calling *to Present!—to Fire!*—

& that, when I raised my Eyes, *unto the Hills, from whence cometh my Help*—I saw that the small Company of Redcoats was astonished by this new Enemy and that, thus confronted, they swiveled towards Capt. Draper and FIRED A VOLLEY.

I prayed as Prince & I huddled; and *the Lord delivered us out of our Distress*—for other Militia concealed farther down the Beach had arisen out the Eel-Grass & fired their own Rounds, the Air being liquid with Smoke—

& the Redcoats now, in the first Rank, dropped down to one Knee to fire while the other Rank stepped back.

No longer could I see the Conflict through the Smoke & Evening—who fired, &c.—& Courage having quit me, I did not raise my Head again as the Air thundered. I heard a Scream, which was John, still disordered with Pain.

[275]

After some Time, I perceived that the Enemy was draw-ing away & firing at a Company farther down the Line of Hills on my Shore; & from this, reckoned that the Flood was become too deep for them to cross to annoy us with their Bayonets. They made their way down the Beach on Noddle's Island towards the Bay, firing as they went.

Prince quivered with some torment of Spirits; but now looked about too; and we both rose from the wet Sand; & we made our way to the Water's Edge to fetch up poor John.

He could not stand, Shun, & when we raised him between us, he could not move the one Leg, which dragged after him, bobbing across the scallops of the Mud. Prince supported the Bro-ken Side of the Boy, I his Other.

So struggling, we reached our pitiful Revetment.

We laid John on the Ground, while he howled. We bound him with his own Shirt & staunched the Bleeding. His Hip was shattered. We fed him Rum to dead the Pain, & then lifted him & began walking back double-file through the Eel-Grass across the Isle to the far Shore.

Some twenty Minutes later we heard Sounds of Jubilation & a Detachment of Militiamen come over a Hillock, saying that they had all but driven the Redcoats up the Length of the Isle & that the Parliamentary Schooner & Sloop had been bombed so exceedingly that they fought simply to remain afloat.

When we was arrived to the Shore near where we had forded in the Morning, Scows with Fisher Boys were come to greet us, & we laid John in one Boat & sent him & Shem & Prince across to Chelsea.

We spent an Hour or so beating more Livestock out of the
Brambles, where Pigs & Sheep were fled. We drive them onto
Boats & waded back to the Island & they was taken over to the
Land. Prince returned, his Errand with John complete; he said
the Boy slept & was like to live. Prince joined us in shuttling
the Beasts across the widening Channel to Chelsea.

At long last, we led the last of the Livestock onto the
Scows.

On the Waters, we passed into the Channel. Behind us, the
Tide rolled in, as did the Waters return and *cover the Chariots of
Pharoah, & the Horsemen, & all of Host of Egypt* to their desper-
ate Confusion as the Israelites fled across the denuded Deep—

> *He turned the Sea into Dry Land: They went through the
> Flood on Foot: There did we rejoice in Him.*
> *O bless our God, ye People, and make the Voice of His Praise
> to be Heard:*
> *For Thou, O God, hast proved us: Thou hast tried us, as
> Silver is tried.*
> *We went through Fire & through Water: but Thou broughtest
> us out into a wealthy Place.*
> *Blessed be God, which hath not turned away my Prayer,
> nor His Mercy from me.*

And do you, O Best of Sisters, wake in the Night, and
find our Mother woken too, as by some Presentiment, & do you
descend the Stairs & out into the Dooryard, holding each other,
& does the Voice of your Soul inform you, as you stand beside

our Gate, that far from the thick Fever of Crickets in the Hills
and the Silence of Mountain Stars, your Brother is engaged in
Battle? And do you, standing together, *Pray?*

> *For if you do, I overhear you. And I am Safe.*

& I am

your humble & affectionate

Brother & Son,

Private Ev. Goring

Dulwich, Massachusetts
May 31ˢᵗ, 1775

My dear Fruition & Mother —

Enclosed is the letters from the Others, which I have taken down
most particular at their Command & some writ on their own; &
they would be gratified, could you pass them on to their Houses.
Please would you also give my special Regards to Liz? I wonder
whether you ever shewn her these Letters, especially the Last,
with my Heroism, which you might do, should she inquire for
my Safety.

     If you wish to Reply, as I hope you'll do, you should send
your Letter to the Encampment at Cambridge, as we will likely
March there Tomorrow or the next Day, & get our first Glimpse
of the whole Patriot Force.

     After our Drill yesterday, the Captain having commended
us on our great Success in our late Sally, Shem, Prince, & me
conducted ourselves to Chelsea to visit John, where the Rascal is
laid up in an House, surrounded by Ladies most solicitous for his
Recovery. The News: He lives, if he don't prosper, & his Leg
shall be Sawn Off. He was in Horrors at the Thought of this
Loss & it was a Doleful Day, with him Weeping & telling us of
what he should miss, back in the Village — the Skating & how he
should help his Father at Harvest &c. O Shun, it was Pitiable to
see. It han't happened yet, but will on the morrow, says the Doctor. John already desponds for the Limb, but he can't feel it now.
He has no Sense there. It is a Dead Thing already. He was
further full of Misery for his violent Fit which conduced to such

Confusion, & he asked I should beg Capt. Draper for Forgiveness. I do aver Capt. Draper shall grant it, for Capt. Draper is the kindest of Men, & in that Ditch, we all lay Confounded, and should not judge one another.

With many Fond Words we bid John Farewell & hope that his Recovery is Swift & that the Maker of his Limbs will Support him in the Sadness to come. You & Momma could keep him in thy Prayers.

Being upon the Docks of Chelsea, we halted to admire the Spectacle of the burnt Schooner grounded out near Hog's Isle, which charred Carcass lays there rolling on the Straits for all to see, its Ribs blackened. There has been further Raids upon those Islands in the last Days, & most of the Livestock is got off them now & furnishes Meals for Patriots.

We set off again towards Dulwich, & I see Prince wishes to say something to me, and I ask him does he wish to disburden hisself, and with utmost Humility, he says in his usual Style, "Private Goring, sir, you are, I trust, sensible of the Gratitude I owe you for your Intervention in my ill-advised Diversion."

"Your Diversion," says I.

To which he replies, "There can be little Doubt that without your timely Interference, I should have been dispatched by the Musketry of the Regulars."

"Prince," says I, "you cannot divert me. You planned a Martyrdom as plain as a Catholic."

He diverted his Eyes in Shame.

I did not wish to make him Miserable, so with some Repentance for Words he might have took unkindly, I said, "Sweet, humble Being, don't Fret. You drew off Fire that might have finished John," & said that John shouldn't be lying there Alive, surrounded by the Ladies, had Prince not stood up; and I said that it was Heroism & it don't matter a Bean what his Reason was.

"Your Kindness is—"

"You are most heartily welcome."

"Private Goring, I am indebted in so total—," and I stopped him, wishing no more Gratitude for doing no more than he had; though I han't done it to try and *Die*.

We walked farther, & skipped Stones in a Saltmarsh, & the Sun set over the Hills. When we reached the Shore, the Tide was low, & there were Children there disporting themselves with Chum. There was a whole Mess of Entrails spread upon the Sand; & Shem—you know your True Love—dived into the Children's Game & grabbed Parts & made to rub them in their Hair & his. They laughed & then ran to Prince & studied him, having seen few Negroes, I reckon. When they was gathered by him, he pointed to each Organ of the savaged Fish & he told them of its Use, & he demonstrated which were not from Fish, but Sheep.

They were interested by his Lesson—though wary, i'faith, because of his dusky Skin. They asked him Questions about the Gills, & he answered them & gave us the Names of Things in *Latin & Greek*.

I cannot imagine the peculiar Circumstances of his Life, & I fear to wonder at it. Know only that we had a pleasant Evening as your delicate Lover Shem & the Children horsed with the Entrails, hurling them at each other by Handfuls, & the biggest

of the Boys, being struck, slung them around his Neck like Jewelry & pranced far out onto the Strand, greeting the Sea as it slid
forth sighing, as if it welcomed him.

So did we play, while above us all, the last Illumination
folded in Judgment Scrolls across the Horizon.

Remaining —

your dutiful Brother & Son —

Ev

Cambridge
June 2nd, 1775

My dear Fruition—

We are come at last to Cambridge & the Great Encampment.

    Receiving yesterday our Orders to march here, we broke Camp in Dulwich & marched the Day through, & now are favored with our first View of our Patriot Headquarters. We have been but in the Provinces of Freedom; & now are come into its Heart.

    Fruition—it is not to be imagined. 'Tis perpetual Activity here, joyful almost in its Bustle—with the wide Avenues of this Town, the fair Mansions, their Gardens & Arbors & Parterres overrun with fine New England Rebels—on the Common, Tents—if some could be called Tents—nay, Blankets hanged on Poles, Kerchiefs strung up with Baling Twine, Shacks bound together of Sumac, & mobbing it all (Faith! Would you could see it! The *Blessed Confusion* of it!) thus: New Hampshire Men in Deerskin Leggings & Connecticut Men shaving in the Trees & Pocket Orators preaching Government in overbig Hats & Stockbridge Indians stalking among us painted & Farmers in their Blouses hefting Blunderbusses & Fathers and Sons enjoying Jests together, burning Toast or Syrup on the Fire—

    Our Spirits is in a continual *Ferment*.

    The Lord expounds here upon *Variety*.

    We have builded our Camp anew, & as it saith in Genesis, "*I dwell in the Tents of Shem.*" Now we wait simply for

Engagement, & hear continual Word that Gen. Gage shall march from out the Town and try to *whelm us all.*

Boston sits upon the Water, & is Unknown; & we await for it to vomit forth its Hordes, which makes a Man *uneven in temperament.* 'Twould be no little Piece of Foolishness for the Regulars to delay Attack upon us much longer, as we strengthen every Day, with Addition of new Companies, adding Numbers to Zeal.

This Waiting is terrible, & the Men would be most gratified by Word from their Families,

as you have received from your brother,

Ev.

Cambridge
June 12th, 1775

My dear Fruition—

I much appreciate the Lines you sent me.

    Here, we simply await Calamity. No Action; simply Prepa-
ration. We hear of Foraging Raids on the Islands—Deer Island,
Pettick's Island, a Mansion burned, Cattle conducted to Shore—
but no more than that. The Army sits yet in the Town, waiting
& biding for we know not what.

    We drill & drill & drill. I long ardently for Activity
for my Hands is Commissioned to Build & to wet & to warp &
to bind. Friend Prince has been requisitioned for a Work Detail
of Negroes & Irishmen which is much relied upon to dig Ditches
& hoist Abatis. We have, in full Sight of the Parliamentary
Army, strengthened our Fortifications at Roxbury with Ditches
& Breastworks & other such Devices; & as we scurry like
so many Ants, Parliament's fine Army hath cut through
Boston Neck & entrenched there within scant Distance of
our Fort at Roxbury. *How thrives a City when its Neck
is slit?*

    I see Friend Prince upon occasion, at the Earthworks or
sometimes in the Evening, when we conduct him to our Camp
to mess; which me or Shem must do with him as he cannot
without Difficulties seek out our Fly, some Officers looking with
the Eye of Suspicion upon a Negro who wanders the Camp
without Orders & Errand. I find his Company *delightful,* as

[285]

must your Brother find Anyone who listens to his Sermonizing &
Raving without speaking, fleeing, slapping, or feigning Fits. I
find I may speak to Prince as I can speak to no Other because
he *listeneth*. Our Converse at these Times is exceeding
Diverting; him relating curious Stories of Animals or Roman
Iniquity, & me relating Tales of the Village, the Cooperage, &
the Mill.

Prince sees more Activity than the Rest of us, his
Detail being frequently employed. He is much changed,
now that he has Purpose.

The Lord hath given to Each his especial Gift & Work;
& I reckon that when that mysterious Work is taken up, we
finding it at long last, then do we most fulfill what we Need
Be. I have my Volubility, which is enflamed; Others have their
Drinking songs or their Sops regarding the *Sweet Lisp of their
Children or their Spouse*; others whisper to their Livestock; or
hold Meetings for the Public Roads; or swell as Demagogues.
These things Illuminate them.

Prince seemed to Desire *Nothing*. He sunk from one
Sadness into Another.

What then does his Joylessness become, when Active?
I have learned: It is Anger.

Now he has this new Anger & he spends his Days
fiercely Digging & felling Trees & splicing them as Haz-
ards to Infantry & sluicing Mud off his Hands &, with his
Detail, building up the Bulwarks & Glacis.

He builds for Freedom — & this is his grim & unsmiling Joy.

So 'tis that we spend our Days. The City sits in the Bay
upon its Piers like a Spider. I observe it from the Rushes but there
is no Activity & nothing conduces to Change. Such is being a
Soldier.

Your Valiant,

Private Goring

Cambridge
June 15th, 1775

My dear Shun—

Nothing of Note.

There are always Sallies—burning Houses, shooting out
the Windows of Taverns. We see the Redcoats crawl on the
Mudflats at Low Tide.

At Night, there are Cannonades without Reason. It is not
clear that they aim at any Target. There appears no Strategy.
Ships pass to & from the Island Town bringing—we know not
what—engaged in silent Errands.

We awaken, & there is a Rumor of Redcoats marching,
& men scurry to their Arms & Companies—to find, instead, the
Blank-Eyed Sentries on the Walls of Boston Neck, & no Sign of
Marching anywhere. Farmers leave our Camp at Night to return
to their Fields.

My Spirits are low . . . I am so hypp'd & full of Fear. . . .

Your humble & affectionate

Ev

Cambridge
June 17th, 1775

My dearest Fruition—
& my dearest Mother—

I will not hesitate: Our Commands came last Evening, when they
were least expected.

There was no word of Destination or Purpose. There was
a great Motion in the Camp & we all fell out & our Company was
placed beside a line of Wagons.

The Wagons had in them empty Barrels; occasioning my
Thought, *that it would be a Paltry Thing, to die for empty Barrels,*
both for the Futility of the Prize, & the sobering Likeness, for
the Dead are always empty Barrels, the Casks being unbunged &
the Soul released.

We were led along Roads in the wake of Troops that
marched with Shovels on their Shoulders. We came to Cobble
Hill & proceeded down to the Charlestown Mill Pond, where we
filled the Barrels with Fresh Water, & brought it to the Hill
above the Town.

The Moon was near Full, & by its Light, I could see
Figures laboring all around us on the Crest of Breed's Hill. There
was a Huffing & the Chip of Blades on Dirt & also the Smell of
wet Soil afreshening the Night. Men were heaving at their Work
& I could see their Faces caught against the Moon-Track on
the Bay.

We were fortifying the Hill in one Night.

It was a Labor like those old Pagan Gods used to delight in,

throwing up a Palace out of Dew, but performed here with
Spades & Logs & the Stones of old Walls. Men were laboring
with Mattocks & Axes & Picks & rustic Grubbing Hoes—&
together they digged out & built up the Breastworks & Redoubts
at the Eminence of the Hill. This all was executed with utmost
Silence; orders being given in a Rasp; even Grunts muffled.

There, at the Base of the Hill, was Charlestown, & the
Channel beyond that was crowded with Parliament's Ships of the
Line, a-bristling with Cannon & still a-slumber; & across the
Channel was Boston, & the Common lined with sleeping Soldiers
who would soon be roused from their Hives— and hence our
Silence.

My Company carried Water from the Mill-Pond to the
Work Details. Some had Canteens, but most had not thought of
those Useful Objects, & drank from their Hands.

Once, in the Midst of it, I saw Prince; he was engaged in
digging. I did not call to him because the Silence was so great. He
and his Brethren labored at the Command of a white Man in dark
Duck who pointed with a Cane.

All Night, Men built their Works on the Hill.

In the early Morning, armed Regiments began to take up
Muskets & move about the Fortification; & many who had labored all Night now prepared to defend their Works all Day. We
brought them Water, too; sensible that soon, they would be engaged in Mortal Battle, & would greatly desire even one Drop of
what now flowed in Profusion. The Men were but half finished
with the Entrenchments when the first Light trembled upon the
Horizon—and they paused—their Shovels in their Hands. . . .
Men leaning above the Trenches were sensible of Visibility

spreading across their Backs. . . . They stood, uncertain. . . .

And then, the DAWN, Fruition—the miraculous *Dawn*—when the Sun rose above the Eastern Sea, & our Fortifications were REVEALED.

Below us in the Bay, the Waters were still & yellow; & in the Channel, Parliament's Warships rode at Anchor, their Masts all calm in the rising Light: the *Somerset,* the *Falcon,* the *Lively,* the dreadful *Symmetry:* all stupefied with Sleep. Beyond them stood the Town of Boston, emerging out of the Gloom, with the Smoke of the first Cook-Fires pulling away from the Alleys & Steeples.

As the Sun rose above the Harbor, we could see figures onboard the Ships—a desperate Call—the Watch first scrying us upon Bunker Hill.

For there they saw us—a Fortification where None had been the Eve before—and now, Rank upon Rank, Company upon Company, standing in our Trenches, we faced them. We did not speak in the morning Wind which rose with the Sun. Staring down upon them, our hard Faces—silent—Shovels & Firelocks resting upon Shoulders—as the Seagulls cried above us—Tinkers, Cordwainers, Shopkeepers, Doctors, Farmhands, Coopers, Gooseboys, Innkeeps, Sawyers, Cobblers, Freemen & Slaves—we faced them—ranged about our native Hill, our Eyes clear in the Morning—looking down upon their Antics on the Bay, as if to say: *This is our Homeland. We shall die, but you shall not take it from us.*

And the King's Cannons began to fire upon us.

Shun, there shall never be another Dawn like this one in all the History of the World—never another Morn like this.

The Adjutant commanded those of us who labored provisioning to pull back to Cambridge. As we passed along the Road, we heard the Battle commence in Earnest, the Field-Pieces answering Parliament's Cannon.

On the Road, I passed Prince in his Detachment. He spied me & held out his Hands to me. They were blistered & red with his Blood; & for the first Time, Shun, he *smiled full upon me;* for he has finally found his Cause & his Work.

I held out my Hand, that we might Clasp, & he reached for me, but his Corporal ordered him back in Line.

I am back now in Camp, & it is well past Noon. We hear confused Word of the Battle. The Redcoats have landed in Charlestown, & we hear they attempt to storm the Hill.

No more, Shunny. Soon this all shall be decided.

O LORD—THE WORK OF OUR HANDS—ESTABLISH THOU IT.

Fruition—

The Camp is full of them—the Dying. We are driven out by the King's Army—they took our Fortification—though the Word is, there are heavy Losses upon their Side. But we stood firm—my God, Shun, I shall weep—we stood firm.

But now—the Companies falling to their Knees with Thirst & the Wheelbarrows filled with red, screaming Boys & the Stretchers dumped on the Grass & Flowers of a Garden— & Men hobbling between their Friends—I have never seen the Like.

& by the Surgeon's Tent, where the Shrieking is continual—we all saw a Basket with Twelve Feet in it—the Soles still covered in Mud, where Minutes before they carried the Weight of Men.

& I am still,

Wholly,

Your Ev.

My Spirits being much depressed by this Spectacle, so soon as I had Discharged my Duties, I sought out Prince's Work Detail, that we might Sup together. I returned with him to our Camp, bidding him to bring his Violin, for we had need of Cheer.

That Night, we all *desponded,* a Melancholy Crew, all overtaken with a Vision of what it would mean for the Camp to be over-run, did the Army sally forth from the Town, say, at Dawn the next Morning, & we had to confront their Pitiless Ranks, who are the foremost Men for dispensing Death in all the World.

It is their Inevitability that most we fear: the Scream, terrific in the highest Degree, & the Unstoppable Ranks of them, the Blare of their Uniforms, & the Bristle of their Muskets, offer-ing their Bayonets, & the Slow Approach, first in Ferocity, when they reach our Ranks, & begin to stab & to stab & to stab.

Our Company were low, much hypp'd by the Bloodshed of the Day. We sat by the Fire.

Mr. Symes raised his Voice & bid us remember Worcester at the Close of last Summer, he being there, in those glad Ranks, when the Men came down out of the Hills to see that there should be Fair Play in the Courts; & the King's Lackeys were made to march from out the Court-House; the Judges & Sheriff & Gentlemen of the Bar parading before the joyous Crowds, their Hats in their Hands, their Pates hung low for their Crimes & Preferment; & amongst that Clamor, it was determined that WHEN JUSTICE IS ADMINISTERED, IT SHALL BE ADMINISTERED BY

OUR COUNTRYMEN, SELECTED FOR SERVICE, & NOT BY THE
TOYS OF MINISTERS & DISTANT DUKE.

I rose then, on an Inspiration; & I spake of what we fought
for—Our Homeland—and the Beauty of my New England, of
the Hills & Forests; & the Broad Fields cleared for Bounty & the
Vales with Pools where Boys kick at each other's Shins to force
a Slip

& the Rock of the Coasts

& the Summer

& the Winter

& my Cooperage in the Morning, when the Work is sharp
& neat

& Clabber-Girls with their Skirts tucked into their Waists
for Work

& Threshers catching breath against Stone Walls

& the Orchards where the Apples sour

& the Affability of our Insects

& Birds walking up Spires

& Our Devil-haunted Woods

& our Lakes

& our Coves

& our Barns

& our Groves

& I invented a Thousand Idiocies, speaking faster & faster,
laughing, as if it were all *Delightful,* but almost in Tears, until
finally I burst out, *"Sirs—Prince—Does New England SNOW
not make you hungry? Pray tell me if I am alone: Does it not
look most delectable to eat?"*

"Mr. Goring," says Prince; & his Voice was kind. "You bid me always to speak; yet there are times when Sorrow is best spoken through Silence."

Bless you, my Friend—for he knew exactly why I run antic—and I ceased. And in the End of Speech, we found Companionship at last.

He picked up his Violin & began to fiddle upon it; one of his Sonatas; & those resting around the Fire come closer to listen; & as he then played country Tunes, I joined in Song, & we played the music of my Meadows and the City's Alleys; & from other Fires, Men came—the Men of my Homeland, Shun—& we sang together as Prince played. When he did not know a Tune requested, he quickly conned it, & we all begun singing together; & so, singing of Village Maids & of Men on Drays & Nags headed into Battle, we felt the whole of the Nation beneath us—the Birches of the North—the quiet Lakes— the Rivers that lead to the Sea and the Roads that wind to the Mountains—the Villages—the Smoke—the Air.

Is this not worth dying for?

So thinks

thy Timid & Affectionate Brother,

Evidence Goring

Cambridge
June 19th, 1775

My dear Fruition—

I have done my Good Work for today & shall set it down.

    In the Morning, I heard that a Visitor sought me out, & 'twas an envoy from the Cambridge Committee of Safety. The Gentleman said that he had heard reported by several men of the militia that I had a Negro friend played excellently upon the Violin, who had given strong Proof of his Skill the Night Previous. I, being jealous of Prince's Safety, gave the Man no Straight Reply. He pressed, & eventually discovered his Commission, *thus:*

    Strong Report alleges that within the City Walls, the Officers of the Parliamentary Army have raised a Band of Music to play at their Dramatical Orgies—Overtures & Symphonies & such Stuff—Music to swell their Breasts & Vanity. In this same Band of Music, only the Winds are Regular Soldiers, the Rest being common Citizens, many of them Negro Fiddlers. One of the Fiddlers has sickened & will retire from the field, & so our Committee of Safety believes that could we slip a Negro Musician within the Gates (& they say such is not so impossible a Work of Subtlety) he should be placed in a most Excellent Position to spend some Hours of each Day with the Officer Class, with their *Confederation of the Damnable*—and report their Doings back to us outside the Walls.

    Me having heard this Commission, "Sir," said I, "indeed I know such a Fiddler—a Negro Boy who I reckon fiddles like the Seraphim. Yea I know of such a One; & I assure you that none could be more firmly attached to the Cause of Liberty & to the toppling of Slavery from her Basalt Throne."

My Zeal seemed somewhat to cool his Zeal. He hung back & requested Proofs of the Boy's Dedication to our Cause. I told him at some Length what I had witnessed of Prince's Heroism; & I added that they could find none more suited to this Commission, as the Boy was quick in his Wits — as examples — with Pride — telling him of Prince's Latin — his History — his Knowledge of the Entrails. This quieted the Man's doubts, & he asked me to accompany him to speak to his Superior; to which Request I assented. We proceeding to a Tory House that had been confiscated as an Headquarters, he took me into a Parlor now hung with Maps over some few gawky Portraits of Shrivel-Pizzled Loyalists, and asked me to repeat the Tale for one Mr. Turner.

Mr. Turner listened to my Account with all due Gravity & having heard the Story, confirmed that Prince sounded the very Boy he sought. He was most Grateful to me for bringing the Youth to his Attention, as the Militia who had heard the Divine Fiddling around the Campfire last Night had been unable to recall Prince's Name, owning however that he was a Friend of Private Goring, of Kedron, which indeed, I had confirmed in all Particulars most satisfactory. Having said this, Mr. Turner bid me fetch Prince at his Work Detail posthaste so he might be offered this interesting Opportunity & ushered within the Walls of Boston momently, personating a Drover or a Gooseboy or some such Trade.

At this, the Gentleman turned to the Side — throughout the Discourse, he turned always from one Side to the Other — an unsettling Habit which made me almost *giddy,* he being named Mr. Turner—and addressing the Wall, he dictated Orders for an Escort of Four Soldiers for us, & asked me to accompany them & aid them in identifying my dear Friend, & to recall that there was need for (a) Utmost Secrecy and (b) Celerity.

Such I did with Speed, finding Prince some Half-Mile off, in a Ditch. Surprise yielded firstly to Suspicion, & he asked me the Name of the Man who had issued this Commission; but, he having heard of Mr. Turner as a Dancing-Master in the City before the Conflicts, he assented to listen to the Rest of the Request.

I rendered its Outline & then urged it upon him, saying, "Prince—here your gifts shall not be hid beneath a Bushel—but you shall render Signal Service to our Cause, the Cause of Freedom, with that Instrument dearest to thy Heart."

He baulked, i'faith, at the continual Deception he would needs support; the danger of the initial Entrance into the Town & the Consequences of being Found Out, which could not be more Dire—but it was, I trow, because of the Brutality of the Commission & its unforgiving Nature that *he agreed.*

"Now," said he, "I shall strive."

"Indeed, Friend," said I, and well can you imagine with what Fervor I shook his Hand.

The Escort came forwards to conduct him to Mr. Turner. I walked a Ways with them. Prince's Eyes were quick and green— as did they already spy the Gates open before him & the City a-glitter & hear the Whisper of Trumpeters ripe with Secrets & the Fall of all this that had gone before *& the Glorious Advent of Liberty.*

The Spectacle of his Resolve & Bravery melted me, as does it now — O Prince, noblest of Men, willing to risk thy very Life for thy Country, when thou been Enchained these long Years, & know all thy People to wait for Liberty!

Moved by such Transports, I caught up his hand & asked him *what in Life he wished for most.*

He did not reply at first, saying, "I have few Desires, sir."

This Modesty was too much, & I urged him that he must reply. "All Things — all — are open to you — and you need not deserve, but simply Pluck."

Prince then, collecting his Wits, & with Resolve said softly, "I know what I wish. I wish some Day that I might live by a River — one that is strong of current & silent; & above it, in the Pines, the Hawks shall call; & I shall live there in a small House of one Room & play the Violin, & Someone Else shall play the Harpsichord, & we will be far from all Human Habitation. We shall walk by the Banks of that River, & listen to the Buzzing of the Rushes, & that alone shall be our Company."

One of the Escorts begun to laugh, saying, "Rushes don't buzz."

Another said, "Just the simple Things, Friend: Your Harpsichord." And they both exchanged Looks & laughed.

But O Prince — Prince — good Heart — for thee the Rushes shall buzz — for thee shall Forests abound with sylvan Harpsichordists — for thee be *Peace & Justice* — & so for all.

& thus we parted Ways, me & Prince, and he was taken into the Garden of the House where Mr. Turner awaited him, & his bright and glorious *Future.*

I forwent Supper and walked by the shore of the Charles until I could see Boston.

Already, at that Hour, the Sky over the Sea was dark. The final Part of the Sun set to the West. There was some Wind, as I think that a Storm arises up. The floating Artillery Batteries heaved on the Water. The Sun caught the Spires of the South End, the gray Water that roils under the Docks, the Grasses on Beacon Hill; & all was in Motion & Ferment.

Above us all—Patriot & Tory, Citizen & Soldier, our tiny, covered Heads—the Clouds in their Herd browsed the green Skies.

As above the Tricorne of

your Humble & affectionate Brother,

Private Evidence Goring

*[From Mr. Richard Sharpe, of the Novanglian College of
Lucidity, to Mr. Clepp Asquith, Esquire, of the Virginia Colony.]*

Canaan, Massachusetts
June 29th, *1775*

Dear Mr. Asquith—

'Tis with the greatest pleasure that I report the return
of the fugitive slave-boy Octavian Gitney to the fold of
the Novanglian College of Lucidity, though no pleasure
should be gleaned from an act so strictly necessary and,
given the expertise of our body and the kind emoluments
of our Trustees, so assured in its execution.

Some three days hence we heard a report from a member of the Canaan Militia encamped at Cambridge that he
had witnessed a rousing performance on the fiddle by a
Negro youth of considerable achievements, who displayed
a familiarity not only with melodies of common truck—
contra-dances and such like—but also with the work of
European masters, with whose flourishes he endeavored to
entertain the soldiery at the completion of their martial
supper.

Hasting speedily to the scene of the encampment,
I distributed agents to determine which Negro work
detail employed said fiddler; being frustrated in this design,
I eventually drew in one Private Evidence Goring of
Kedron, cooper, reputed to profess friendship to the fiddler.

His description of the youth and the dates all assured me that the matter was beyond doubt; at which, I dispatched my agents to draw Octavian away from his detail into a secluded place and clap irons on him and conduct him to my carriage, which we rode post-haste back to Canaan.

I do not believe that this Pvt. Goring colluded in obscuring Octavian's identity for these months; legal retribution against him would, I believe, gain little and lose much, the confusion of the courts being such as it is, and the dangerously leveling sentiments of many Massachusetts jurists being so opposed to the right to own human chattel. Prudence occasions us to restrain where anger might bid us assault. The man is, in any event, by all accounts a fool: too fantastical of temperament and childish of observation to merit trust; but too trusting to merit confidence.

Octavian had no occasion to struggle. His hands and feet were bound quite quickly in a grove hard by a house seized by the Cambridge Committee of Safety; and, after initial aggression, he fell into a grave quiescence which has not lifted nor lessened. During the coach-ride back to Canaan, he several times moaned; but gave up even this paltry attempt at protest, and has since remained almost inert. It appears that his senses are disordered.

We have nonetheless restrained him with (a) shackles on his hands, (b) shackles on his feet, and also with (c) an iron mask with a bit that prevents him from biting or speaking. We maintain a constant watch over the chamber where he is held, and I have every felicitous expectation that within a week, his senses will be restored and we may resume our course of study and experimentation. It has occurred to me that, far from being a setback only, this interlude affords us a chance for reprimand and correction which might themselves be observed, with an eye to establishing general regulations for chastisement and reform, and the observation of which disciplinary actions most efficaciously bid fair to reformulate the creature and establish submissive principles.

Once again, it is with entire satisfaction that I report the issue of this episode. I might make a special mention of the gratifying compliance of several key Patriot functionaries to our inquiries despite the qualms of some whimsical officers; from our sizeable donations, they know us staunch supporters of the twin causes of (a) liberty and (b) property, and impressed thereby with our zeal, they offered every assistance which could be requested. You may find it eases the anxiety of our other Virginian trustees to inform them that even here in Massachusetts Bay, amidst revolution, the principles of property are upheld with such assiduity; officers keep strict account of which Negro soldiers are free, and which bonded; and of the bonded, who is the owner, that they may be returned upon the cessation of hostilities.

While I must own that there is a spirit antithetical to the continuation of bondage in this Province—especially among the rank-and-file of the citizens' army—the institution is so fundamental to the health of the whole of these colonies that I foresee no contest in assuring its continuance. Our only fear at present is that the Crown seeks to

stir up the Negro against his master, and that those enlisted in our ranks might employ our own firearms against
us; for which reason, there is much hope that our Patriot
army will disbar the African race from service soon—
which, though sadly diminishing our assaultive force, will
be of great relief to us all.

I present you, sir, with our compliments, and our hopes
that we shall soon throw off the yoke of Tyranny and enjoy the exercise of reason and the pursuit of our interests
untrammeled by the interference of kings or foreign
courts. At such a time, however, as far as degree shall persist, I shall remain,

> Your humble & affectionate servant,
> Richard Sharpe

[A letter between slave catchers]

Canaan, Massachusetts

June 29th, *1775*

Lew—

We ketched him. Mr. Sharp and me. There ain't no need to kepe serching.

He dont have meny fine wayes now. He dont eat. He dont move. He dont do anything. He lyes on the floor with his hands shakled and his feet shakled and a metal mask over his face.

I shuld like to see him playe a minuette now.

And P.S. who is £*5* richer? It is

yr great friend,

Davey

[IV.]

THE GREAT
CHAIN OF BEING

drawn from the
Manuscript Testimony
of *Octavian Gitney*

In this world we are condemned to be an anvil or a hammer.

— Voltaire, *Philosophical Dictionary*

They bound me hand and foot; they placed me in a solitary darkness. They put a mask upon my face, with a metal bit between my lips to silence me.

They gave me a tongue; and then stopped it up, so they would not have to hear it crying.

PSALM 88: *DOMINE, DEUS*

O LORD God of my salvation, I have cried day and night before Thee: Let my prayer come unto Thee. Incline Thine ear unto my cry; For my soul is full of troubles, and my life draweth nigh unto the grave. § I am counted with them that go down into the Pit. I am as a man that hath no strength, § Free among the dead, like the slain that lie in the grave, whom Thou rememberest no more. § Thou hast put away mine acquaintance far from me; § Thou hast made me an abomination unto them: I am shut up, and I cannot come forth. § Mine eye mourneth by reason of affliction: § LORD, I have called daily upon Thee, I have stretched out my hands unto Thee. § Ever since my youth, I have been wretched and at the point of death; § I have borne your terrors with a troubled mind. § Thy fierce wrath goeth over me; Thy terrors have cut me off. § They came round about me daily like water; they compassed me about together.

Lover and friend hast Thou put far from me;

and darkness is my only companion.

T hat the body, thrown, hath solidity, extension, resistance, measure, motion, color; hurtled into the darkness, or set there by the unseen hands of boys, still it hath these qualities; chained in shackles; vizarded with metal; that a body continueth thus to exhibit these qualities in the absence of sense or sensation — this in itself is perhaps not remarkable.

That in the absence of motion, I should lie unmoving and become unaware of floor and wall, sky and earth, and all the forces that bind; that after a time, even the sensation of the iron bit projecting into the mouth, biting the palate with every motion to gag — that even this sensation should vanish — this is of interest to those who treat not simply of pain and punishment, but of perception and essence themselves; for the mask itself came, after a time, to seem an extension of the flesh; the space between the lips occupied by the bit no more foreign in its intrusion than lip touched to lip, or wrist to wrist, or floor to belly, once the mouthpiece had warmed and the sour tang of metal had suffused the mouth, pacifying the clamor of the tongue. There was no position in reference to matter or objects; not the recognition of surfaces; the senses themselves collapsed and abrogated their wonted distinctions; and the body was left aware but bereft. In this way, matter's division ceased, and, as the ancients professed, substance was returned to its originary unity.

At long last, you may no longer distinguish what binds you from what is you.

A lesson on solidity from my childhood: Mr. 03-01 sits before me, and holds an egg near his ear. "How," he asks me, "do you know it exists?"

"You're holding it," I answer.

"Because," says he, "it has solidity and form. Matter extends in space, and within this coordinate space, it offers resistance." He taps the shell with his ring.

"It will offer less resistance if served with bacon," says my mother. "May we eat?" They all sit around the table, their plates before them.

Mr. 03-01 hurls the egg at me. Unsuspecting its abrupt motion, I do not catch it, but it hits upon my face and falls to my lap, cracked and oozing; my lip and cheek sting, and are wet.

I put my hand to my cheek and press.

Mr. 03-01 shows no sign of amusement or remorse. He asks, "Is it a chicken?"

I look down, confounded. I shake my head. I want to cry; indeed, I want greatly, very greatly, to cry, but I know I must not.

Mr. 03-01 explains, "It hath the *substance* of a chicken, but not the *form*."

They told me of substance and form; they told me of matter, of its consistency as a fluxion of minute, swarming atomies, as Democritus had writ; they told me of shape and essence; they told me of the motion of light, that it was the constant expenditure of particles flying off the surfaces of things; they told me of color, that it was an illusion of the eye, an event in the perceiver's mind, not in the object; they told me that color had no reality; indeed, they told me that color did not inhere in a physical body any more than pain was in a needle.

And then they imprisoned me in darkness; and though there was no color there, I still was black, and they still were white; and for that, they bound and gagged me.

Oh, to be cast back in that house—with all the motion away from it, the escapes and flourishes of freedom, wholly negated—as if I had gone nowhere—as if there were no motion. Oh, to be back in that house where my last sight had been the ~~████████████████████████████~~ ~~████████████████████████~~

When last I had been imprisoned, in my childhood, she had been at my side; we had been stashed in the ice-house. I was not, then, alone, for she loved me; she was with me then and spake comfortably to me.

Oh, to be returned to that house of death—

~~There is no~~

*H*e is gaping," said one of the boys.

"*Leave it*," said the other.

They put something before me.

I felt something hit my teeth, and discovered it was the bit for my mask. It swung up before my eyes. My mouth was at liberty; my lips worked in the air. I smelled warm pudding.

"*Is he awake?*"

I do not recall the remainder of this interview.

I was become so Observant that I could observe nothing. I know not whether my senses were shut, or thrown so far open that there was no latitude for thought and recognition.

As my senses returned, I became aware of light all around me. Perhaps previously, I had awakened only at night; or perhaps in my distraction, my sight as well as my other faculties had been rendered inoperative.

I was not shut up, as I had thought, in a cellar, but rather in an upper bedroom. The heat in the room was great, it being the height of summer. I could hear the sour histling of the cicadas in the trees around the house, the crickets in the field. I imagined that should I look out through the shuttered window, I would see the willows that stood at the back of that desolate estate.

Outside, the country men called to each other on the road that went by the house, and I heard, too, the daily round of the servants and family.

That I was dragged back to the place from which I had fled; back to a scene of the utmost degradation and horror, was a fact constantly before me. In my Observant state, I had even fancied that the sensation of shame inhered in the manacles, I could feel it so acutely in them; I had believed the manacles an extension of my wrists, and shame a quality radiating from them like the heat from the walls. I had been sensible of its pulses spreading throughout my arms, across my chest like the ramifying systems of artery or nerve.

My arms were shackled before me with only three links of chain between them; my feet had to suffice with four, making perambulation impossible. That I longed or rather thirsted to put my arms out straight, to swivel my legs—with a physical ache not simply the discomfort of the musculature—this may be said without surprise; yet it was the simplicity of this need which confounded me so. In other days, to raise an arm, to lower it, would be the merest twitch; to yawn, to stretch would be accounted no great freedom; and now, as in thirst we dream of water, the body told me tales of what comfort those simple actions would provide, but they were rendered the most impossible phantasy.

We believe that the body hath its rights—to move in a reasonable ambit—to raise, to lower its limbs—but across the face of this earth, there are every day those who suffer unforgivable torments, strapped or chained, confined in boxes or in the holds of ships. May the Lord remind me of this always as I walk free upon paths, and may I thus always give thanks unto Him for the strange, small gifts of gesture, of simple tasks done with requisite care and sphere of action.

Once, as I have narrated, Mr. Gitney punished me for penetrating the secret chamber of the College by forcing me to hold wide my arms, with volumes recounting the data of my life stacked upon them; and at the time, he spake of punishment as freedom. Now, imprisoned with the weight of my childhood ever more dismally heaped upon me, I longed for that earlier stint with the arms spread wide.

Such a punishment, indeed, would have seemed a freedom.

You have not eaten for three days," they said.

"I am Observing," I replied, "as you taught me."

"What have you observed?"

"The solidity of shackles. They increase the solidity of the body. When I walk free, I am not conscious of my solidity."

"Yes. Shackles, like all matter, are defined by resistance."

"Do not tell me," I said to them, "what is defined by resistance."

I should like to be able to pronounce that I ate none of their food; that I drank none of their water; that I remained absent from their inquiries and entreaties; but after the space of some four days, when oatmeal was placed before me, I could not resist it, and I broke my fast, figuring that abstention to the point of death was an heroic, but withal a futile, stratagem, perhaps more cowardly to affect than manfully to face the adversities that surrounded me.

Lying without motion, I had nought to do but consider how I was arrived at such a pass. My suspicions in this matter were terrible to consider.

Nothing was clearer than this: I had been returned to the Collegians and to captivity as a favor by Sons of Liberty grateful for the College's donations to their cause.

I had spent several weeks applying myself to the cause of liberty. I had dug trenches and hacked at roots with mattocks. I had worked upon my hands and knees, stooped it seemed for days, fortifying Breed's and Winter's Hills, raising works upon the scarred streets of Roxbury near Boston Neck. The hafts of the tools were stained black with the sweat of us all, our contributions, black and white alike.

Black and white together, we ate our rationed meals; both black and white received the same portion, and if we sat near the fire of those of our own race, it was by dint of habit, rather than stricture of government.

We did not speak much as we labored. Heaving dirt from a pit, I would hear on another man's breath some song half-sung in time to his swing; the engineers called their instructions, wending their way through our deep, loamy fosses. When we ate, we did not much speak, but rather watched one another or the fire.

Quite often, the King's Army launched their artillery towards our works without hope of the shells reaching us. After the first shell in the distance, calls would go out from the crest of the hill that we should seek shelter; and we would file behind the half-built fortifications and hunch in the dirt, arms limp at our sides. Some would sleep while the shelling, futile, echoed along the summer roads; some would wind stalks of grass around their fingers; some would mutter to friends.

I was never free from dirt. It was on my hands and in my mouth, and my food crackled with it; my eyes were full of it, after days of examining it, exhuming stones like bone. I smellt dirt in my dreams. We were constantly begrimed.

Some nights, a friend and drinking-companion of mine of the

Patriot forces, a Mr. G——ing, would seek out my fire and would conduct me back to his regiment, with whom I had briefly served. We would form a small band of music and play songs requested by our fellows. These were sweet times. Mr. G——ing would look about him and would proclaim the joyous equality of all, the liberty that would soon overtake us.

And was he right to celebrate?

Indeed, we worked side by side, white knuckles as scored and darkened as brown; and yet as we labored for liberty, applauded by men in silk waistcoats who came to observe our unity and diligence, I noted thus:

The Africans amongst us risked our lives for liberty, and yet had no assurance liberty would be ours; our pay, in many cases, came not to us, but to our owners — for it was reckoned that we belonged to them, and so *our labor was theirs,* so they should receive compensation for our absence from their farms, their dining-rooms, and their cellars.

Mr. G——ing might speak in sanguine tones of imminent freedom, but he did not know of the secret colloquies we held when no white men were by, where we whispered to each other the rumors we heard: that the other colonies would only join the rebellion if it were declared that "property" was secure — that there should be no general emancipation. Mr. G——ing talked with fire of the Continental Congress in Philadelphia, a noble experiment in human dignity; we heard it was peopled with slave-lords, men who bewailed their enslavement to Britain while in their rice fields, thousands of their bonded servants toiled without pay in the mud, the sun above, the air swarmed with insects, and the water red with scum. We heard of their fear of slave rebellion, women bereft of their husbands sleeping with their grandfathers' blunderbusses shrouded in the bedsheets, children weeping and running at the sight of footmen who had stood by them since infancy, afraid of the hatchet or razor. We heard that such an insurrection was planned, though the reports never mentioned the same colony, nor the same date, but only details obscured by hundreds of miles and the hearth-tales of countless households: a name such as Pompey or Quash; an outrage, as the whipping to death of an infant for wailing or some unspeakable indignities practiced upon a slave by his lustful master; and sometimes, a hint of a sign by which we should know the time was come, such as the cry of the conch or tracks from a horseshoe inscribed ARISE.

The times, the seasons, the signs may have been mythical; but the sufferings were not. I lay in the dark with the breathing of men around me and knew that then, at that selfsame moment, where dawn groped across the sea, my brethren lay bound in ships, one body atop another, smelling of their green wounds and fæces; I knew in dark houses, there was torture, arms held down, fire-brands approaching the soft skin of the belly or arm; and still — there is screaming in the night; there is flight; mothers sob for children they shall not see again; girls feel the weight of men atop them; men cry for their wives; boys dangle dead in the barn; and we smoke their sorrow contentedly; and we eat their sorrow; and we wear their sorrow; and wonder how it came so cheap.

It was for this that we labored and fought, risking our very lives. And yet some of the men who worked alongside of me or who died upon the bayonets of the British at Bunker Hill had been enlisted by their masters without promise of freedom; with no offer of emancipation; and they fought in lieu of their masters, who were acclaimed generous patriots for supplying men for the cause.

My companion Mr. G——ing hath a generous heart—a heart so filled with light that I could scarce desire to cloud it—but he did not think on this much when he came to visit me in the evenings. He little noted the lists of slaves made up by regimental commanders, that no runaways should enlist, or the careful tallies of monies to be paid to men who stayed at home and sent their bonded Negroes to the wars instead. He little noted the notice that was taken of Negroes who moved about the camp at night. Had he seen such, his heart would have melted; he should have bellowed with outrage; and for that, may God bless him; but still, it would have been the outrage of a white man, unthreatened by these hypocrisies.

After the battle was fought atop Bunker Hill, I saw a Negro man upon the road from Charlestown. He was tall and stout of build, and he had a hole so broad upon his chest that the bone of his skeleton was shown. He used his musket for a walking-stick. His smock was scarlet with his blood. He stopped in his ragged pilgrimage only to lift his hat to white men who fled past him.

A passerby stopped and required directions of him. I saw him gesture and explain a route.

Being satisfied with the response, the passerby thanked him profusely and went onwards, toward the tea-room he sought; and I took the slave by the arm and helped him limp to the physicians' tent.

There, we sat him upon the hay and the doctor examined his wounds. Being questioned by the doctor, the man responded that his name was Hosiah Lister, the last name being his master's name, and that he fought in his master's stead, but that he should, upon the completion of the war, be freed. The doctor recorded his regiment and company and dressed his wounds, but without much hope of success; the loss of blood being great, it was supposed he would soon give up the ghost.

I went to sit by his side. He watched the flies.

"You have fought bravely, sir," I said.

He recited from his youth a recipe for a concoction to dull flying insects; he told me that he stood on chairs with a glass full of this ammoniac water sweetened, and pressed it up against the ceiling where the flies sat, they falling into the concoction, drunken. So, said he, did he spend long boyhood afternoons; this was his duty.

I asked him a few questions regarding his family, that I might take a message to them, but he gave no certain answer, and fell silent. I called the surgeon. He came and stooped by our side, feeling Hosiah's wrist. After a minute, he shook his head; he lifted his thumbs to Hosiah's eyes and closed them.

Rising, he went to his table and opened a great account book, dipped his quill in the ink, indited a company and regiment, and recorded this, the man's only epitaph:

Hosiah Lister, now dead, rec'd his freedom.

*O*ctavian," a voice demands. "Octavian Gitney."

I do not respond to that name.

"Octavian, have you received any communication from Pro Bono?"

I shook my head.

"He is fled his master in Virginia."

This is cause for rejoicing; but I do not call it so.

"It is believed that he has fled to the palace of Governor Dunmore of Virginia. We find it a matter for surprise and interest that his flight coincided so closely with your own. Did he at any time advert to such a plan in a letter you might have received? Or did you at any time post a letter to him once he was delivered to his Southern master?"

I could not but shake my head; knowing not where Pro Bono had been this seven months.

"Octavian. You will tell us if there has been some collusion?"
When I again did not reply: "Will you relate where he has fled, to the
Governor's mansion or some other retreat?"

Alas, my wretched brother, torn from me so quickly!
Now and forever, hail and farewell.

It is not entirely clear why the College of Lucidity held me so long in such brutal conditions, hobbled and yoked, save to break my will so I should no longer attempt to flee even this scene of desolation. I know not what further scheme they would have enacted upon my already distracted frame had events not transpired which changed considerably the issue of this incarceration.

As it occurred, I was told by one of the Irish boys who they had, it appears, hired in my absence, that in the afternoon they would see me and speak with me about my future in the house; and that I should prepare for this interview.

How might one prepare, locked in most complete immobility? I prepared only through the gathering of rage. I thought on their hypocrisy, too easy a mark, even, for argument, so howling it was — that I had been apprehended as slave through the capitulation of those who fought for liberty.

I thought of the deaths of those slaves who fought in other men's steads; I thought on Hosiah Lister, whoever he had been, who tasted only the freedom of negation; whose dark body received the death meant for his master, the scripted wound, as if he were the doom-shadow of that man, divided through some blasphemous design from the white man's body so the death might die and the man live on.

There, where I saw them, toiling in lines, the bonded, they were like ranks of white men's deaths, substitutes, the shadow that was to come upon a master, waiting to take the contagion within them, or the bullet, the blow, or the final cut.

The Latin for "slave" — *servus* — as rendered in English literally is "the spared one"; slaves being those taken prisoner in battle, who should, therefore, by all the rules of engagement, have been slain. In antiquity, slaves possessed no rights as citizens because, though spared, they were accounted dead, and as the dead, could not be admitted as living men; and so, for generations, the dead toiled and bred in Rome; the dead taught Rome's children the secrets of philosophy; the dead built Rome's great monuments and tombs; until the Romans themselves joined the dead, and all that remained were tombs, and monuments, and half-remembered terms.

So were too these men I worked beside: transformed against their will into the dead; and asked to die again so that they might be free.

Hosiah Lister, now dead, rec'd his freedom.

Consider, then, the full measure of my sadness, reading this inscription; not merely for Hosiah Lister, but for all of us; consider the dear cost of liberty in a world so hostile, so teeming with enemies and opportunists, that one could not become free without casting aside all causality, all choice, all will, all identity; finding freedom only in the spacious blankness of unbeing, the wide plains of nonentity, infinite and still.

This it was that Hosiah Lister had found.

I thought on this, lying in my shackles. Thus, my anger mounting, I awaited my interview.

I waited but a few hours. The Irish boy appeared again, helped me to my feet, and led me shuffling forward.

"They will see you now," he said.

They met me in the experimental chamber. Lately, we had danced there, skeleton and snake pressed against the walls. Now, amongst the apparati, there were couches and settles and, on a table, things for tea.

The Irish boy led me into the room. My heels scraped across the floor in short stints, hobbled by links of chain, as it is said that the young gentle-ladies of Japan walk, hobbled by subservience and feminine humility. The Irish boy helped me sit, and then withdrew. The windows were mostly shuttered. Outside them, in the yard, someone played a country tune on a whistle, a melody redolent of orchards and sun.

Mr. Gitney went to the door and locked it. Those present were Mr. Gitney, Dr. Trefusis—who sat against a wall, his chair tipped back on two legs—and Mr. Sharpe, who rose as I sat, ready to begin a lecture, I perceived.

They regarded me for some time. In my rage, I had found a new insolence, and surveyed each of them without remorse for my forwardness. The look on Dr. Trefusis's face was wry and amiable. Mr. Gitney could not meet my eyes.

Mr. Sharpe gazed as only he could, with an air of assessment and calculation.

Mr. Sharpe and Mr. Gitney exchanged looks, as if in brief converse. I awaited with interest some hint of their motivation and intent.

Abruptly, Mr. Gitney began. "Phaëton, son of the god Apollo," he said, "decided once—against his father's orders—to steer the sun's chariot one day across the sky. That most brilliant of parents remonstrated, urging his son not to attempt the crossing . . . because the boy was not yet ready to struggle alone with such vast forces. Yet the youth persisted . . . ," said Mr. Gitney, looking at his thumbs, and not at me. "The youth persisted. . . . He launched the chariot on its fiery course through the sky. . . . But he could not control the flaming steeds that pulled him . . . and he was dragged left and right . . . and he fell . . . and as he fell, he burned the earth, too, until forests were kindled and seas turned to steam. . . . It is recounted by Ovid that in this conflagration, the peoples of Africa were all seared . . . their skin scorched. . . . Which is why, said the Romans, that the Africk nations were black. . . . So Phaëton fell, and the world burned. . . . And all of that, my boy, all of it because he could not curb his juvenile desire for speed and escape." Mr. Gitney measured one thumb against the other.

I had read this story; I had no desire to hear this story; I felt fury so great at this story that I gladly would have tumbled the chariot and consigned the fields of New England to the flames. I asked, "What do you intend to do with me?"

Mr. Sharpe spake. "You have considerably inconvenienced us and caused us a great deal of expense we cannot well afford."

"You support the cause of liberty," I said.

"We do," agreed Mr. Sharpe.

"Then—"

"Are you going to rail about ironies? Hypocrisies?"

"How can you call yourselves—"

"Sons of Liberty? Because we support an experiment in government that is like to revolutionize not just this nation, but the world. A country where we may follow the dictates of nature without the interference of tyrants or princes. Where we are free to pursue our business without the artificial strictures of dukes and lords."

"This is outrageous," I said. I could scarce contain my invective. "How could you think—"

Mr. Sharpe held up his hand for silence. He had turned, as was his wont, to the side, and was preparing for his talk in profile, when Mr. Gitney, wracked, it is clear, with guilt, broke in: "Octavian, we do not believe in slavery any more than you. We would abolish it, if we could. I would free you and the others tomorrow, if I could. . . . But you must understand, there is an expense for everything. . . . To manumit you, I would have to pay a bond . . . grievously expensive. . . ."

"In short," Mr. Sharpe interrupted, "there are complications of national œconomy far too complicated, involved, and tenuously balanced for a sixteen-year-old youth to comprehend. Did we all free our slaves, America would be thrown into the most abject monetary crisis, commerce would become impossible, and, in the midst of that chaos, we would have roaming about the streets thousands, hundreds of thousands, of Negroes without home or employment, themselves starving."

Mr. Sharpe turned in the other direction. He continued, "It is our duty, now that you and your dusky brethren have been brought hither, to ensure that you are given employment and sustenance. There is considerable evidence to suggest that the African is, by nature, (a) shiftless and (b) rebellious, requiring constant supervision to remain productive. Indeed, reports written on your progress in my time at the College—"

I saw the end of this sentence, and groaned.

"Reports written on your recent progress have, in fact, aided in the scientific establishment of the inferiority of your race. You have done us a wonderful service, through your failure. We have publicly noted the decline in your abilities—"

"Octavian," Mr. Gitney pled, "we never intended that—"

"You will allow me to finish, Mr. Gitney. Octavian, you have been instrumental in the effort to understand African capacities and propensities. You must understand, God has determined—"

"Shall I pour the tea?" asked Dr. Trefusis.

"—that some creatures are less, and some more, potent on this earth, and has given to us the stewardship of all, according to our place in the Great Chain of Being."

"I need not be informed," I said, "about chains."

"It is common sense—"

"There is nothing commonsensical about what you have done to me."

"We have all done what we needed."

"Needed for what purpose?"

"To maintain the stability of the nation, boy. You do not understand the subtleties of business."

"This is not business."

"If a nation's profits shrink, then it is every man's business."

"Where is my profit?"

"In the common good. Which is common sense."

"Kindness is common sense."

"Kindness is nothing of the sort. Kindness without the promise of profit is an impossibility. It is a physical impossibility. You must want something if you are to act. Otherwise, it would be like movement without motivation. Reaction without action. Kinesis without stimulation. Motion without energy. Kindness without profit is like a teapot hovering over a table, held by nothing."

"Yes. Tea?" said Dr. Trefusis, holding out a cup.

Mr. Sharpe snatched it and drank. Dr. Trefusis dispensed one to Mr. Gitney.

"Am I offered tea, sir?" I said, now simply insolent.

"You should not have tea in your state," said Dr. Trefusis. "You appear already to twitch."

"It is easy for dreamers to speak of abolishing slavery," said Mr. Sharpe. "It is easy for women of leisure to sit in their mansions, singing harpsichord-tunes about slave-girls and reading sentimental novels of injustice. They have no knowledge of common realities — how the market works. They give no thought to the Africans themselves — to the chaos and riots which should ensue, the starvation, the burning of public buildings, the invasion of Indian tribes, if the people of your nation —"

"What nation is that?"

"Perhaps you should tell me."

"Am I not an American?"

"Are you not? To what nation do you belong, then?"

"I belong," I answered in voice shrill and tight, "to the nation of whosoever—without profit—pursues the good and the right."

"Then," said Mr. Sharpe, turning from me, "you are a member of an even more bedraggled and inconsequential diaspora than I had imagined."

He poured his tea into his saucer and sipped it loudly.

I rose from my chair and, like one distempered, began shouting, *"This is insupportable!"*

"Octavian," said Mr. Gitney, with a note of warning.

"These crimes—"

"They are not crimes," said Mr. Sharpe. "Your escape is a crime."

"How?"

"It is theft of my property. Your labor belongs to me."

"When did I sell it?"

"Your body belongs to me."

"When did I—"

"Good God! How!" yelled Mr. Sharpe, striding to the door and unlocking it. "Put the mask back on him! I do not need to argue points with a specimen."

Two Irish boys came in and placed the metal mask over my face, and I screamed something—I cannot now recall what—as they swung down the bit and it struck my teeth and scraped the flesh of my mouth. The bit intruding, I was bent almost double with gagging, and could not get a breath; and as I labored there, Mr. Sharpe ushered the two guards out and locked the door and looked upon me with some satisfaction.

I fell then to my knees; I fell upon the floor where my mother had fallen, sick with the fever; and I commenced to vomit through the mask, choking all the while on the dirty and acidic issue which clogged the mask and my mouth.

Mr. Sharpe stood above me, speaking in profile, declaring, oblivious to my convulsions, "The world, Octavian — the real world of objects — and not the phantasies in which you have been indulged in the outrageous luxuries of your upbringing here — is engaged entirely in commerce. Make no mistake of this. Look everywhere, Octavian, and you shall see nothing but exchange and consumption."

I heaved on the floor by his feet.

"We have labored too long under a government that has sought to curtail exchange; such interference is unnatural. We shall see a brave new day, Octavian, when the rights of liberty and property are exercised, and when all men are free to operate in their own self-interest. And as each individual expresses his self-interested will, so does the democratical voice speak, the will of the common people, not kings or ministers; and when the self-interest of every citizen speaks together, then and only then does benevolence arise."

He paused and drank. He then continued, "Look about you, Octavian. We are all part of a web of finance and exchange from which we cannot extricate ourselves. Consider the most pleasant scene of pastoral repose. It is nothing but a vision of consumption. Consider" — and he began to enumerate points on his fingers —

"(a) yes, consider, my boy, the lilies of the field. You know as well as I that they toil, engaged desperately in drawing nutrition from the soil and straining toward the sun; and the birds, (b), the birds, which twitter in the trees, a music that lays to rest all of the strife of the human breast—but could we record that speech and translate it, we should see that it is a record of hunger, display, and terror, cries for help, shouts of warning, the boasting of males eager for fornication, vying in power; the cry of chicks demanding that grain or other living things be shuttled to their open mouths; as (c) the small squirming things of the field are snatched for their food, or writhe in their own operations of hunger and excretion.

"And the farmer, (d), the yeoman farmer working the field, dependent on the flight of bees and the circuit of worms and the drifting of seed, the farmer, will he not sell the grain of that field at the market, and will he not require for his own sustenance the devouring of chickens, and pigs, and cattle, all of whom will also require feed; and is he not beholden not only to the worm, but also, through labor's division, to (e) the blacksmith who made his scythe and (f) the weaver who made the linen stuff of his smock and (g) the spinner of linen thread from flax and (h) he who heckled the flax and (i) he who made the heckle and (j) the button-maker making buttons from the bones of (k) an ox, which mayhap was fed by (l) grain grown upon another farm by other farmers with shirts, and buttons, and scythes, and worms, and merchants to purchase all of it and distribute it across the country—and so the whole fabric of society is predicated upon need and exchange. And even (m) this speech itself; is it not a form of market, at which I display my goods to you, taking pains to best arrange them so that they shall be purchased by you and owned? And even within me, are not my very organs (n), as I speak, and yours, as you writhe there, spitting, all your body in disorder, are not these very organs involved in exchange — the stomach hungering in its lickerish decoctions, the heart drawing and expelling blood, which circulates, carrying its half-exhausted freight, and so, inwards and outwards, the organs and the skin, the lungs and the air, the energies of sun and flesh, in all things, we are involved in commerce; and all things, Octavian, devour, and all things are for sale; and all things have their price; and all things vie and kill; and that is all we do; and all things must support themselves, or be consumed."

I was crouched and still upon the floor; not moving except to heave my breaths, which gargled in the mess I had coughed into the mask. At intervals, in my efforts to breathe through both vomit and iron, I convulsed again in spasms; and choked more; and vomited; which foulness ran through the mask, stopping up the nose, and dripped from the eye-slits, as if, defeated by Mr. Sharpe's harangue, I wept.

"It would be a tragic world," said Mr. Sharpe, "if at the top of all of this, at the apex of this system of use and ingestion, there were not God Himself, (o) — or rather, (a) and (o), alpha and omega, first and last — who grants us desires and pleasures and motivates us to action."

I looked up now, and saw a curious thing: Behind Mr. Sharpe, Mr. Gitney was trying to rise out of his chair, but seemed unable so to do. He saw me glancing at him, and wiggled his hands. His mouth was open. His limbs moved convulsively.

"God Himself," continued Mr. Sharpe, oblivious, his eyes fluttering, "engaged in all this vast commerce, this destruction and use ... Triune overseer of this one, monadic, universal œconomy:

at once Investor, Capital, and Profit. . . . He who invested His only begotten Son for the gain of all . . . He who . . . instilled in us . . . our individual desires . . ."

Mr. Gitney had sagged to the floor, his mouth opening and closing. Mr. Sharpe's arm, previously raised with fingers outstretched to enumerate, again and again, the little stock of what devoured what, had fallen to his side. He said in dullard tones, "He who leads us now . . . to follow Him . . . He has instilled in us . . . individual desires . . . and pleasures. . . . Did I already . . . ?"

Mr. Gitney made a long, lowing noise, the speech of a cow. I sat up fully and watched them. Mr. Sharpe had not ceased in his pontification, though weaving unsteadily now in his deportment.

"America . . . shall respond finally . . . to the self-interest instilled in all men by our God . . . now untrammeled by the unnatural devices of princes and . . . tyrants. . . ." He coughed. He scratched at his throat. "And as each individual will . . . expresses itself through commerce . . . the good of all shall be promoted . . . and mankind . . ." Mr. Gitney glided behind him like a large white slug. "Mankind shall reach . . . its native perfection . . . and perfect . . ." He stepped backward over Mr. Gitney. He sat. "Felicity," he said.

Turning to Dr. Trefusis, he said, "The tea."

"Yes," said Dr. Trefusis.

Mr. Sharpe shook his head as if to clear it of contrarieties. He rubbed his eyes with his hands, and, drawing them away, blinked slowly. He regarded no one thing in the room, but rather gaped at whatever lay before him. His words somewhat deformed, he said, "I have been in heaven."

Dr. Trefusis said, "You've earned your wings."

Mr. Gitney was crying on the floor, the whine pitched high.

Mr. Sharpe reported, in words uneven and slurred, that angels had no arms. Dr. Trefusis agreed.

"They lift . . . with hope," said Mr. Sharpe.

"That's a pretty sentiment," said Dr. Trefusis.

"I need . . . my gravity," said Mr. Sharpe.

Mr. Gitney gave a sudden cry, and trembled briefly with all his frame; then fell still. Mr. Sharpe slept, his head upon a trestle-table laden with mounted oyster-shells.

I knelt upon the floor. Outside, through the shutters, someone still played a country tune upon a whistle. The vomit dripped through my mask.

Mr.'s Gitney and Sharpe were now without motion. The patterns of their breath were disjunct, and hissed in the experimental chamber. One rose, one fell. I was in a pool of my own foul expulsions. Dr. Trefusis sat on his chair, smiling faintly and looking at his colleagues where they slouched.

"It seems," he opined, "a very pleasant day for a walk."

I nodded slowly, the alloys of my helmet rattling.

"An opiate," explained Dr. Trefusis. "I have never before poisoned, but I find it extremely agreeable."

He rose up and went to Mr. Sharpe's body; with a flourish, he drew forth a set of keys and, from another pocket, a handkerchief. He came to my side. "For one last time, you shall be requested to lower your head before me," he said. I did so. I felt the entrance of the key in the lock; and the report of its revolution.

With that, the mask came away. Vomit splashed to the floor. I gasped for air, finally untrammeled (as Mr. Sharpe would have it) by the strictures of tyranny.

Dr. Trefusis gave me the handkerchief. Bringing both of my

hands up to my face, I wiped at the vomit there. While I thus cleaned myself, Dr. Trefusis hunkered down, his thin shanks tucked beside his neck, and he fiddled with the lock at my ankles until my feet were free. He rose and took the manacles to Mr. Sharpe, who he shackled to a table-leg.

He turned back to me. I held out the handkerchief and my wrists. He came to me and took the handkerchief. He searched the ring for the key to my metal cuffs.

Watching him, I realized that the subterfuge should be greater still, did I not exhibit the freedom of my hands to the household as we departed, and I lowered my arms. Said I to Dr. Trefusis, "No, sir. It is a fashion that suits me."

He looked at my wrists, and then at me. "Ah, indeed," said he. "*Le bon goût.*" He tucked away the keys in his waistcoat, hands trembling giddily.

He took a profound breath, smiled briefly at me, and said, "The Stoics prescribed that we should be indifferent to external events. Nevertheless, at this moment, I must admit I find I am not in full possession of my hard-won *ataraxia.*"

He went to Mr. Sharpe and worked at tying the wet handkerchief around that reprehensible man's head as a gag. "My emotions at the moment," Dr. Trefusis observed, "are scarcely intelligible. I wonder why we insist on naming them. Hope at this instant is indistinguishable from fear; joy looks much the same as anger; and anxiety," he said, "cannot be divided from pleasure." He shifted the handkerchief, the vomit smearing on Mr. Sharpe's jaws. With a jab of the thumbs, he pressed the sodden cloth between Mr. Sharpe's lips.

The venerable *philosophe* surveyed his handiwork. "Pleasure,

Octavian," said Dr. Trefusis, wiping his fingers on Mr. Sharpe's coat. "We must learn to enjoy our little pleasures."

Together, we shrugged Mr. Gitney out of his robe — he not having a handkerchief — and used it both as gag and binding — the arm for a gag, the tail of it, wrapped tightly, to tie him to the mantel column.

With that, Dr. Trefusis pushed me before him to the door. He unlocked it and I stepped into the corridor. He called back into the chamber with the two inert bodies, "I understand, sir," and shut the door behind him. He locked it. To the two boys who stood by the door, he said, "Mr. Sharpe has asked he not be disturbed before he is done. On no account. You, secure the Negro. We are taking him to the carriage."

They took my arms roughly and led me out of the detested house.

Outside, the verdure of field and tree was overwhelming. The green was opulent; and I almost fell upon my knees with thanks.

A day, an hour, of virtuous liberty
Is worth a whole eternity in bondage.

They led me to the carriage house. Dr. Trefusis demanded that the groom prepare the equipage for a journey to Worcester. To the boys, he said, "Mr. Sharpe and Mr. Gitney will be working in the experimental chamber until later this evening. Tell the cook she need not prepare them anything. They wish no intrusion."

It was not an easy wait for the horses to be harnessed to the carriage. Dr. Trefusis and myself both lacked the instinct for subterfuge; and so we both worked uneasily with flaps or pockets. I drew my shackles up and down my wrist; he wrapped his fingers in the lace of his sleeves and paced about the yard.

One of the Young Men came out of the house. "Do you have word of Mr. G.?" he called to Dr. Trefusis.

"Which . . . Mr. G.?"

"Uncle."

"He is in some mysterious colloque with Mr. Sharpe in the experimental chamber. They asked not to be disturbed."

"He and I were going to try some soldering."

"I think he has put soldering quite out of his mind," said Dr. Trefusis. "I would not disturb him for solder."

"Soldering, lads?" said a second Young Man, projecting his head out of the door. "Is the word 'soldering'? Capital. Don't begin without me."

"Uncle's in the experimental chamber, plotting with Mr. Sharpe."

"I say let's rouse him."

"Famous. Let's!"

Dr. Trefusis said, "He asked —"

"What happened to the Negro, made him spew?"

Dr. Trefusis held up his hands. "Boys, do not . . . — Mr. Gitney would fain not be disturbed."

"'Fain'? What's 'fain'?"

"Sir," said the groom, "your carriage is ready."

"Do not disturb your uncle," said Dr. Trefusis.

"We will give him ten minutes."

"Two or three hours, at least," said Dr. Trefusis, "to transact their business." He ushered me quickly to the carriage.

I mounted the steps; and Trefusis having shut the door

behind us and rapped upon it, we set out. Though I was jolted by the ruts of the road, I was infinitely gratified to see that house—that execrable house—dwindle behind me. The Young Men stood about in the yard, watching us go.

Once the noise of our transit was too great for the coachman reasonably to hear anything that passed between us, Dr. Trefusis plucked at his eyebrows, his spirits disordered from the dangers that still lay before us.

"What waits for us in Worcester?" I asked.

"Naught," said he. "I shall momentarily request that we turn for Cambridge. We lay a false trail." He smoothed his eyebrows with some agitation. "It shall not be long," said he, "before they discover our subterfuge and send riders after us."

"I shall not submit to capture," I said simply. "I cannot go back."

"There is no fear of that," replied Dr. Trefusis. "When we are caught, you will be hanged for murder attempted and treason and I will be hanged for the theft of you."

I thought on this, then asked, "Why treason?"

"A slave who seeks to kill his master, as through poison, is always hanged for treason. In attacking your master, you attack the system of sovereignty itself. Do you find it is difficult to breathe when there is commotion? I do."

We rode for a while through the countryside. We saw boys training on village greens. They stood in rows which elongated and revealed new actants in military geometry as we passed them. Their calves were crossed; rakes held at ready like guns; their faces full of the seriousness of fight.

Elsewhere, there were men working in the fields, and women

carrying water in yokes across their shoulders. We heard no pursuit.

"What waits for us in Cambridge?" I asked.

"Naught," he said. "The tides today will be low at eleven o' clock in the evening. By dark, we will flee across the mud-flats into Boston."

I thought on this; and then offered, "We should cross to the south, at Roxbury or Dorchester."

"Why?"

"There is a floating battery off the shore at Cambridge. They are more likely to spy us there than if we approach the city from the south."

Dr. Trefusis smiled and clapped. "A strategist!" he exclaimed.

He opened the sash and leaned his head out of the carriage, shouting up to the coachman, "I have made an error. Take us instead to Roxbury." He drew back inside. He offered, "Things have come to an entertaining pass, when a city under siege — the spot of greatest danger in the colony — is the only place that might offer us safety."

We rode across the countryside towards Boston, and the encampment of the enemy.

As we rode on, the day grew more chill, the sky's blue more hardened with silver. We stopped at an inn to bait the horses, sup, and arrange that I should be sluiced with water to clear off the vomit; being washed, I felt the dampness of the afternoon even more acutely. Dr. Trefusis arranged a horse-blanket to be draped over me, and we continued upon our way.

When we arrived at Roxbury, night was falling, and so also

was drizzle. The coachman ducked beneath his cape as we clambered down.

Dr. Trefusis gave the coachman a small purse of coins and bid him find an inn to stay at overnight before returning to Canaan, saying that Mr. Gitney had instructed he should have no need of the coach until the next day.

An unaccountable serenity had stolen upon me; I felt the operations of my wits as clean and mechanical, aiming only at that which needed to transpire: the flight at the appointed time across the mud. I knew now also what I should do once we reached Boston: that we should first find an inn near the wharves; that on the morrow I should seek out a position with the military orchestra, the late bait used to afford my capture. I should receive a small sum from that employment. We should use the salary I made thus to find lodging. I had no doubt that other solutions would present themselves as clearly to my sight.

We waited beneath a willow-tree down near the shore. It provided us but little protection. Dr. Trefusis and I huddled beneath the same horse-blanket as the drizzle grew to rain.

At perhaps ten, we heard a great number of militiamen approaching, speaking in accents boisterous and jocular—and so we quit our position and crouched some several rods away, in the grasses by the shore.

The grasses were no shorter than we, and provided excellent protection. The rain fell upon us; and we waited in the mire for time to pass so we might make our dash across the flats.

It astounds the recollection, that we waited as we did, as fearful as we might have been, as cold, as shivering, as wary of danger as we were; and it cannot be imagined, what our thoughts must have been in that time.

"Strength, Octavian," said Dr. Trefusis. "You will not be the first royal son of a slave to be secreted in the bulrushes."

"You do me too much honor, sir," said I.

"I do not. You are a prince, are you not? And you are in the bul-rushes."

"These," I opined, "are not rushes, sir. They are grasses."

"Obstinate child. How do you know?"

Grudgingly, I admitted, "Mr. Gitney instructed me. 'Sedges have edges and rushes art round. Grass hath a joint that grows down to the ground.'"

Dr. Trefusis began to shake mightily, which convulsions I could feel beneath the wet horse-blanket we shared. I thought he suffered from a chill, but recognized then that he laughed.

"Octavian!" cried he. "Octavian, you are a gem of rare price. You are worth every ell of the rope that they shall hang me with." He slapped my back awkwardly and stumbled, I catching his arm before he pitched into the mud. "My boy, you are brimful of prom-ise. Someone should say this to you before we are shot." He ges-tured grandly. "It shall be an honor to accompany you, Octavian, on the next chapter of your extraordinary pilgrimage." We looked about us; and recognized, I believe, in the same moment, that the time was nigh, and that there was no purpose to remaining hidden; the next chapter had begun. For a moment, we gaped at the im-minent futurity of it. "And without further flourish —," said Dr. Trefusis.

We trooped through the grasses out onto the mud, where the

rain fell densely all around us. Dimly could we see the hearth-fires and candle-auras of Boston. I put the blanket about Dr. Trefusis's shoulders alone. We looked about.

"There is nothing now for us behind," said Dr. Trefusis. "So we must go forward."

With this benediction, abruptly, he set off running; and I, caught unawares, ran after him, and within a few steps had mastered his pace.

The sand was ribbed beneath our shoes, and the puddles often deep where we plashed. The shells of crabs snapped under our heels.

We passed a campfire on the mud, steering well clear of it, for we saw that men in uniform tended it.

Once we passed a cabal of figures in black cloaks and tricornes carrying torches and whispering together. They swam out of the darkness and the rain, and were as quickly swallowed up in it again.

The storm grew heavier. But still we could see the city before us, though it was limned only by glances of light through windows, guttering signal fires, a glimmer of ovens.

I knew not what I ran toward; I knew not what freedom meant, though it seemed at that moment to mean the quickness with which we leaped over rivulets; I thought on the word *freedom*, and could picture nothing that it might be, beyond freedom to die; I knew not what the hours held, nor the years; nor whether I would one day sit beside my river; nor whether I would hang, nor fight, nor what man I would be, nor what woman I would take to wife; nor what would be the fate of this nation, birthing like a

Cæsar, tearing its mother midst blood and travail. I knew only the rain and the old man who toiled to keep pace with me; and I knew our goal. We left the Patriots behind us.

Together, we fled across the bay towards the lights of the beleaguered city.

End

— *of* —

VOLUME I

It is worth a quick note on the use of history in this novel. Though much of the material is Gothic and fantastic in mood, it is founded on fact.

The College of Lucidity is, of course, a fabrication, supposed to be a provincial and incompetent version of, for example, the American Philosophical Society. The lesser experiments undertaken by the Collegians are either inspired by or drawn directly from works on scientific and philosophical speculation in the period. Educational experiments gauging non-Europeans' ability to absorb the Classics and other disciplines were really pursued: In the late seventeenth century, Harvard University supposedly attempted the experiment with several Native American boys. In the eighteenth century, the Duke of Montagu sponsored a Jamaican student's education at Cambridge University with an eye to determining his capacities. When the student, Francis Williams, did remarkably well, flourishing and becoming both a mathematician and poet, outraged critics of African equality—including the philosopher David Hume—attacked the attempt as being inconclusive, just as Thomas Jefferson, later in the century, would refuse to acknowledge the equality of African capacities when confronted in a similar situation by freed African American Benjamin Banneker and his excellent almanac.

As for the Revolutionary War material, it should be said at the outset that this is a novel, in which context it would be impossible (and even undesirable) to present all the available material in its full complexity. It was my purpose to try to re-create a moment when we did not know that the war would be won by the colonists — or what that victory would bring about. To my mind, attempting to understand the conflict as an uncertain revolution, as a civil war of Englishmen against their own legitimate government, restores awareness of the real bravery demonstrated by those provincial farmers and craftsmen who took up arms against the most powerful empire in the world.

The issues of Loyalism and patriotism, populism and class, and of the role of race in the Revolution are tremendously complex, and readers interested in these questions should turn to histories of the period to learn more. Historical narratives, untied to a single fictional point of view, will inevitably render a fuller picture of the subtleties and nuances of the conflict than a fictionalized account such as this may do.

Readers should keep in mind that the opinions expressed and the anecdotes related by these characters are reflections of what was *believed* to be true at the time by one group of people or another — not absolute fact. So, for example, I report a rumor that at the Battle of Old North Bridge, a soldier was scalped. The rumor is authentic, but the episode itself is not — it is now thought that a Patriot killed a soldier with a hatchet or tomahawk, and other soldiers reported it as a scalping. Similarly, Octavian's mother understands the precedent of the Somerset Case to free all slaves in England, an understanding that apparently circulated among American slaves at the time. In fact, the reality was much more complicated.

Though I tried to stick as closely as possible to eighteenth-century diction and grammar, of course I adapted period style to modern fictional ends. As an example: In my treatment of clothing, I referred to a "banyan-robe" instead of simply a "banyan," because otherwise the term would have been meaningless. I refer to a "tricorne," although the word supposedly only appeared once the hats themselves were out of fashion. I felt it was necessary to be more specific than simply speaking of "a hat."

Several of the scenes of mob unrest in Boston are composites, rather than specific real events. Take, for example, the tarring and feathering on page 75. The details are drawn from reports such as this, by Loyalist Anne Hulton:

> The most shocking cruelty was exercised a few Nights ago, upon a poor Old Man a Tidesman one Malcolm he is reckond creasy, a quarrel was pickd wth him, he was afterward taken, & Tarrd, & featherd. Theres no Law that knows a punishment for the greatest Crimes beyond what this is, of cruel torture. And this instance exceeds any other before it he was stript Stark naked, one of the severest cold nights this Winter, his body coverd all over with Tar, then with feathers, his arm dislocated in tearing off his cloaths, he was drag^d in a Cart with thousands attending, some beating him wth clubs & Knocking him out of the Cart, then in again. They gave him several severe whipings, at different parts of the Town. This Spectacle of horror & sportive cruelty was exhibited for about five hours.
>
> The unhappy wretch they say behaved with the greatest intrepidity, & fortitude all the while. before he was taken, defended himself a long time against Numbers, & afterw^ds when under Torture they demanded of him to curse his Masters The K: Govr &c which they coud not make him do, but he still cried, Curse all Traitors. They bro^t him to the Gallows & put a rope about his neck say^g they woud hang him he said he wishd they woud, but that they coud not for

God was above the Devil. The Doctors say that it is im-
posible this poor creature can live. They say his flesh comes
off his back in Stakes.

(He did, as it happens, survive, and sent portions of his skin to Parliament to show them how he had suffered on their behalf.)

The origin of the Revolution is fascinating, and I recommend that
those interested in exploring it further go beyond my brief précis of circumstances to examine the documents themselves and historians' inter-
pretations of these momentous events.

ACKNOWLEDGMENTS

Thanks to Liz Bicknell for editorial advice; thanks to J. L. Bell for his invaluable historical advice; thanks to Laura Murphy and Erika Gasser for reading suggestions; thanks to Curt DiCamillo and Dianne Haley for information on specific obscurities; for support, thanks to Vincent Standley, Tina Wu, Alison McGhee, Leda Schubert, the Cambridge Social Club, and the faculty and students of Vermont College; for a quiet place to retreat, thanks to my parents. Invaluable assistance in my research was rendered by the staff of the Boston Athenæum; thanks are due particularly to Lisa Starzyk, Mary Warnement, Reva Pollard, Sue Terry, Doug Caraganis, and of course Monica Higgins, who supplied the ham sandwiches and harpsichord.